THE GIRL AND THE
WINTER BONES

A.J. RIVERS

PROLOGUE

January 1982

THE FINGERTIPS THAT RUN DOWN THE SIDE OF THE MAN'S FACE aren't deterred by the decomposing skin or the areas of bone now visible through the patches of flesh that have already degraded to nothing.

The eyes that follow the curves of his shoulders, gauging to make sure he's sitting up straight, don't see the expression still frozen on his face or the gruesome fluids discoloring his clothes.

"We might have to dismiss early today. It looks like it's going to storm."

The cold snap in the air hadn't made them hesitate when they headed out on their camping trip. In fact, Mark and Sasha relished the idea of spending time out in nature when most people would run away from it into warm shelter. They loved the thought of experiencing that rush of doing something challenging, of exploring what most would never see.

This is something that brought them together when they first met. Each has their individual love of camping, hiking, and all things outdoors, but it only flourished when they found each other and began feeding off their mutual need to conquer the untamed and the unknown. They're still young, but the years they've spent together have been more filled with life than three or four of the lifetimes of the people they know.

But they want more. They want to see it all, to do it all, to discover that next incredible experience they'll carry with them for the rest of their lives. Whether venturing across the world or just wandering into the woods near their hometown, they are always the happiest when out in nature.

This camping trip was supposed to just be a simple getaway into the woods where they could relax, recharge, and spend some time alone together away from the constant interference of their roommate Melissa. They won't have a roommate forever. They keep telling themselves that. One day they'll have a place of their own and it will feel like they are actually a married couple. But for now, the only way they can afford the adventures they crave is to share their home. For now, they feel the most married when they are away from home, outside of sight of anyone.

And that was the very feeling they were chasing when they drove to the edge of the woods and hiked in. They set up a primitive campsite with only their tent and a fire ring built from the rocks they were able to scavenge from the surrounding area. It's not enough, and Sasha has a slight heavy feeling in her stomach looking at the large gaps between some of the rocks. The rocks are there to prevent the flames from spreading out and catching the rest of the forest on fire. She worries it's not safe, that the fire is going to move between them and lick flames across the dry leaves and piled limbs just outside their small clearing.

She has to tell herself it's going to be fine. The fire is necessary. Without it, they won't have warm food or coffee, and they'll likely freeze before they even make it into their sleeping bags for the night. They need the fire. They'll just hope for the best.

THE GIRL AND THE WINTER BONES

This is their second night out in the woods. The first brought them at least three miles away from where they left their car and was a much flatter, smoother clearing with signs of recent campers having passed through. Last night's fire ring was already waiting for them, and even a few bits of wood had already been sitting nearby, burned through enough that it caught far more easily than the new wood.

Today's hike took them five miles deeper into the woods. It's not a tremendous accomplishment. They aren't going fast or trying to carve a new path through the woods. They're just enjoying the quiet and the peace. Even with the sting of the air and the wind they're trying to ignore getting faster and harder.

They have their emergency weather radio ready to receive messages as they feed the fire and start heating their supper. It suddenly crackles to life and sends out the message that snow is expected in the area overnight.

"Do you think we should try to head back to the car?" Sasha asks.

"In the dark?" Mark asks incredulously. "We're almost ten miles from there. It's going to be fine. We'll just hunker down here for the night. We'll add the extra tarp over the tent and it will be fine."

She believes him because she wants to, and because she doesn't want to face the thoughts that will go through her mind if she doesn't.

They unpack the extra tarps from the supply bag and fight against the rapidly dropping temperature to tie them in place so they hang over the tent, providing an extra layer of protection against any snow and ice that might start to fall. As they finish, the smell of burned bacon tells them they turned their back on the fire for too long. Mark spits out a few profanities and grabs the pan out of the flames, hissing when the cloth he snatched hastily to cover his hand isn't enough to block the searing heat soaked deep into the black iron.

Sasha does her best not to laugh. His fits always strike her as funny. He hates that. She stops herself from telling him he should be wearing gloves. It won't do any good. He'll throw his tantrum, but he'll be better in a few minutes. He always is.

Mark folds the cloth and pulls the pan the rest of the way out of the flames. The wind has started to whip up, bringing with it the smell of snow, but she doesn't mention it. If she doesn't say anything about it, maybe it won't be as bad as the radio said it would be. She picks up a pair of wooden tongs and starts pulling strips of bacon out of the pan.

"They aren't that bad. We can save them. They'll just be a little crispy."

Mark is too busy digging aluminum-wrapped baked potatoes out of the hot coals. They'd partially cooked them ahead of time and packed them in their cooler so that they wouldn't need to spend as much time in the fire. It made for a quicker meal, which was always welcome at the end of a long, bitterly cold day. He drops the potatoes on a plate in front of her and Sasha scoops one up with her gloved hands to hold close to her face and ward off some of the chill.

Next onto the fire is a pot for coffee. Water boils fast on the edges of a campfire, and by the time their food is distributed onto plates for each of them, Mark is pouring steaming coffee into tin mugs. As they eat, the first tiny snowflakes start to fall. Just little flecks floating around in the air around them. Sasha feels them on her cheeks and on the strands of her hair touching her neck. She pulls her scarf up and ties it closer to cover as much skin as she can. It rises up over her chin, bobbing with every bite she chews.

The snow falls heavier when they finish eating. Not enough to make the fire struggle, but enough for them both to want to get out of it. They follow the same routine they always have when getting into the tent. Boots off while standing outside the door, each foot stepping inside onto the cold, slick floor, then the boots set just inside where they won't get filled with snow or creatures seeking shelter.

The unwelcome visitors in the toes of their boots are more of a risk during the warmer months, anyway—when the ground can sometimes seem alive with bugs and slithering creatures—but even in winter, neither of them is willing to risk putting their feet in with a snake, rodent, or venomous insect. This far out in the woods, an injury like that turns tragic quickly.

They don't bother to change out of their clothes before climbing into their sleeping bags. When Sasha was young, the Girl Scouts taught her never to do that. It's tempting. Not wanting to face the chill of the air inside the tent during the transition from one set of clothing to the next. Or even during the heat of summer being so tired and worn to the ground, not wanting to go through the effort of changing before falling over asleep. But nights are cold even after hot days, and sleeping in damp clothes creates a chill that can drop your body temperature and become dangerous. Those lessons still make her feel guilty as she wriggles down deep into the bag and reaches beside her to pull another blanket over herself.

Mark gets into his own bag and maneuvers over so he's pressed close against her, adding his own extra blanket as well. Both still wear their hats to hold in as much body heat as they can. Sasha knows she should take off her scarf. It's not safe to sleep with it looped around her neck. But her eyes are already drooping. Getting warm makes it harder for her to will herself to move and take it off.

He's saying something to her. She doesn't know what it is, but she murmurs acknowledgment anyway. She's vaguely aware of the flickering of the fire fighting against the snow just outside their tent. They shouldn't have left it burning. They should have extinguished it before getting in the tent. The wind is too strong. It could grab up bits of flame and toss them into the woods. The snowflakes are battling the flames down, but maybe they aren't enough.

Sasha doesn't think of anything else. Her body fights to stay warm in the cold. All the exertion of the hike and hauling the extra equipment has caught up with her. She tries to stay awake, but there's just no energy left.

Her next moment of awareness is of biting pain and a startling, high-pitched scream. Her chest aches like her lungs are struggling to fill with any air, everything is dark, and for a few delirious seconds, she wonders if she's dead. It's a frantic, dizzying thought from somewhere at the edge of sleep, sharp with the memory of the scarf and the feeling of the tightly stitched yarn against her neck. Then she feels herself being shaken and Mark's voice coming at her through the darkness and fog, and she knows she's alive.

Emma

"Don't move. Don't make a single sound. If you do exactly as I tell you, I won't hurt you."

I know it's a lie. Never have those words been uttered by a man wielding a knife and been genuine. It doesn't matter if I follow every one of his instructions to the absolute letter and grovel at his feet. The tip of his knife is pressed into the side of my neck, just over the throb of my pulse, and at any second, he could bury it in and splatter my life on the floor.

CHAPTER ONE

"GET UP!"

Sasha doesn't fully process what he's saying until Mark has her by her arm and is dragging her out of her sleeping bag. She scrambles with him out of the tent and grabs at the scarf around her neck, pulling it loose but not taking it off because of the sharp cold that hits her.

"What's going on?" she asks.

"A limb from the tree fell on the tent," Mark says. "It tore right through the tarp and the side of the tent and snapped the support poles. Are you okay? Is it bad?"

She looks at him quizzically. "Is what bad?"

Mark reaches up and touches the side of her face. The touch stings and his fingertips come back dipped in red. As soon as she sees that, the pain resonates.

"Part of the limb hit you," he explains. "It came down right over me and on my chest, but not too much."

He says something else, but the sound of the wind, the high-pitched sound that Sasha realizes she thought was screaming as she woke up, carries his voice away. She shivers at the intense cold chewing through her clothes and thinks about the sweat close to her skin freezing against it. She should have followed the Girl Scouts.

She turns toward the fire and realizes it's down to embers. The orange glow is gradually disappearing beneath a coating of snow already far deeper than she expected. The tattered pieces around the torn area of the tent flutter like broken wings in the whipping air.

"We have to get out of here," she says. "That tent is destroyed. We can't stay in there tonight."

Mark nods, lifting up his hands to breathe warm air into them. He's put his gloves on, but she can feel the stiffness in her own hands and knows he's feeling the same. She hadn't brought her coldest weather gear. She didn't know she was going to need it. Her mind goes to the old shelves in the basement. The ones that used to be in the corner of the den, sagging under the weight of a collection of books that got too big too fast. They'd probably still be sitting there if Melissa's niece hadn't come to visit and used as many crayons she could hold in her chubby little hand to scribble across the entire wooden side.

The marks are still there, now pressed against the rough dark cement wall in the corner, and a new shelf is upstairs in the den, handling more books in more space. Now those shelves hold camping gear. And right on the bottom, close to the wall, is her pack of gear designed to resist the lowest temperatures. Thicker waterproof gloves, a lined hat, coveralls made of material that makes her feel like she's wrapped in a dense gray quilt. None of them are doing her any good now.

"We need to try to get the sleeping bags and blankets and some water." The wind blows harder and he ducks his head down, trying to bury his face in the collar of his coat as he waits out the swirl of stinging snowflakes. "Come on. We need to move."

They gather the supplies they can salvage, stuff their feet into their boots, and try to ignore the intense chill and wet feeling from their snowed-on socks, and head away from the destroyed camp. Visibility is almost nothing and Sasha's legs ache almost immediately.

"We're not going to make it back to the car," she calls over the wind.

Mark continues pressing on for a few more yards, his determination bending him forward at the waist so his shoulders can plow through the thick snow and wall of icy air. But he knows she's right. There's no way they will be able to hike all those miles in the dark and cold. He pauses and looks around.

"We need to find the markers. Give me a second."

He's more familiar with these woods than she is. He hiked and camped here when he was younger, when the hiking trails were still heavily used and the campgrounds were always booked. That was when the relatively small park was still seen as a destination, before the larger campgrounds were established and bigger attractions opened.

Mark has a soft spot for these woods. He can see the memories when he looks into the trees, can still hear his brother's voice laughing, can see his mother determined to make a cake over the fire and never managing to avoid it from burning on one side. They don't come here often, choosing to explore new places when they go on their adventures, but it's the perfect spot for spontaneous trips.

This time he decided to bring her to a different section of the park than he had before. Sasha is used to the other side, where there are still standing cabins that haven't fully been taken back over by the woods, bath houses with pumps outside that still run with water from nearby wells. On one of their trips, they even found an old canoe still waiting at the edge of the woods, wedged between two trees that have grown since the canoe was put there.

That side of the park was the one that used to bring in families and young people thinking they wanted to try their hand at camping but weren't ready for the commitment of actually being at the mercy of the woods. They wanted a structure that looked like it belongs among the trees and a nice lake with a sturdy dock leading out into it, with all the modern amenities and plumbing. It's technically spending time out in nature, but it's not really the real thing.

This side of the park, separated from the other by hundreds of dense acres, was always more or less left to itself. Old trails have been cut through the woods and rough-hewn markers are set at irregular intervals to give some guidance to the more experienced hikers and campers choosing to roam this way. These are the campers who welcome what the forest has to offer them and relish the opportunity to explore and discover.

The two halves are of the same park, but little connected them then and even less does now. Two separate entrances dictate what experience visitors will have from the moment they arrive. While it's technically possible to get from one half to the other, it was difficult even then. A hiker needs exceptional understanding of where they are and how to navigate terrain not prepared for passage while also knowing how to avoid the occasional manmade obstacle of pump houses, equipment sheds, and ranger cabins.

Now it's even more difficult. The forests are grown up thicker and deeper, abandoned by the rangers and care teams who used to come through and thin the undergrowth, collect the fallen wood, and clear other debris. Some of the visitors who have passed through in the last several years haven't been kind to it. Trash and discards are scattered among some of the thickets, making Mark's heart heavy, but also making the passage through these areas more dangerous.

According to the town, this park is officially closed. It's no longer accepting any reservations for the cabins and summers no longer see young people in khaki uniforms tromping through the woods with bands of children who will earn little badges proclaiming them junior rangers. For a while, barricades blocked the entry roads and chains discouraged entrance to campgrounds, cabins, and old recreation buildings.

Those didn't last long. People still came. Not the ones who had spent their time in the cabins, weighed down by way too much stuff. Those ones moved onto the newer, shinier facilities. The ones who still came were the hikers and campers who loved the trees and the dirt, who wanted the open sky and the smell of the rain. But along with them also came people who appreciated being out of sight. They didn't want to be watched. They didn't want to be seen. They wanted the trees to give them privacy and shelter and they showed their appreciation by leaving behind their destruction.

Sometimes the police come through. They check to make sure no one is trying to burn the forest down and no one is in danger. But other than that, the forest has been left to reclaim itself and anyone who goes in is on their own.

Some, like Mark, still know how to get themselves around. Not all of the markers are still there. And the ones that are aren't all fully legible. But there's enough of them to combine with recognizable milestones to keep experienced visitors oriented to their location. And the ones who know it the very best, the ones who spent long hours there over the years, know something else, too: the park has a secret.

Emma

I don't respond. I don't change the expression on my face. I resist the urge to even swallow. Not because I want to appease this man's sick desire to control everything I do, but to spite it. He wants to see me afraid. He wants to see the beads of sweat form on the edges of my hairline and roll down over my face. He wants to see me cry. He wants to feel me shake. He wants to know that he has gotten under my skin and has me dangling from his fingers.

He doesn't.

I won't give in. I never have. I never will.

CHAPTER TWO

I T'S A SECRET THAT WAS ONCE WIDELY KNOWN. EVERYONE WHO
lived in or frequently visited the area knew about the empty school
just beyond the boundaries of the park. But over time that knowledge dissipated and now the crumbling old building seems all but forgotten. It's rarely spoken about. It hasn't been turned into anything or
reopened the way some speculated it would. There are stories about
that school, the way there are stories about nearly every place that is
no longer new and abundantly useful. As soon as it closes and its rele-
vance dips, a location becomes fodder for legends and creepy tales, the
backdrop for stories that blur the line between fantasy and reality. Some
know the difference. Some don't.

That's what's on Mark's mind now. He's heard all the stories about the
abandoned school and the once sprawling grounds that are ever-shrink-
ing as the surrounding woods close in. He's told his fair share of them,
too, even if he's never really believed any of them. But he always loved
to join in as guys bandied tales of terror and boasts of bravery back and

forth across the lunch tables, or murmured them over campfires, knowing having the building seem so close only heightened the effect of the details he spun out of his own mind's shimmering threads of imagination. He just enjoyed being a part of the tradition. It felt like his birthright coming from this area.

Sasha doesn't have that same link to the area. She moved here a couple of years before they met, bringing along her own memories of woods and dark corners and empty buildings echoing with stories. One day, he'll see those places, the ones she left behind. They've talked about it. She says she misses that place and everything she knew there. Yet they've never been back. There's always something that stands in their way. Something else that gets planned and happens instead. She doesn't complain. He doesn't ask.

"This way," he says, finally finding the green-painted remnants of a wooden sign that once marked a juncture of three paths.

The branching of the trail is no longer evident the way it used to be. The largest of the three, the one they are standing on, has gotten narrower and less distinct, and it's hard to tell where the two others separate off and lead into their own places in the woods. Young trees, ground growth, and debris have taken over to camouflage these trails into looking little different from the rest of the forest floor. But Mark knows where they used to be; he knows which one to take that will bring them to the back of the park and the edge of the woods as fast as possible.

"Where are we going?" Sasha asks.

"Dawn Day School," Mark tells her.

She's heard those words before, but they're floating around in the back of her mind in the same way as the names of distant relatives rattled off during a new boyfriend's family event. They're there. They could probably be brought up to the front if she really dug deep to find something that would remind her. But right now in the chill of the storm blowing up around her, they stay where they are just out of reach. She doesn't have the energy or the care to try to recall anything they might mean.

"Why?" she asks instead.

"This is only going to get worse," he explains. "Going back to the car isn't an option and the closest buildings are through thicker parts of the park. They would be hard to get to and I can't guarantee the condition they are in. A couple of them were built with bricks or cement, but most of them are wood. They might have already collapsed, which isn't something I'd want to find out after already hiking there. And even if they are standing, they probably won't offer too much shelter from a storm like this. The school is a bit of a distance from here, but not too far, and there's a path. It's made of stone, so it's going to be able to withstand the storm. We'll be safe and warm there."

Another gust of wind lashes their faces with snow and frozen rain, stopping any response she might have given in favor of tucking her head into her chest and squeezing her eyes closed against the sting. She keeps them closed as the wind continues to whip, relying on the sound of Mark's boots crushing down into the undergrowth to keep her going in the right direction.

The self-enforced darkness creates an eerie feeling as she walks. Without being able to see anything around her, her other senses heighten but seem to blend into something different. It's sensing rather than perceiving, feeling something around her rather than actually being able to see or hear it. Her skin prickles and her muscles tense with the feeling that someone is coming toward her. It's the feeling of being watched, distilled.

When the wind calms for a moment, she opens her eyes again and sees Mark ahead. He steps onto a sapling bent over the path to force it out of the way and uses another crush of his boot to flatten undergrowth blocking their way. Sasha gets close behind him so they can push through the dense part of the forest together.

It feels like they've been walking for hours as the snow gets deeper and the temperature seems to drop more with every minute. She's thirsty but doesn't want to take a sip of the water she's carrying at her hip. She worries about it freezing on her lips. Finally the trees ahead thin out and she can see open space beyond.

"Is that it?" she asks.

Mark nods. "There's an old road we have to cross and then we should be able to just go up the driveway of the school. There's a gate, but the lock on it got broken a long time ago and was never fixed. But even if they did fix it, there are plenty of places around the perimeter that are easy to get over."

"How long has it been since you've been here?" Sasha asks.

They push through the trees and walk out onto a grassy shoulder at the side of a sun-grayed, cracked road that looks like a river of ash. It gives her a slight chill, the kind of uneasy feeling that keeps children from trick-or-treating at the darkened house at the end of the cul-de-sac. Not really fear, but a kind of hesitant instinct that slows your steps and sharpens your thoughts.

"The guys and I actually came out here on my bachelor weekend before we got married," Mark tells her. "We just stayed one night in this park, but we'd come a bunch when we were kids, so we thought it would be fun to visit again."

She nods but doesn't have much of a response. They pass over the old road and walk along the other side toward the driveway leading up to a massive gray stone building set back a few hundred yards from the road. What he described as a fence is actually a heavy iron gate blocking off the driveway a couple dozen feet from the entrance. The rest of the grounds that are visible are surrounded by a brick wall with decorative finials that are likely meant to be beautiful but come across like spikes on columns set at regular intervals along it. The wall is only about six feet high, making it more than possible to scale it if they absolutely have to, but neither wants to. Not even in good weather conditions, but certainly not in the wind and snow.

They get to the driveway and find the gate closed, but the large chain that had encircled the halves hanging loose and a large padlock secured back in place on one of the halves. It looks more like someone unlocked it, went through, and didn't lock it again rather than broke or cut it. Mark pushes the gate open and they step through onto the grounds.

A shiver goes down Sasha's spine, but this time it's one of excitement. They aren't supposed to be here. That's obvious. And there's thrill in that. She likes the little bit of risk, that tiny bit of stepping outside the bounds. It brings up hints of memories from the back of her mind. They come from a long time ago, but not so long that she doesn't remember that feeling. The rush. The tingling at the base of her spine and shiver in her stomach.

Walking through the unsecured gate onto the grounds of a school that looks like it hasn't been in operation in decades doesn't have exactly the same effect as those days, but she's glad for the tingle that takes away the foreboding.

The driveway looks long as it weaves and winds its way from the road through an overgrown lawn up to the building. There's a small building off to one side; probably a shed when the school was in use. As they get closer, she catches sight of a playground off to the other side. The old-fashioned merry-go-round turns slightly with a new gust of wind and swings hanging from rusted chains sway and twist. The sight draws Sasha in, making her pause and not notice that Mark is continuing on without her.

"Come on, babe," he calls.

She looks up and sees him several yards away. She jogs to him and they continue toward the building. It's bigger and more foreboding when they get close to it, but Mark doesn't hesitate. He's comfortable with this building, with the surroundings. He knows this place and doesn't feel any reason to slow down as he takes the stone steps two at a time to get to the protective shelter of the overhang on the wide porch.

Sasha can imagine classes of pristinely dressed children arranged on the porch for a photograph to mark the school year. It appears in her mind in sepia tone, though she doesn't actually know when the school was last operational.

Just stepping under the overhang of a balcony above the porch makes her feel safer from the elements. If their tent hadn't been destroyed, they could have just set it up here, against the stone wall of the school and out of the wind, and ridden out the rest of the night without going inside. But Mark doesn't stop. He reaches for the handle on the massive double doors and pushes one open into a foyer that is far smaller than Sasha expected.

She has to remind herself that this is a school and not a sprawling house as they step inside and he shuts the door. It's so dark inside she can barely see anything in front of her. Mark reaches into the supply pack he was able to salvage from the ravaged campsite and pulls out two flashlights. They aren't just the flimsy plastic-shelled kind that his mother always keeps stashed in every room of the house for sheer terror of the electricity going out. These were built with heavy metal casings that let them withstand weather and the battering that can come from days out in the wilderness. One of them has the scrapes and chinks in the metal from a tumble down a rock ledge to prove it.

He turns on his light first, then hands the other over to Sasha. They shine their beams in opposite directions, then bring them back together to create a halo of illumination around them.

"Is there any electricity in here?" she asks, shivering.

He wants to laugh, but he can see how cold and tired she is and keeps it in.

"No. The school closed thirty years ago. There hasn't been electricity in a long time. But at least we're inside," he offers. "And we have our flashlights."

"And a couple of blankets," Sasha adds. "Not being out in the snow and wind will make it easier to stay warm."

"We have something better than that," he says.

"What do you mean?" Sasha asks.

"Follow me," Mark tells her and heads down the hallway in front of them.

Emma

The man came up behind me before putting the knife to my throat, so I didn't see his face. I'm not sure which one he is, but it doesn't really matter. There's no difference between them. Not in the greater scheme of things. It doesn't change the grotesque heat of his body pressed up against me or the hand gripping the back of my waistband to keep me in place. It doesn't change the stale breath rolling down the side of my neck as he buries his face in my hair and draws in an exaggerating, skin-crawling inhale. Or the tip of the knife pushing just a little harder now so a pinprick of pain tells me it is very sharp and he is very serious.

"I've read about you, Emma Griffin," he snarls. Then he pretends to stumble over his words like he's embarrassed by what he said. "Oh, I'm sorry. I mean *Agent* Emma Griffin. FBI. I know what people think of you. You're the jewel of the Bureau, aren't you? Their little surprise weapon. No one would expect someone who looks like you to come with a shield. Have you ever heard the phrase 'don't bring a knife to a gun fight?'" He chuckles at himself, obviously extremely amused by his own perceived cleverness. "And here's the thing. There's something else I know about you, too. I know you don't like to follow the rules. You don't like to go along with procedures and policies, do you? You like to do things your own way. You like to go places alone."

The knife twists just slightly. Not enough that it seems like he's trying to cause any serious damage, but enough to underscore his words. I still stay silent.

"And that means I have you all to myself."

CHAPTER THREE

MARK LEADS SASHA DOWN THE HALLWAY TO THE BACK OF THE huge building, explaining as they go. "When the school closed, it had already been around for about fifty years and the building was around even before that. It was originally built as a house. Some super-wealthy business tycoon or something designed it for his wife. The Boudreauxs. The story goes that they moved in planning their big, wonderful life together, and everything was good for a while."

Sasha peers left and right. There are no classrooms here, only supply closets and admin offices, and small apartments to house staff who once lived there. They pass through an open area at the apex of the hallway containing the former staff quarters and the one leading from the front of the school, and continue on toward the two kitchen spaces.

"They were happy," he continues. "They loved each other very much and the plan was to have tons of children. But he worked a lot, and it took him away from home for long stretches of time. And each of the children they'd had died at birth or shortly after. And with each one, his wife got sicker and weaker. She would walk around the house, not eating, barely speaking. All alone in this huge place. One day, her husband found her dead at the bottom of the stairs. He didn't know if she had fallen or if she had thrown herself. Maybe she'd just died of a broken heart."

"That's horrible," Sasha said absently.

Mark nodded. "He didn't make it for long after that. He killed himself in the same spot where he found his wife. After his death, his family found his will and a letter he wrote describing his desperate love for his wife and how horrible it was for him to watch her go through the deaths of each of their children. It was so painful and awful for him to lose them, but it was only compounded with the loss of the wife he lived for. He couldn't continue on in the house they'd had such big dreams for and been so happy in together.

"But he did have plans for the house. He and his wife had always wanted the house to be filled with children. It was the one thing they dreamed of and ached for more than anything in the world. And he wanted to make sure that happened. So he made it his final wish that the house be turned into a school. He left his entire will and estate to dedicate to opening the school and running it for as long as possible.

"At first, it operated as a private boarding school where students lived alongside the staff. It was meant to be a wonderful place, but there were rumors that there was a lot of abuse that happened inside these walls. Beatings. Mistreatment. Horrible things. That's why, as the story goes, the spirits of that original couple came back to haunt the halls. They hated how the children were being treated in their home. They built it with the intention of children being loved and happy there, and the abuse broke their hearts."

"People really thought there were ghosts?" Sasha asks.

"It's what they say," Mark tells her as they enter the large main kitchen and then walk through a door at the back that leads to another, smaller room. "People started hearing strange noises and seeing things they couldn't understand. Teachers who mistreated the students were involved in mysterious accidents no one could explain. One even went missing and was found dead in the storage shed outside. There was no obvious cause of death. Rumor was, he was literally scared to death."

Cold ripples along Sasha's skin and she sweeps her light around the room, taking in every corner, the simple wood cabinets on the walls, and the tables lined up in the center.

"What is this place?" she asks.

"Like I said, they had big plans, not just for a family, but for entertaining and being a pillar of the community. They always invited people around to dance in the ballroom."

"There's a ballroom here?" Sasha asks.

Mark chuckles softly and nods. "Yes. It isn't a ballroom anymore. They turned it into the school gym, but it used to be a ballroom. There are also two kitchens. This one was used mostly for prep, to keep it out of the way of the rest of the place. The big draw of it for us tonight is that." He shines his flashlight across the room to show her the large fireplace taking up a considerable part of the far wall. "We can get a fire going and it will keep us warm."

"Is that safe?"

A sudden loud sound somewhere outside the room makes her jump and gasp. She turns her light toward the door to the smaller kitchen space, which they left open, but she doesn't see anything. She wants to go close the door, but doesn't want to seem like she's afraid. Mark is never afraid. He smiles at her now.

"It's fine. There are probably a few animals that had the same idea about getting out of the storm that we did. They're not going to bother us any more in here than they would have if we were sleeping out in our tent."

Sasha knows that's true and it makes sense, but it somehow seems more threatening to think of being in a closed building with wildlife than it does to just be out in a tent. She doesn't hear anything else, so she turns her attention back to the fireplace. Mark is already crouched down in front of it, shining his flashlight inside to look at it and the chimney.

"What are we going to burn?" she asks. "I guess we probably could have brought the remnants of our tent."

He chuckles at her snippy sarcasm and points his flashlight to the corner where someone has piled wood. They aren't evenly cut logs, but obviously branches, twigs, and parts of fallen trees that were gathered up from the forest floor and brought in.

"Remember, we aren't the first ones to visit here," he tells her. "I figure not as many people come out here anymore, but clearly someone has recently. The last time the guys and I were here we brought some wood in from our hike up here. There were a couple of pieces already in here and we left what we didn't use."

"It's like the take-a-penny, leave-a-penny jar of illegal overnight accommodations," Sasha remarks.

"Something like that. I prefer to think of it as members of the same outdoorsman community coming together and cooperating so more can experience these places," he says.

"Of course, you do," she says.

He builds the framework of the fire and pulls a starter out of his pack. It's made of wax melted down over a lump of dryer lint with a cotton swab dipped in nail polish remover and coated in wax as a wick. The device looks strange and doesn't exactly fit with the guidelines and rules the Girl Scouts taught her when she was young, but both know the odd-looking lump will go up in an instant. Then it will burn hot and powerful enough for a few moments to catch anything it's around, making it perfect for getting a strong fire going fast even in not the best of conditions.

This is the kind of starter they bring along with them when there's a forecast of rain. Last summer, a starter just like this one got a fire roaring when the clouds were rolling in and droplets were starting to fall, then the fire kept going right through the downpour. They stood in the zipped mesh front portion of the tent they'd had at the time, watching the fire fight to survive the onslaught of water. The manufacturer had the gall to call that little space with its total mesh surroundings and zipper flap leading into the rest of the tent the "living room."

And they loved it.

It was ridiculous. It kept bugs away, but only if they never opened that part of it. They could stand in it and watch the rain, but only if they didn't mind getting misted with the cold remnants of the droplets split by hitting the mesh. But they loved it.

And it gave them the perfect place to watch that fire fight through the rain. The storm eventually battered it down to only glowing embers down deep in the mound of wood they'd built up, but it was still impressive to see that fire still going. She carried that memory with her, bringing it up sometimes when she felt like there was something insurmountable in front of her.

The fire jumps to life and almost instantly the warmth starts to ease the sharp chill on her skin. Sasha steps up closer to it and takes off her wet gloves so she can hold her hands out toward the orange glow. When her shivering has stopped and she feels more relaxed, she looks around at the small kitchen. She can feel the history in the stones. She can see the staff scurrying around preparing elaborate meals for the happy, loving couple that didn't know they were doomed so long ago, and then another staff preparing far simpler food for the children and administration that turned this place from a home to a school.

"What else do you know about the school?" she asks.

Mark sits down on the stone floor in front of the fireplace and absently pokes at the wood with a long stick burned black on one end from being used for this purpose many times before.

"After the teacher was found dead in the storage shed, the conditions of the school became public knowledge. Staff and former students started to talk. People found out what was really going on inside the walls. Of course, some families didn't believe what they'd heard. They said it was just rumors, and their own children didn't say anything was wrong.

"Some families were pretty dismissive about it. They figured discipline builds character, and that was why they'd sent their kids here in the first place. They would point to how they have these kinds of schools in England and the success there. They thought the horror stories they were hearing were just exaggerations, even if their kids told them about the conditions.

"Then there were the families who were horrified by what happened. They didn't know anything like that was going on at the school they thought was going to be the best thing possible for their children's education and lives. They wanted their kids to be successful. They had no idea their kids were being mistreated like that."

"Didn't they ever visit?" Sasha asks.

"Not often. They had family weekends twice a semester and they had holidays, but the administrators had threatened the children. They'd tell them their parents didn't care what they were experiencing, that they sent them to the school knowing what was going to happen, and they deserved it. And if they complained about it, their parents would just be angry and things would be even worse, so they stayed quiet."

"Jesus. I can't imagine that the parents liked hearing that."

"Oh yeah, they were furious. They forced the school to close and I've heard some of the administration was even arrested. The school was empty for a while and then it reopened as a private kindergarten through twelfth grade school that catered to the wealthy people around here. But just as a day school. No one was interested in another boarding school and the people reopening the school didn't want to revisit any of that history. I've seen some of the brochures and stuff from when the day school was still in operation. They talked about the building being a home, but never talked about the deaths, and they talked about the former boarding school, but just said that it closed after many years of operation."

"Just glossed over everything, didn't they?" Sasha asks.

"Yes, they did. But apparently the new school was everything the Boudreauxs would have wanted it to be. The students were happy, the parents loved it."

"So, what happened? Why did that one close?"

"That's another mystery. Supposedly there was a teacher here who got too friendly with some of his students. Other people say a girl was murdered and it was covered up," Mark says. "I never really looked into it that much and I guess it's not as interesting as the earlier stories, so people don't really talk about it. It's possible the school just closed because fewer people enrolled their kids in it. A reclusive private school for all the grades up until college might seem convenient, but it doesn't exactly fit in with what most people think of when it comes to their children's education."

"But it didn't close recently," Sasha points out. "You said it closed, what, thirty years ago? Something like that? School was different then. My grandmother talked about how she went to a school that taught all the grades from the beginning of school up through eighth grade. And my grandfather went to one that was all the grades, like this one. They came from really small towns, but I'm guessing around here didn't have exactly a booming population decades ago."

"That's true. All I know is it closed decades ago and hasn't been used for anything else since. A while ago there was some talk about an investor wanting to turn it into apartments or something, but it never went anywhere."

"I can't really imagine people wanting to live in an apartment in a building like this out in the middle of a technically closed park," Sasha points out. "It's not like there's a whole lot around here to build up the appeal."

"There are a few houses a couple miles behind the school and one or two actually in the limits of the park, but, yeah, you're probably right." Mark laughs. "You want to go look around?"

Sasha peers over her shoulder at the dark outline of the door. She's caught in a moment of internal conflict, going back and forth between the uneasiness the building immediately caused her and the curiosity that always comes back. It's not much different than the woods, rock formations, and grottoes they've explored before. The curiosity wins over. She looks at him with a grin.

"Let's go."

Emma

The man's hand tightens on my waistband, giving me a little tug as he does it. I subtly move my feet a bit further apart so my hips put pressure on the rest of the band, keeping it close to my body. He moves to the side just enough that I'm able to slide my eyes over and catch a glimpse of him out of my peripheral vision. I can't be positive, but I think I know who he is now.

He doesn't have a name. At least, not one that is ever spoken among the people he's chosen to spend his time with. I'm sure there's one floating around in his memory, one that maybe his mother still says if she has anything to do with him. I don't know if she would, if she knew the kind of person her baby boy turned out to be. And yet, there have been plenty of families knit together on the premise of greed and blood. Children born and raised to be a part of what the generations before them started.

Whoever he was before this moment, I only know of him as Bam Bam. It's what his boss referred to him as, and what the other guys called him. A name that has to have a story behind it, and one people probably don't want to know. One I can make a guess at.

"You think you're so brave coming out here by yourself trying to stand up to us," Bam Bam sneers. "But you should have thought about it better. You don't know the kind of trouble you can get into without someone there to back you up. But you're here now. So let's have some fun together."

CHAPTER FOUR

THEY STAND UP AND SASHA LOOKS AT THE FIRE. "SHOULD WE PUT that out before we go anywhere?"

Mark shakes his head. "It's fine. The floor and the walls are stone. It's not going to catch even if an ember jumps out of the fire, and I highly doubt that's going to happen."

"What about that wood over in the corner?" she asks with a sarcastic note.

"If the fire gets out and walks over there to light that wood on fire, then it deserves it," he says. He winks at her. "Let's go."

Both armed with their flashlights, they leave the small prep kitchen and walk back into the larger kitchen. As soon as they step through the doorway they leave the warmth and glow of the fire and seem to walk through a tangible division into the dark and cold of the rest of the building. The few minutes they spent thawing out and knowing they are inside rather than facing the storm outside, though, gives them both a feeling of security and confidence, making it easier to tolerate the chill as they venture into the dim hallways to see what they can discover.

"How much of this place have you gone through?" Sasha asks.

"Quite a bit of it," he says. "It was changed a lot over the years with all the different purposes the building had, so there are some strange configurations of the rooms in places. And there are a lot of things that were just left when they closed the school. At least, there were the last time I was here."

"Just left? What do you mean? What kinds of things?"

Mark shines his flashlight on the nearby wall of the hallway, illuminating framed photographs and sketches hung every couple of feet that are now covered in dust and cobwebs.

"There's a trophy case around here, too. Academic trophies, mostly, but some for things like archery and rowing, too. There isn't a lake on the property, so I'm guessing they used the lake in the park for that. The last time I saw it, there were only a couple of trophies in there. It looked like they took the other ones when the school closed. Maybe they gave them to the families of kids who had won them," Mark says.

They continue down the hall and Mark points out a door to one side. They try it and it opens easily. Sasha steps in first, shining her flashlight around. She's excited now, enjoying the tingly thrill of exploring the building where they shouldn't be, seeing these things that had been left behind with the thought of never being seen again. She wonders about the last person to walk through what she realizes now is the front office of the school, the domain of the principal, vice principal, and secretaries.

She walks around the massive desk at the front of the room, the first imposing piece of furniture anyone coming into the office would have encountered. She imagines the secretary who used to sit there, all prim dresses and hairspray-cemented updos with dark-rimmed glasses and lipstick she carefully dabbed each morning and after lunch so it was there but not too much.

"I wonder who the last person to use the office was," she muses, coming around to open up the drawers on the other side of the desk. "Think it was the secretary?"

"Maybe," Mark says. "She might have been responsible for getting the records and everything sorted. Or maybe it was the principal. Kind of saying goodbye."

"Let's check out his office," Sasha says.

They go past the secretary's desk and the little odds and ends of office materials she'd left in her drawers all those years ago—paperclips and pens, a couple of loose staples—and into the hallway to the side she figured would lead to the private office of the head of the school. She's right and is rewarded with a heavy wooden door with deep scrollwork that gives her the impression this might have once been the study of the man who designed this as a sprawling house for the woman he loved so much.

This door is closed and Sasha hesitates for a brief second before taking the doorknob. It almost feels like she's interrupting something by going inside. Unlike the front part of the office, this private chamber has two large windows, providing some respite from the deep darkness. The snow outside is still falling heavily, but the flakes and the thickening blanket forming on the ground are reflecting the moonlight, amplifying it so it seems like the grounds around the building are lit up.

"It feels different in here," Mark whispers.

He's not sure why his voice dropped or why he doesn't feel like he can make it any louder while they're standing there in the cavernous office. It's not like the principal's offices he remembers from when he was in school. He wasn't a frequent flier of the administrative offices, but he'd had a brush or two with the principals as he was growing up. It was all harmless. Skipping class. A senior prank. Sneaking into the girls' locker room after school. There weren't even any girls in there. Just the janitor who came in and ratted them out to the principal the next day.

There are no terrible memories of his visits to traumatize him into being uncomfortable in the office, but he can't deny the eerie feeling that settles over him as they walk around taking in the discarded pieces of furniture and the frames still hanging on the wall. A couple of them are empty, which strikes him as odd. The others have pictures of men he assumes held leadership positions throughout the various eras of the school. Others have documents he can't quite read in the darkness but might be degrees or award certificates. A bookshelf against one wall has been largely emptied, the few remaining volumes tipped over like they've been picked through and hastily discarded.

"You'd think they would have emptied these rooms out," he says, fingering the spines of a couple of the books.

His sister collects antique books and he wonders if she might be interested in any of these if they are old enough. Almost as quickly as that thought goes through his mind, he pushes it away. He doesn't want to steal from the school. He can't explain why, but it was left this way for a reason. Even if he doesn't really buy into the whole idea of ghosts lurking around the old building, it feels like this place has its own life. It's sacred in a way. It shouldn't be damaged, and if he was to take anything from it, he feels like something, he doesn't know what, would come along with it. He doesn't want to find out what that meant.

"If they were just closing up the school and not moving to a new facility, they really didn't need any of it," Sasha says. "And even if they were moving to a different facility, it would have all new stuff. You said the school catered to wealthy families. If that's the case, then they wouldn't need to bring old furniture and things around with them. They would get everything new with the new building."

"I guess that makes sense," Mark says. "But what about the pictures and stuff like that? You'd think they'd at least remove that."

Sasha opens the top drawer of the desk and finds it empty. The next has a few old office supplies much like the ones left in the secretary's desk. The third has metal tracks along the sides to hold up folders she assumes once held student records. There are still a couple of folders, but they don't have any documents inside. It seems the records either went to a new school facility or were destroyed. The large bottom drawer on the other side holds a single, large leather-bound book.

"Look at this," she says, taking the book out of the drawer and setting it on the desk so she can hold her flashlight over it and get a better look. She reads the embossed letters in the thick leather cover. "Dawn Day School. It looks like some sort of scrapbook or something. Why would they leave this?"

She opens the cover and looks inside. An inscription in old-fashioned handwriting is faded by the years and more difficult to read.

"In gratitude for dedicated service to the families of Dawn Day School," Mark reads. "I can't read the name, but I'm guessing it was the principal at the time."

"I guess he wasn't but so dedicated if he left this here," Sasha remarks.

They flip through the pages of the book, scanning over old pictures of smiling children, progress of renovations being made to the building, and other chronicles of the days of the school. Toward the end of the book a caption explains that several items were found during some of the renovations that show the history of the school. The next pages contain various items that look like they come from the private home of the Boudreaux couple.

Handwritten notes and lists are even more difficult to read than the inscription in the front of the book, the whispery handwriting soft and gray against the thick cream-colored paper like mosquitos. On some of them, a date is visible, putting the writing of them back more than a century. It fits in with the story Mark told Sasha about the creation of the school, and his eyebrows lift slightly when he sees the dates and the few scattered words he can decipher that seem to align with the details he'd been told.

"These look like receipts. Can you imagine trying to heat this place with coal?" he asks, pointing out a collection of slips attached to one of the pages with little black adhesive corners, which remind him of the photo albums that sat on his grandmother's coffee table when he was little. They're probably still there, untouched, but appreciated for their existence. "Look. This one is for a delivery of wine and champagne."

Sasha brings her light closer and leans down to read the receipt for herself. "Wow. That's a lot of bottles."

"It must have been for one of those galas in the ballroom," he says. "Looks like it was in February. Maybe they were celebrating Valentine's Day."

Sasha smiles at her husband. "Awww. That's sweet."

He smiles back and leans in for a kiss. Their lips are melting into each other when they hear the loud sound they'd heard when they were in the kitchen. Sasha gasps involuntarily and grabs onto Mark, pulling back away from him at the same time as pulling herself closer. His hands go to her hips, squeezing them in a protective gesture that turns comforting when the sound doesn't happen again.

"I want to know what that is," he says. "Come on."

For a second, she thinks she should protest. This seems like it could be dangerous. They have no idea who else could be inside the building, or if there's an animal that has gotten trapped and is angry. it probably isn't the best idea to hear a strange sound and go toward it. And yet, it's that very suggestion that keeps her curiosity front and center rather than allowing any of the fear that had trickled in to take control again.

"Let me put this back," she says, picking up the book.

She goes to set it back in the drawer and realizes there's something else in the corner. She reaches in and her hand touches something with a strange, almost indescribable texture. It's spongy and firm, yet somewhat soft at the same time. When she pulls it out, she immediately drops it on the top of the desk.

"What is it?" Mark asks.

"Oh, god. That is so disgusting. Is that real?" Sasha asks.

The lump on the desk looks like tissue. Even in the dark the shape and uneven texture on the top tells her with no uncertainty what it is. She cringes and turns slightly away as Mark leans closer to it.

"No. It can't be," he says.

"Why not?" she asks.

"How would a *tongue* get in a desk drawer in a school that's been closed for decades?" he asks.

"You say that as if finding a tongue anywhere else would make perfect sense and would be no cause for alarm," Sasha says. "And where did the wood in the kitchen come from?"

"I know, other people brought it in. But that's being helpful and offering something that other visitors will be able to use. It's not a *tongue*. And look at it, it's not even the right color or anything. I really don't think it's real. It's probably some sort of prop," Mark offers.

"A prop?" she asks.

"There have been a couple of times when people decided to use the school for different projects because of the creepy atmosphere. I know that at least one bad no-budget horror film was partially filmed here, and a group put on a Halloween attraction one year. The Halloween attraction was authorized, but it was only put on for that one year. I wonder if it was just too intense or too much of a possibility of damaging the structure.

"The horror film production didn't even ask permission to make their movie here. They just showed up and set up shop. They only got part of the movie made before the police came and shut it down. The group ended up on the news talking about how the whole property should be accessible to the public because it's so useful and could be turned into something, but it's instead just being left to fall apart. Of course, that meant literally nothing to anyone in control and it's still empty," Mark says. "But I'm going to venture a guess that this thing was from one of those projects. Then somebody found it and thought it would be funny to put in the desk. Or maybe it was even in the desk for the movie. It's fine."

"Well…"

"It's fine," he repeats. "Come on. I want to go explore more."

For good measure, Mark tosses the tongue back into the drawer and sets the book down on top of it. Sasha continues to stare into the drawer, swallowing hard to force down her nausea.

Emma

I let Bam Bam pull me backward, away from the wall where I was standing just inches from the corner I'd been looking around before he walked up. The movement is enough to lessen up the pressure on the tip of the knife and ease the pain. I don't feel blood coming from it, so I don't think he's broken the skin.

I'll take that as a bonus for now. I have a feeling it's going to change soon.

As he pushes me in front of him so that I walk down the dark hallway, I take a moment to mentally scan my body, making sure I can feel everything I need to feel. Bam Bam doesn't say anything but guides me with the pressure of his hand on my pants. Everything in me wants to fight back against the feeling of his hand there and the push of his knuckles into my lower back. But I stop myself. I need to control every movement and every reaction. If I am going to get through this, I have to handle myself carefully.

CHAPTER FIVE

"That's seriously sick," Sasha says, shuddering again as the thought of the tongue, fake or not, goes through her mind again.

"Horror movies aren't generally designed to be heartwarming," Mark says.

They leave the office and move deeper into the building. Sasha notices the lack of windows even more as they walk through the darkness. Even in the classrooms that are standing open, windows are few and far between. The ones that are there are curved like turrets and surrounded by metal cages. In a way it seems they're meant to be decorative, but it doesn't change the fact that they are bars.

It makes the building seem even more like a castle, fortified and impenetrable. They venture into one of the classrooms and find the desks still in a row, facing the chalkboard at the front. Signs of other visitors fill the board, signatures and little messages, some symbols likely meant to look frightening in some way. Pieces of chalk sit in the tray at the bottom waiting for others to come and add to the living mural. Those pieces aren't from when the school was in operation. They were brought there with this in mind.

Mark walks up to the board and picks up one of the pieces of chalk. He writes their names in a small empty area of the gray slate and doodles little caricatures of them, adding their wedding anniversary. Sasha takes the chalk and adds her own note, surrounding it with a heart. She loves their little shared moments like this, when they can be silly and cute and not worry about anyone thinking they need to act more like adults. She never really understood that admonition, anyway. They are adults. Any way they act is acting like adults.

The next couple of classrooms show more signs of the school being shut down. The desks had been piled up at the back of the room rather than still being set out. There are fewer decorations up on the walls and the teacher's desk has several boxes set on top of it as if the instructor had started to pack up in preparation of bringing their things with them on that last day and then changed their mind when those final moments passed.

It seems like former visitors had chosen that first classroom and reconstructed it on purpose rather than it being left that way.

The eerie feeling of thinking of the last people to use these rooms returns as they walk into the nurse's office. Sasha feels a little shiver pushing back a dark green curtain that separates the waiting area from two brown upholstered cots in a dark corner. She thinks of the children who used this area, the ailments they dealt with. She wonders how many of them were there just to get out of their classrooms for a few moments and how many were seriously ill.

That thought is particularly sobering when she remembers the years the school was operational. There were so many childhood diseases at that time that could have horrific consequences. She can't help but imagine children lying on the beds, suffering from something they might not have even understood, and think that a couple of them might not have ever had the chance to recover.

"Hey, check this out," Mark calls over, breaking Sasha out of her thoughts.

She finds him in front of an old metal filing cabinet. It's positioned in a corner behind the simple wooden table that acted as the nurse's desk as if being guarded. Mark has one of the drawers open and is shining his flashlight down into it as he flips through folders inside.

"Are those records?" she asks.

"Yeah, it looks like it. The principal must have made sure that the records of the students were taken out of his office when the school closed, but these ones were just left," he tells her.

"Great job with the privacy protection, huh?" Sasha mutters as she joins in searching through the folders.

"But that's not going to stop you?" Mark teases.

She looks up at him and blinks. "No."

It's like peering into the past as they peek at the names and complaints of the children who passed through this clinic, resting on the cots, receiving medication and first aid from the nurse. Some of the files are thicker than others, revealing the children who were either perpetually sickly or the ones who leaned hard into hypochondria. The amount of students who appeared in the office frequently in search of cleaning and bandaging for scrapes and scratches, or ice packs for bumps and bruises, is concerning.

"This one just says 'distress' as the reason this girl came into the clinic," Mark says, showing her an old form from one of the folders.

"This one, too," Sasha says, holding another sheet next to the one he's holding to compare the two notes. "Look, they're from the same day."

"1956," he murmurs, reading the date at the top of the page. "That's around when the school shut down."

"Distressed because another girl at the school was murdered?" Sasha suggests.

Mark shrugs. "I don't know."

Before either of them can say anything else, there's a strange thud out in the hallway beyond the clinic, followed by a series of smaller popping sounds. They look at each other and put the papers away before heading for the doorway.

"Hello?" Sasha calls out into the hall.

Her voice grows in the emptiness of their surroundings, seeming to travel in all directions and disappear around corners and into open rooms. There's no response. They swing their flashlights back and forth and Mark sees something toward the end of the hall. He reaches out and grabs hold of Sasha's arm to get her attention.

"Look."

She follows his gaze and sees something a few yards away, near a bend in the hall that leads deeper into the school.

"Is that a ball?" Sasha asks. They move toward it. "Like a playground ball?"

They walk up to it and see that it is indeed a blue rubber ball sitting on the floor in the middle of the hallway.

"Where did that come from?" Mark asks, glancing around like there's going to be some easy explanation of the ball's origin.

"Was that the sound?" Sasha asks. "I don't think it was here before."

"We probably just didn't notice it," Mark says.

Sasha pins her flashlight between her arm and body to free up her hands and reaches down to pick up the ball. She holds it for a second, then drops it onto the floor. It creates the same thud they'd heard and as it bounces a couple more times, moving away from them, they hear the same little pops.

"That was the sound we heard," she says.

Mark turns, sweeping his flashlight into every corner, trying to penetrate as much of the darkness as he can to find anyone who might be lurking there watching them. He doesn't see anything.

"Maybe it was in one of the classrooms propped up against something and we jostled it while we were in there. It could have just fallen."

"And come out into the hallway?" Sasha asks. She shines her flashlight around the corner where the ball was sitting. It's another hall of classrooms leading down toward a set of large doors. "Is that the ballroom?"

Mark snickers. "Do you think the ball came from there?"

She shoots him a glare and starts down the hall. Something behind them sounds like a door closing. It doesn't slam, but it's loud enough to make them stop and turn around.

"Did you notice any broken windows? Anywhere wind could have come in?" Sasha asks.

"There had to be one," Mark says. "That has to be why it's so cold in here."

They both know that doesn't make sense, but neither acknowledges it.

As they move further down the hall, a smell enters Sasha's nose and makes it wrinkle. It gets stronger as they continue. She holds the back of her hand up to her nose to block it.

"Do you smell that?" she asks. "What is that?"

The sickly sweet, oppressive smell seems to be coming from further down the hall, and despite the sick feeling in her stomach, Sasha follows it. Like the rooms in the first hallway, the doors along this hall are standing open. Near the end of the hall, however, the door to one is mostly closed. Mark steps up to it and shines his flashlight directly in front of him as he presses his palm to the door and pushes it open.

At first, nothing seems different about this room than any of the others except for the strong smell. He knows the smell. It's one he's encountered before in his camping trips and hiking expeditions. It's not one that anyone wants to run into, but it's usually nothing more than something unpleasant to come upon. The smell of death and decay. Mark's first thought as he steps over the threshold into the classroom is that an animal came into the school looking for shelter and either got stuck inside or was already hurt and ended up dying in the corner of the classroom.

It's a sad thought, not something he particularly wants to come face-to-face with, but also something he can't just walk away from. Sasha's curiosity mirrors his own. The strange smell, the sounds, the uncomfortable feeling. It is only making him want to venture further and find the source of it all.

He never felt this way when he came during his younger years. There were scribbles on the chalkboards, and sometimes they found things like beer bottles sitting in the corners or food wrappers they collected so the building wouldn't be destroyed. Once they found someone sleeping in piles of sleeping bags, surrounded by supplies like he'd decided to just move into the school.

It wouldn't be so unexpected to find something that ended its life here. What he didn't expect was Sasha's scream.

Emma

I can hear the voices of the other men before I can see the glow of light around the edges of the door ahead of me. They are laughing, getting louder and bolder as they compare notes of their most recent conquests and the plans they have for the money they got from the job they just finished. It's the one code they use. *Job.* They didn't do any work. They didn't earn the money now probably stacked in front of them.

"Hey, guys," Bam Bam calls out when we're a few feet away from the door. "Guess what I got? Somebody open the door."

He knows he can't let go of my waistband or the handle of the knife to take the doorhandle, or it will give me the opportunity to escape. He doesn't know I already have the opportunity. I always have.

CHAPTER SIX

THE SOUND CUTS THROUGH MARK AND INSTANTLY SPARKS A feeling of protectiveness in him. There is nothing that could make him back down if Sasha is in danger. It is the only thing in the world that makes him feel that way. But she isn't in danger. Nothing is threatening her. Nothing is chasing her. She's standing in the same place she had been.

Only now she's staring at the desk in front of her and the badly decomposed corpse propped up in it.

The body is in such bad condition it's difficult to tell whether it was once a man or a woman, though the clothing suggests it's a man. The cold will have thwarted some of the decay, but it doesn't stop it; the body is discolored and breaking down. There's nothing that immediately suggests what happened to the person, but Mark highly doubts they walked into the classroom, sat down at the desk, and simply died.

"We have to get help," Sasha says. "We have to get somebody."

Mark nods. "Come on. We'll go toward the neighborhood. I think that's the closest place."

They run down the hallway and turn the corner to run down the front hall. They reach the front doors that they walked into just a couple of hours before, but they won't open. Mark makes sure the doors are unlocked and tries again. He can feel some give behind the resistance and pulls as hard as he can. He finally puts his boot against the wall to give himself leverage and another hard pull forces the door open.

Immediately a harsh rush of wind blasts stinging snow into their faces. The cold and the flakes push them back into the building. There's no way they'll be able to walk anywhere. They shut the door and Mark looks at Sasha.

"The storm wasn't supposed to last all night. It will stop soon and by morning we'll be able to get out."

"Morning?" she sputters incredulously. "You think I'm going to stay here with a body until morning?"

"You don't have a choice," he says. "Neither of us do. We wouldn't be able to see anything out there and we don't have our cold weather gear. We wouldn't make it even to the nearest house. We have to wait until the snow stops and the temperature goes up a little so we can survive the walk. It's not going to do us any good to go out there and die in the snow."

"Then what the hell are we supposed to do?" she asks.

Mark takes her by her upper arms, the movement making the beam of his flashlight shoot up toward the ceiling and illuminate half of her face. The tears pooling beneath her eye sparkle in the light.

"I need you to calm down. Just take a deep breath and settle down for a second."

"Calm down? Don't tell me to calm down," she snaps. "There's a corpse in that classroom. A dead person just sitting in one of the desks and I promise you, they didn't put themselves there. Someone *put* them there. Or made sure they didn't move from there."

"I know," Mark tells her. "I know. But that is not a fresh body." Sasha groans and Mark gives her a slight shake to force her to continue paying attention to him. "He's been dead for a while. We're going to just hunker down here for the night and leave as soon as we can. It's going to be fine."

It's the same words he'd used earlier when they were in the kitchen. They don't sound the same now.

"Okay," Sasha says. "We'll just…"

The rest of the sentence disappears into her cry as a crash like an explosion echoes from down the hallway. Mark wraps his arms around her, squeezing her tight.

"Shhhh. It's the desks falling. Remember? Remember the desks stacked up? One of them must have shifted and it caused the rest of them to topple. There's no one around here. If they were here, they would have come out. Right? Right?"

He's trying to convince himself as much as he is her. He sharpens his awareness, paying close attention to everything around him without letting Sasha see it. He wants her to see him calm and in control. He doesn't want her to know how much fear is pumping through his veins.

"Right," Sasha finally relents.

"Good. Alright. Let's go back to the kitchen. I'm getting cold. Aren't you cold?" he asks. She nods. "Okay. We'll go back there and sit by the fire. It'll feel good to warm up and maybe we can get some sleep before morning."

He's pretending everything is normal even though he knows it's not. But it's all he can do. He has to push the reality of what they saw away. He has to ignore it and focus on just this moment. They start back toward the hall that leads to the kitchen and Sasha hesitates.

"The clinic," she whispers, holding tight to his arm. "The door was open when we left."

The door is closed now, latched into place.

"I must have closed it on my way out," he tells her even though he knows he didn't. He was the first to walk out and she followed behind him. "We just weren't paying attention."

They start walking again when the familiar thud and popping sound makes them stop. They freeze in place, their backs to the sound, unwilling to move. Her breath rattles in her lungs and his blood rushes in his ears. They stand like children. If they can't see what's there, it isn't.

Finally, they draw in a simultaneous deep breath and turn around. Another rubber ball, red this time, rolls across the floor. They watch until it comes to a stop and its lack of movement triggers them. They run for the hallway, their flashlight beams bouncing and shaking erratically with their frantic pace.

As they run through the kitchen, Mark miscalculates the space and smashes into the corner of a metal counter in the center of the room. Pain races from his hip down his leg and he stumbles. Sasha grabs onto him, dragging him the rest of the way into the smaller kitchen and slamming the door behind them. There's no lock on the door and she grabs one of the large wooden tables and starts to pull it across the floor. It's heavy and she struggles trying to move it, the feeling of whomever else is in the building with them making her heart race.

She can feel them coming. She hears something that sounds like footsteps in the kitchen.

"Help me," she pleads.

Mark fights the pain to get on the other side of the table and push the table forward. It finally starts moving and they're able to get it across the door, barricading it so it can't be opened from the other side. They both expect to hear the door slam against it as someone tries to open it. They step back from the table, backing toward the fire, waiting for the door to move.

It remains still.

The silence only intensifies her anxiety. The anticipation makes her stomach twist and her heart pound so hard in her chest it makes her feel dizzy. It gets to the point where she wants the door to move. She wants it to open and hit the table, to hear the sound, to hear the person on the other side. It horrifies her to think of it happening, but if it does, she doesn't have to wait for it anymore. The anticipation will be gone, the tension broken, and all that will be left to do is react.

Emma

The door in front of us opens and I see several men sitting at a large table covered with bound bundles of money, drug paraphernalia, and weapons. The firearms don't scare me. I know they aren't loaded. Those aren't for battle. They are for sale. The ammunition is kept elsewhere, handled much like the accessories for children's toys. Sold separately. They take this approach for several reasons. One is purely profit driven. They can make more money by selling the gun and the ammunition as two separate pieces than as a set. It's also a safety precaution. It's generally not a good idea to hand someone a high-powered weapon that is already loaded, but it is especially dangerous when there is a large amount of money involved. The kinds of people who do business with these men are the same kind who would be more than happy to accept the gun and then use it to steal back the money they just handed over.

The man who opened the door looks out at us and raises his eyebrows. He looks as surprised as he should. The last thing he probably expected to see when he opened the door for his associate is Bam Bam holding a knife to the throat of the FBI agent who has been tracking them.

"What's going on?" a voice asks from behind the man whose name I don't know. He must be fairly new to the group.

But I know that voice. I've heard it through surveillance equipment and recordings over the course of months. The new man steps aside and I see the face belonging to the voice. Lyle McCormick. High up in the hierarchy, though not quite at the top, and bulging with the arrogance and over-confidence this gave him, Lyle leans back in his chair and gives me a grotesque smile. He runs his tongue across his teeth, sucking at them as he looks me up and down, undoubtedly concocting any number of horrific things he'd like to do now that he has me in his grasp.

"Oh. We have a guest. I didn't realize we were expecting company. Come on in, Agent."

Bam Bam pushes me forward so I stumble a few steps into the room. I glance around without moving my head enough to worsen the press of the knife blade. It's a delicate balance between wanting to collect as much information as I can and knowing my time is limited, and I'm very aware of walking along that thin line. As Lyle pushes back from the table, I ready myself.

I don't know if it's something in my expression that unwittingly gives me away or if he is just abundantly cautious, but Lyle hesitates when he gets to his feet. He looks me up and down, narrows his eyes, and looks to Bam Bam.

"Did you check her?" he asks.

The beat of hesitation from the man still holding onto me is enough to change the energy of the moment, of the entire room. Lyle's posture changes. His head leans slightly toward Bam Bam.

"No."

And that's it. Time is up.

CHAPTER SEVEN

NOTHING HAPPENS. MARK AND SASHA LOOK AT EACH OTHER. They hope the other can say something that will make this better. Neither can explain it. Neither can say what will change or when.

They don't say anything, but move backward toward the fire, eventually finding each other and melting down onto the floor. The measly blankets they were able to salvage from the destroyed tent are dry now and feel warm between them and the slate floor, but they can't rest. The room feels far safer than being out in the rest of the school, but not truly safe.

Mark knows this building far better than Sasha, but even he hasn't been here in years, and before that his visits weren't exactly frequent. He'd come a few times and explored, but for no more than a couple of hours at a time.

Someone is in this building with them. Someone who has likely spent far more time in the school than Mark has. That means they know it better; they are familiar with it in a different way. They might know something about the room they are in now that Mark doesn't know, something that makes them less safe than they even thought and with nothing they can do about it.

He dreads morning.

When morning comes, they have to try to escape. They have to find a way out of the school and then through the grounds and to the nearest phone they can find to call the police. He brought Sasha here because he thought they would be protected. He thought they would be comfortable and warm, and in the morning when the storm had subsided and they had gotten more rest, they would be able to make their way out of the park and back to their car. It shouldn't be that hard.

Now he's afraid they won't get out of the school without whomever is here descending on them. And that is if they make it until morning.

Mark doesn't know how long they've been sitting there, staring at the door, when he realizes that Sasha is sagged against him. The cold, exhaustion, and adrenaline dump have gotten to her and she has collapsed into sleep in his arms. He's still on edge. False energy — nothing more than the protectiveness coursing through his body preventing him from relaxing—brings him to ease his wife onto the floor, cover her up, and start to pace.

As long as he's pacing, he feels under control. As long as he's pacing, his mind and body are ready to defend them both.

He paces for as long as his legs will support him, then sits back down beside Sasha to wait.

He feels like he's checked his watch a thousand times to count the seconds ticking by when he finally sees it's morning. The sun is likely not fully up outside and the temperature will still be unbearable, but they can survive a short walk if they move quickly. It's their only choice. They have to get out of here.

He wakes Sasha up.

"Come on, babe. It's morning. We've got to go."

They collect the few supplies they brought along with them and stir the weak flames that remain into the ashes and wood to extinguish them.

"How are we going to get out?" Sasha asks.

Mark looks around the room. Weak early-sunrise light is filtering through one window on the wall shared by the fireplace. But it has the same bars as the windows toward the front of the school.

"Do you think you could fit through those?" Mark asks, indicating the bars. They aren't right up against each other, and he thinks it might be possible for her to get through if she squeezes hard enough.

"I might," she nods.

To get to the bars, the glass has to be gone. Mark takes one of the logs left in the corner and smashes out the window glass. It takes more force than he expected, but eventually he has an open space giving access to several of the bars. Stepping aside, he gives Sasha room to try to push through the bars. She steps up to the window and peers outside.

The snow is beautiful. Pristine and fresh, it sparkles in even the faint light. It's the kind of snow that always makes her want to make snow angels and collect it for snowcream. The rich concoction made by sprinkling sugar and vanilla over snow has always been one of her mother's favorite ways to mark rare snowfall. But right now, Sasha is looking for footprints, for blood, for anything that might reveal someone has already been walking around in the early morning hours.

She doesn't see anything, and with the snowfall obviously over, she's confident no one is right outside. Climbing up onto the table just beneath the window, she puts her head and shoulders through the gap between the bars first. Somewhere she heard if you can get your head and shoulders through a space, you can get the rest of your body through as well. She doesn't remember where she heard that or if she believes it. Right now it doesn't matter. She has to try.

She tries to avoid the broken glass as she climbs through, but she feels it bite into her hands and push through at the ends of her sleeves. The cold of the metal is intense when she grabs onto the bars to try to pull herself through. Her upper body fits and she moves forward slightly to test her hips. When it seems like they may fit, she moves back across the table and turns to look at Mark.

"You try. I think I can get through," she says.

"Then you need to go," he says. "If you can get through, just go. Head for the back of the building and find the old..."

She interrupts him.

"No. I'm not going anywhere without you."

Mark lifts his voice a little higher.

"Go to the back of the building and find the old parking lot. Go through it and..."

"I'm not going without you."

"Go straight through the woods and it will eventually bring you out to a neighborhood. There's also an old access road. I can't confirm the condition that it's in or if cars ever use it for anything else, so your best bet would probably be to go through the woods. But if you just stay on the road, you should be fine."

"Mark, I am not going anywhere without you," Sasha repeats. "It doesn't matter if I can fit through that window. If you can't, then we both stay. We find a different way out."

"What if whoever is here is waiting right outside that door?" Mark asks.

"Then we figure it out. Together. I won't leave you," she says.

Mark reaches out and takes hold of her, pulling her in for a tight hug. He kisses the top of her head and whispers that he loves her. This wasn't supposed to be this way. This was supposed to be a chance for them to get some time together, to enjoy being just the two of them. Guilt swells in his chest. If he hadn't decided to bring her out to this park rather than going to a different campground, they wouldn't be in this situation. The storm wouldn't have caught them and they wouldn't have ended up here in the school.

He allows himself only a few moments of that feeling. It's not going to do him any good to wish he had made a different decision. He can't change it now. All he can do is try to get them out safely.

"When we get out of this and get back to the house, I want to start looking for a home of our own," he says. "I don't care if it's small. I don't care where it is. I just want something for the two of us. For you and me."

He takes hold of either side of her face, cupping her head so he can look intently into her eyes.

Sasha fights the tears welling up in her eyes and nods, gripping his wrists.

"You and me."

They share a kiss and Mark starts looking around. "I don't think I'm going to be able to get out that window. It looks too small."

"Try."

He climbs up on the table and tries to ease himself through the same bars that Sasha just tested. These aren't the type of bars installed on apartments and shops in cities to prevent theft. They're designed to protect the delicate, expensive glass of the windows rather than to keep people from accessing the building. Or from getting out. They are positioned further apart. But he still feels himself squeezed on either side and knows he can't fit himself all the way through. He shakes his head as he backs out of the window and drops back to his feet on the kitchen floor.

"I'd get stuck," he says. Daylight is getting slightly stronger outside and he sees the outline of a door on the opposite side of the room. He hadn't noticed it last night. "That probably leads outside."

He crosses to it and grabs onto the handle, giving it a strong tug, but it doesn't move. Sasha comes up behind him and tries it but gets the same result.

"It's not moving. And that's a thick door. There's no breaking through it," she says.

"Then all we can do is go back out into the main kitchen and see if there's another way."

"And if there isn't?"

"We figure out what to do next."

Together they move the heavy wooden table away from the place where they pulled it in front of the door. They pause, waiting to see if the sound of the table moving will cause anything to happen.

Everything stays quiet and Mark steps up to the door. They don't have the time to hesitate. They need to move as quickly and deliberately as they can. Nothing happens when they open the door and walk out into the kitchen. The only windows in this room are narrow ventilation points up high on the walls. There's no way either of them would be able to get to those, much less through them. There are no other doors. The only option is to go into the main school.

They brace themselves and move into the hallway. All around them, everything is quiet and still. But it feels oppressive. Like the walls themselves are watching them. There are so many corners and rooms, small alcoves and shadowy faces. They don't know enough about the design of the building to know if hidden passages and servants' hallways still exist behind the walls. The thought of someone peering out through the eyes of paintings or the slats of a vent would have sounded wild and ridiculous before last night, but now it's far too plausible.

Holding onto each other with one hand and their flashlights with the other, Mark and Sasha move swiftly toward the front door. As they cross the entryway, they hear footsteps echoing somewhere in the school and a low, scratching sound like chairs being dragged across the floor. Sasha gasps and they let go of each other, both reaching for the handles on the doors to yank them open. Even as they are doing it, they expect resistance. Instead, they open easily. They run out into the glow of the sunrise, their feet cracking through thin ice and sinking into the fresh snow.

They don't look back as they jump down the stairs and run as fast as the terrain will allow them down the driveway and toward the abandoned road in front of the school.

Emma

Up until this moment, I've been holding my hands down near my hips, my palms flexed to the front like I'm showing my surrender. Now I move them quickly, one going to the front of my waistband where I shifted my gun before going into the building and the other grabbing hold of Bam Bam's wrist as I twist around. The knife cuts into my neck and I feel the blood start to roll down my skin, but it isn't deep. The movement puts Bam Bam between me and his men and trains my gun at him. An instant later, the room erupts in sound and movement as ten other federal agents stream in, their guns drawn, shouting commands. They're followed by a wave of police officers doing the same.

Bam Bam goes to his knees and I stare him in the eyes.

"I'm not like sending a knife to a gunfight," I tell him. "I'm like sending water to a fire fight. I put you out."

CHAPTER EIGHT

"WHY WAS THAT SO EASY?" SASHA ASKS BREATHLESSLY AS they disappear into the trees.

"I don't know, but I'm not going to question it," Mark says. "Keep going."

He directs her as they run, going down overgrown paths to backtrack around and head for the closest neighborhood. He doesn't want to go back onto the grounds of the school but knows the small store right at the edge of the residential area is going to be the closest phone available.

His lungs ache and his face stings as they go, but he keeps pushing, encouraging Sasha when she slows and letting her push him when he starts to lag. Running through the cold, pulled down by the snow, is far more difficult than traveling in milder weather and he can feel the effect of not sleeping the night before. His body wants to give out on him, but he won't let it. He can't stop. They need to get where they can call the police for help, get warm, and find a ride back to their car. He wants to go home with his wife and for this to be over.

The feeling of oppression, of being watched and controlled like a rat in a maze has followed them out of the school. It trails after Sasha as she tries to focus on the trees going past her. If she keeps her mind on them, ticking them off without really counting them, she proves to herself that she is actually moving forward through the forest. She's making progress. It doesn't feel like she is. It feels like any second now, she's going to run back out onto that river of ash and see the towering iron gate in front of her.

But they are moving. They are getting through. The branches of trees and tendrils of ferns taking back over paths left untouched for years claw at them, tangle around them, try to keep them where they are, but they force their way through. Somewhere in the woods is their abandoned campsite and the fallen tree that pushed them to the school. Sasha doesn't know if they'll ever see it again. She doesn't care.

Finally ahead of them she sees the trees thin and a barrier made of wooden boards lining the edge of the park. The sight gives them a boost of energy and determination and they run toward it, leaping over the barrier to get to the road. Within minutes they are in the convenience store and the manager is on the phone with police as one of the clerks presses cups of hot coffee into their hands and heats food for them in the microwave behind the counter.

Neither of them want to eat but they accept the food gratefully. Right now, any kindness is welcome.

The rest of the morning comes to them in a blur. As the sun rises outside, police cars slide into the lot and uniformed men walk into the store. They try to explain what happened and are ushered into the back of one of the cars to be brought back to the school.

They don't want to go in, but they do. They walk in the beam of the officer flashlights, showing them where they went the night before. As they walk down the hall toward the classroom, Sasha looks around and takes hold of Mark's hand.

"The balls," she whispers. "They aren't here."

"What was that?" one of the officers asks.

They explain hearing the balls bouncing on the floor and seeing them in the hallway, but that they aren't here any longer. The officers look at each other incredulously. They don't share the compassion and concern of the manager and clerk at the store.

"Show us this classroom," the other officer says.

They're prepared with their guns in their hands as Mark and Sasha bring them to the hallway and direct them to the classroom. The door is closed now. Neither of them had closed it. They know they hadn't. But they don't say anything right now. The officers direct them to stand back against the other side of the hallway and approach the door with guns raised, bellowing their presence at anyone inside the room. Mark and Sasha know the one person inside that room isn't going to hear them.

One officer reaches forward and turns the knob, using his foot to push the door the rest of the way open. They rush inside. Mark and Sasha hold their breath as they wait. They can taste the revolting smell on the backs of their tongues. It isn't as strong now, or maybe they are just used to it. They wait for the officers to come back out and radio for backup. For the sirens and lights and medical examiner. For a team to spread out and search the school to find whoever did this.

But none of it happens. When the officers come back out, their faces are drawn, their eyebrows tight together.

"Nothing," one of them says.

Mark's hand falls away from Sasha's as he takes a step closer to them.

"What do you mean nothing?" he asks.

"It's just a classroom. Just like all the other ones. There's nothing in there."

Sasha darts across the hall into the classroom, bracing herself to face the same sight that took her breath away the night before. Only when she gets inside the room, she sees the officer was right. There's nothing here.

"It's gone," she says, the words tumbling out of her mouth involuntarily in shocked reaction to the empty classroom. "The body is gone."

Mark comes into the room, his stunned expression illuminated by the bright morning sunlight now shining through the window on the side of the room. There's only one, but it creates a vibrant winter-cold rectangle of yellow light on the floor across the front of the teacher's desk. She doesn't remember there being this much light the night before. There should have been light.

"The window," she says, pointing at it. "The window was covered last night."

"Was it?" Mark asks.

"There was no light. No moonlight. It was totally dark in here."

"Then how did you see the supposed body?" one of the officers asks.

"Flashlights," Sasha says, not even trying to keep the bitter edge from the words.

"Could it be a different room?" Mark asks.

Sasha shakes her head. "No. This is the right room. I know it. But that window was covered. And the body was sitting right there in that desk."

She points out the chair where they saw the decomposing figure the night before.

"We'll check the other rooms," the officer says.

There's condescension in the offer. He's trying to soothe her and it makes her angry.

"This is the right room," she insists.

"Just to be sure."

They leave and she can hear them going into each of the other classrooms, muttering between themselves. They officers don't believe what they've heard.

"This is the right room," Sasha insists to Mark, keeping her voice low so they can communicate without being listened to.

"I know," he says. "But where is the body? What happened to it?"

"I don't know. They need to search the school."

The officers came in with their guns already back in their holsters and aggravated expressions. She knows there's no chance they are going to search for anything.

"Where did you say you spent the rest of the evening?" one of them asks.

They show the officers the kitchen, describing the fire they started and hearing the person on the other side of the door. One of the officers looks at the window.

"What happened here?" he asks.

"We broke it to try to get out this morning," Mark explains. "We didn't want to go back through the rest of the school."

"Where the playground balls were?" the other says mockingly.

"They were there," Sasha says flatly.

"Look, I know the storm last night was pretty intense. You said yourself it surprised you while you were camping. Maybe that tree falling on the tent shook you up more than you thought. Maybe the cold got to you and you started seeing and hearing things."

"We aren't delusional," Mark says. "We know what happened."

"I'm sure you think you do. But there was no body in that classroom. And I don't see any indication there's anything going on around here. Other than the window the two of you broke."

"What about the smell? I know you could smell it, too," Sasha says.

"An animal somewhere. Places like this always have rats and raccoons and things that come in and die. It's not unusual. Especially in the winter. Look, it's done. We won't press charges for the broken window, but we better not find you here again. We're going to bring you back to your car. I suggest you stay away from this place. Trespassing on private land and breaking into closed buildings is dangerous. Not to mention illegal."

"We didn't make this up," Mark insists. "And we weren't hallucinating."

"Let's go," the officer replies curtly.

There's nothing they can do. The officers aren't going to entertain anything else. All they care about is getting Mark and Sasha out of the school and getting back to what they see as work worth their time. They walk out of the front door and toward the cruisers parked at the front of the building. As they climb into the backseat, the feeling of eyes on them ripples down the back of Sasha's neck again.

From above, looking down from the vantage point in the shadows beyond the window on the top floor, they look small. Old, yellowed curtains close as the cars pull out and drive away.

CHAPTER NINE

Three years later...

A GUNSHOT RINGS OUT, MAKING ME PULL BACK BEHIND A NEARBY tree, spinning so my back is pressed against it.

"Damn it," I mutter.

Up until this moment, I'd hoped the man I'm chasing wasn't armed. Maybe he didn't have time to grab his gun before running out of the warehouse my team just raided. It was wishful thinking. They always have their guns on them. It's a disturbing similarity criminals have with the FBI agents who pursue them. Where we go, our weapons go with us.

Mine is held to the center of my chest right now. I can feel my heartbeat against my ribs, but the vest I'm wearing stops it from drumming against my hands. There's another cascade of gunshots and I hear a sharp cry. Someone has been hit.

"Morris is down," a voice shouts from somewhere else in the trees. "Suspect is out of sight."

I curse. It's the last thing any agent wants to hear when in pursuit of a dangerous criminal. The gunshots weren't a threat, they weren't an intimidation tactic. Vincent Broddeus, a drug dealer with ties to organized crime overseas, has been near the top of my list for years now.

Three years ago, we located and eliminated one of his most powerful and prolific associates but weren't able to find him. None of the men we took in that day were willing to give him up even after sitting in prison, and he's managed to stay out of our grasp since. It helps that he's known to have many people willing to do anything he needs, including acting as go-between to make sure that he is not directly associated with other criminals, can't be linked by eyewitnesses or even paper trails to sales of drugs or weapons, and is never seen with any of the victims that end up littering his path.

But now he's ours.

The team I'm leading has carefully investigated his crimes and identified his movements until we were able to locate the warehouse where he'd been hiding since getting wind of us coming for him. And now he has shot one of my team.

I push away from the tree and look for Morris. He's on the ground several feet away, another agent crouched beside him applying pressure to his thigh. The sight makes my stomach sink. Bulletproof vests are valuable tools, but they do nothing when the shot isn't directed at center mass.

"Call for a bus," I command. "Get him to the road."

EMS won't come into an area with an active shooter. They have to wait until the threat is completely neutralized. Meaning the shooter either has to be apprehended or dead before the emergency response team will come in to help. While it's understandable to want to avoid further making things more complicated with additional injuries, this means those who are already injured have to wait for the help they need. Sometimes that help doesn't come fast enough. Moving Agent Morris to the road means the ambulance can get to him faster or one of the other agents can transport him to a meeting point to get him help fast.

Trusting my team to do what they need to do to handle Morris's injury, I continue my pursuit of Broddeus. I know there are other members of my team to either side of me, but I'm not specifically aware of any of them. It's just me and the wooded patch of land where the dealer headed after bailing from the car he drove away from the warehouse.

The car was parked inside the warehouse, making it easy for him to jump behind the wheel and take off when the raid began. He didn't care about anyone he left behind, including the men already brought down at gunpoint. The way the door opened and the car skidded out of sight told me this was a carefully prepared plan. They had a contingency in place for if the FBI ever caught up with them. That fit with the type of criminal I learned Broddeus to be as I dug into his crimes and traced his movements in a network that crosses the world and tangles the nation in his web.

He's the type of criminal who is both arrogant and cautious. It's a dangerous combination.

Some criminals are so arrogant they don't believe they could ever be caught. They believe their intellect far surpasses that of any of the law enforcement agencies after them. No matter who is on their trail, not matter how close they get, these outlaws believe they can do anything they want and will never see any consequences. Even if people know they are the ones who are responsible, they are too crafty to actually have that responsibility proven. They believe they will never be caught, and even if they are, they will stand in a court without any fear because no one can actually prove what they've done.

Others are intensely cautious. They are aware of the risks of what they're doing and the possible consequences they could face. They don't deny the power of law enforcement and the very real chances of getting caught. Rather than taunt those looking for them, they spend their time planning and strategizing. These are the criminals who approach their crimes more like a career than as a lifestyle. They have extensive plans in place to protect their enterprise and know how to react if something goes wrong. Despite this caution, it is often the lack of arrogance and extreme planning that is their undoing. They aren't confident enough in themselves to push the envelope, which keeps them accessible, and their plans are so firm they become restrictive and trip them up.

Then there are the ones like Broddeus. Though he is in no way as prolific or powerful as some of the masterminds I have encountered in my career, like the Dragon, my uncle Jonah, or the men of the Order of Prometheus, he exhibits many of the same personality traits and behaviors. He believes himself to be special beyond others, elevated above society both legitimate and criminal. His crimes are more than a lifestyle, more than a career. He believes them to be his birthright, his destiny. And because of that, he takes them seriously. He makes plans to protect himself and his endeavors.

THE GIRL AND THE WINTER BONES

These are the criminals who have delusions of grandeur surrounding their crimes, believing them to be more than just the criminal actions themselves, but who are also keenly aware of the society nipping at their heels in the form of law enforcement. The fact that they are both intensely entitled and also prepared for things to go wrong can make it seem like these criminals are a step ahead of us. They strategically structure their plans around the idea of security. They plan their crimes with the possibility of a betrayal by an insider or a raid already in mind. They have plans within plans within plans.

They think that means they win.

They don't.

I don't care about the advantages they have or how well they have prepared for anything. If someone commits a crime, especially one of the horrific ones my team investigates, I will not be intimidated by them. I will not be put off by a challenge. I will do what it takes to bring them down without hesitation.

Just like now. The temperature is cold and the branches that I push aside are covered in a coat of ice. I stomp some down to get over them more easily and duck under others. I keep my ears sharp, paying attention to the sound of Broddeus crashing his way through the woods ahead of me. It's not easy to get through a forest like this quietly. It can be done, but it requires care, precision, and a slow pace. None of those are available right now.

"Get down! Show me your hands!" I scream. "Get down!"

He doesn't react, but I wasn't really expecting him to. This kind of chase takes longer than just a few minutes, especially after a gun is discharged. Usually in a chase like this, that's a sign that they are still trying to fight. He won't slow down and give in any time soon. Hopefully he will run until he has exhausted or injured himself and drop. I can keep up with him, though. An entire lifetime of martial arts training under my father, gun skills learned and perfected within the FBI, and frequent workouts means my body is crafted to do this. I'm often underestimated. But that doesn't last long.

Another discharge is probably meant to scare me away, but all it does is betray Broddeus's location. I move behind a tree briefly to check in with the rest of the team. Not wanting to use the walkie on my hip because he could hear it, I instead look around, trying to put eyes on every one of the men I know are there with me. I count them, making sure it adds up. A couple stayed behind with Morris to make sure he gets to the road so the ambulance can get to him, but the rest are accounted for.

Dougherty makes eye contact with me from the tree he's leaned against. I nod my head in the direction I heard the gunshots and he nods in return, telling me without words that he heard the same thing and understands what I want. He darts to another tree while I go in the opposite direction. We continue to move from tree to tree until I can see a dark anomaly among the trees in front of me. It's Broddeus, crouched down among shrubs and undergrowth, trying to remain unnoticed.

"Throw the firearm in my direction and lay down on your stomach!" I shout.

He shifts and I brace myself. I look over at Dougherty where he has taken up a position to the side and slightly behind the suspect. I step behind a nearby tree and the other agent picks up my command. I watch Broddeus turn his attention in that direction. As soon as his body is facing away from me, I rush toward him. My knee hits the center of his back, pushing him down to the ground. His gun discharges, but no one reacts. I kick the weapon out of his hand and he thrashes, bucking me off his back and into a small tree beside him.

My head hits the tree, making my vision swim and bright spots dance in front of my eyes. He comes down on me, his hands coming around my throat. The other agents descend as we grapple. My fingernails dig into his arms, but he doesn't let up. He has the strength of anger and desperation. The kind that comes from a place of knowing he can't do anything. There's nowhere for him to go. Nothing for him to do. No other options. But he's going to go down fighting.

I maneuver enough to force my weight into his chest with my bent leg and smash my fist into the side of his head. The impact seems to disorient him just enough to loosen his grip. I take the brief opportunity to take the upper hand again, flipping him over so I can pin him to the ground. Dougherty grabs the front of his shirt as I get to my feet and we drag him up to standing, getting him cuffed.

"Does someone have his firearm?" I ask.

"Got it," reports one of my team.

"Get him to a car," says Dougherty.

I step back to give them more space. I don't need the help bringing him in, but I don't feel like dealing with him anymore right now. It's the point of having a team. I can get them to do the things I don't want to do.

"You okay, Griffin?" Pierce asks.

I touch my mouth, feeling a slight sting when my fingertips come into contact with a split in my lip I didn't even know was there. My head throbs and I'm still a little hazy on the edges of my thoughts but nothing too bad. I've dealt with far worse.

"I'm fine. Let's get out of here," I say.

Takedowns like the one I did today are usually the result of months of dedicated work that culminate in a few intense moments when I straddle the fine line between going back home at the end of the day and my name ending up carved into a memorial. But the work doesn't stop once the perpetrator is in the back of the car or even when they are brought into the police station. Instead, that's when quite possibly my least favorite part of it all begins.

Paperwork, interviews, statements. It can stretch on and on, and with the drain of adrenaline that happens once it's all over, the whole process can be exhausting. Today it's especially difficult to sit through the process. I can't keep my mind off of Agent Morris and wondering how he's doing. I got reassurance he is alive, which is a relief. That isn't necessarily a given with a gunshot wound to the thigh.

A gunshot to the leg can be a simple through-and-through injury. Even if the bullet lodges itself in place, many victims are up and walking around within a couple days. I've had colleagues get shot in the leg, finish the takedown, then return to active duty less than a month later. When it goes that way, it's a relief.

When it doesn't, it's devastating. That's because a shot to the leg can mean hitting the femoral artery, which can cause the victim to bleed out and die at mindboggling speed. Stopping the bleeding is extremely difficult, even with fast medical intervention. Sometimes the victim will be talking coherently, engaged with what's going on around them, and still die because there's simply no way to stop the bleeding.

I can only hope Morris's injury is nothing that serious. I keep waiting to get word and when I haven't by the time I'm finished with tonight's stage of wrapping up the investigation, I head directly for the hospital. Agent Cavanaugh, the one who swooped in to tend to Morris when he went down, approaches me when I walk into the waiting room.

"How is he?" I ask.

"He's in surgery," he tells me. "The doctors haven't told us anything."

I look into the waiting room and see half a dozen agents scattered among the chairs, staring off into space or holding their heads in their hands.

"Give me just a second," I say.

I approach the receptionist desk and hold out my badge so it's the first thing the woman behind the desk sees when she looks over at me.

"Oh," she says. "How can I help you?"

"My name is Agent Emma Griffin. One of my team, Hugo Morris, was brought in here with a gunshot wound to his leg. I need to know his current condition and when I'll be able to see him."

I don't give her any room to take control of the conversation. I'm not requesting anything or asking permission. I'm informing her of what I need with the full expectation she will see to it. That is how I get a considerable amount done. Particularly when going up against people who don't think I should be in the career I'm in, or that I shouldn't have earned the recognition I have, I've learned to stand my ground and approach the world by telling, not asking.

"Of course, Agent Griffin," the receptionist nods. "Give me just a moment." It doesn't hurt that my name carries weight. She disappears into the back of the emergency room and comes back a few moments later. "Agent Morris was brought into surgery for his wound. The doctor will be out to speak with you shortly."

"Thank you," I tell her.

The wait among the other agents feels long, but it's actually only a few minutes later when a doctor in green scrubs and a pristine jacket comes out of the back and towards me. This is either not the man who actually performed Hugo's surgery or he is exceptionally conscientious about not appearing in front of friends and family in clothing with any reminder of trauma on it.

"Agent Griffin?" he says.

"Yes." I step up to him and reach out to shake his hand. "I'm Emma Griffin."

"I'm Dr. Call, I want to let you know that he's doing great. He got through surgery to remove the bullet from his leg and is in recovery. There is a fracture in his femur, but no major arteries were hit, so he has a long road to recovery ahead. But otherwise, he will be okay."

I exhale a massive sigh of relief.

"He's strong," I say. "He'll be fine."

"I can tell that he is. Give me just a few more minutes and I'll have the nurse come out to get you so you can go back and see him," Dr. Call says.

"Thank you."

An hour later I'm walking out of Hugo's room, tying my hair up into a ponytail and feeling every minute of the last day, when I see my supervisor Eric Martinez rushing down the hall toward me.

"Hey," I say.

"Emma," he says, gathering me into a hug. "Are you alright? I heard you got into a fight with Vincent Broddeus."

I give him a wry smile. "It was more of a scuffle, but I'm fine. The EMS checked me out. Just some bumps and bruises. I'm going to feel like hell tomorrow but nothing serious. Hugo is the one who was shot."

He nods. "I know. I got on the road as soon as I found out. How is he doing?" Eric asks.

"He's on a lot of meds right now, so he's a little loopy, but he's going to be fine. They did surgery and removed the bullet, but it broke a bone pretty badly. You're looking at a lot of leave," I say.

"He just wants vacation after having to work Christmas," Eric teases.

I chuckle. "Yeah, you tell him that. I bet he never thought you'd figure him out."

"Speaking of which, when are you leaving for your road trip?" he asks.

"The day after tomorrow. I'm glad this got wrapped up so I can actually leave on time. Are you sure you, Bellamy, and Bebe can't come?" I ask.

"Yeah. We wish we could, but there's just too much going on. I can't take the time right now. We'll have to plan another one for summer."

"I'm holding you to that." I give him another hug. "Give the girls hugs and tell them I'll see them soon."

"I will. You heading out?"

"Yeah. I've got to get some sleep before driving home tomorrow and getting ready for this trip. I'll see you when we get back," I say.

We wave and I head out of the hospital, feeling so tired and sore I barely feel like driving the ten minutes to the hotel. At least it's not three hours back home to Sherwood. I finally get to the hotel, take a long shower under the hottest water I can stand while I wait for food to be delivered to my room, then call Sam.

"You going to make it?" he asks.

"Yep. I'll be home in the morning. Have you started packing?"

"I have a list."

I laugh. "Good start. I'll see you tomorrow. I love you."

"Love you. Goodnight."

CHAPTER TEN

GET HOME THE NEXT MORNING TO FIND SAM WORKING THROUGH
his packing list. After an ill-fated trip several years ago when he didn't
pack early enough and ended up in Florida with one pair of pants, six
undershirts, a button-up shirt, and only a pair of dress shoes he wore on
the plane, my husband tends to err on the side of over packing. That's
never been a problem for me since I've traveled so much throughout my
life. I'm used to having an overnight bag always packed and ready with
necessities and basic clothes in the trunk of my car, and when I actually
have the time to plan being away and pack accordingly, it's down to a
science.

Maybe that isn't entirely accurate. I have been known to bring far
too many case files and stacks of notes, newspaper clippings, records,
and anything else I can stuff in the car. Everyone around me has put a
considerable amount of effort into trying to convince me that people
can go on vacations without bringing work along. I'm doing my best
to adopt that philosophy. I've even had a couple of trips where I've left

everything behind—which, admittedly, has made for a lot more room in the car. This is not going to be one of those trips.

Not because of my cases this time, but because of Dean. His reputation has grown massively over the last couple of years and he is constantly getting phone calls from people asking for his help finding missing people, proving criminal activity, locating family links, even finding the truth behind unexplained deaths. Where he used to scramble for work, he now sometimes has to turn people away. He tries not to do that whenever possible. He feels like if they are coming to him it's because they need help and he wants to be able to give them that help. He still carries the scars of being on the other end of horrific and unexplained circumstances, and without the help of people who cared enough to dig deeper and find the truth, he would never have gotten through them.

This has him currently wading through several challenging cases and even though the point of our road trip was supposed to be getting a break from everything after a chaotic holiday season, we've planned some of the itinerary around stops for his investigations.

He's in the living room now, his notes and records spread out across the table.

"Did you bring all of that over from your house?" I ask, sitting on the couch beside him. "You know we could have just driven over there and picked everything up."

It has only been a couple of weeks since I signed over my grandparents' house to Dean, giving him the chance to have a place to call home here in Sherwood and also connecting him to the past that was stolen from him by never knowing our family when he was young. He and Xavier spent a week back in Harlan at Xavier's house, then came back here to settle in. The plan is that they will go back and forth between the houses however it works for Dean's work schedule. I hope it means I will be able to see a lot more of my cousin and Xavier.

Xavier loves his house in Harlan. He designed it and has modified it throughout the years to accommodate his quirky ideas and the sometimes brilliant, sometimes bizarre gadgets he invents. These seem to sometimes just pop into his head and he has to create them just to get them out of there. Which is why there are lighting sconces that shoot spears if touched, a wall that spins for no apparent reason, a complex system of pulleys, lifts, and ramps that reminds me of a game of MouseTrap to transport things around the house, and one especially terrifying electrical outlet he rigged for reasons completely unknown to send out intense blue sparks if someone tries to use it.

A visit to Xavier's house can be an adventure.

But it also holds some very difficult reminders for him. The garage is where his best friend Andrew was murdered and the crime pinned on Xavier. The house itself is where he has hidden away from the world, isolated by his own thoughts and perceptions. The front porch is where Dean was abducted and nearly killed.

There are pictures around the house, random objects, odds and ends that don't seem to fit with anything else. That isn't so unusual for Xavier. He places meaning and significance on things that others don't. But I don't think that's the case with some of these things. As I have roamed through the sprawling mansion, which I discovered early on to be a fascinating rainy-day activity, I have come upon many things that don't strike me as originally belonging to Xavier. I don't see him choosing them or buying them. Instead, it's more like they are there because of who they actually belong to.

It's those kinds of things that remind me how much of an intriguing dichotomy Xavier truly is in so many ways. He is unapologetic about who he is. He acknowledges he isn't like other people in the way he thinks and sees things, but he doesn't consider that something to be afraid of or embarrassed about. It is simply his reality and he is open about it. That doesn't mean he can always express what he's feeling or thinking in a way that perfectly translates into our perspective, but that's not his responsibility. It isn't Xavier's job to make the people around him more comfortable or make himself easier to understand. But he tries.

Yet when it comes to his past, there is a big open space. It's almost like he sprang fully formed into adult existence sometime before Andrew's death. Just before then is the starting point of everything we know about Xavier. We know he got tangled up with the Order of Prometheus and ended up the target of their gruesome initiation methods. We know that left him charged with murder and put him in prison for almost a decade.

But there's a void before all of that. We don't know anything about his family or his childhood, even his adulthood more than a couple of years before his incarceration. There have been a few little clues dropped here and there. Anyone who knows him knows how much he loves theme parks. He occasionally mentions foods that he loved growing up or tells stories about places he's visited. We know he was an unmade bed for Halloween one year and that he has a scar on the back of one calf from what he describes as a "sledding incident."

But it's the details of stories like that he leaves out. Who was he trick or treating with that year? Who made him those foods? Where was he sledding?

THE GIRL AND THE WINTER BONES

A few weeks ago we were talking about the composition of bones and he asked if we had ever squished a newborn baby into a Tupperware cake taker. There isn't a single doubt in my mind that this is not only something he has first-hand experience doing, but that the baby was unharmed in any way. He was just doing it for fun, possibly a cute picture-taking opportunity. I have seen the kinds of ridiculous but adorable pictures he has taken of Bebe since she was born, so I know he is the kind of guy who is hanging out with a baby on a beach and just has to put them in a sand bucket.

But the question is who the baby was who Xavier folded up into that cake taker. Was it a younger sibling? Or perhaps a niece or nephew? He's never mentioned having any siblings, but he also hasn't said that he is an only child. I don't let myself think about it much because it makes my heart ache to consider, but I have occasionally wondered if it's possible Xavier once had a child of his own.

I tend not to ask questions about Xavier's past. He openly shares so much that I figure if he's not talking about something, there's probably a reason. I wonder and I wait. Hopefully I'll have a lot of time with him ahead of me and over that time maybe I'll learn more about him.

"Xavier has already declared the house pre-road trip sealed. The rooms have been cleared and nothing else goes in or out," Dean tells me.

I smile. At least there's plenty to already know about him.

CHAPTER ELEVEN

"**H**AVE YOU GOTTEN ANY NEW LEADS?" I ASK, REACHING OVER to shift a piece of paper so I can look at an image beneath it.

A woman smiles up at me from a black and white photo that looks like it was taken at a picnic or outdoor show of some kind. She's sitting on the grass on a checkered blanket, her legs folded to her side and her hands rested beside her. The dark, short-sleeved dress with white Peter Pan collar and large cat-eye glasses she's wearing give a hint as to when the picture was taken.

"Nothing concrete, exactly, but I dug up a few new details that might help. Or they might not mean anything," Dean admits with a heavy sigh. "We'll just have to find out."

I laugh and rub his back reassuringly. "You're going to figure it out. And the road trip will do you good. It will help jostle things in your brain and you'll get to do some relaxing, which you definitely need to do."

He nods. "I'm looking forward to that."

"Who is this?" I ask, pointing to the picture.

"Alma Mulroney," he says, picking up the picture and looking at it carefully. "I was looking into those three girls who went missing right around the same time from near Conway and found an old article from the campus paper at their college. It was an opinion piece talking about the declining safety of young women on campus and mentioned Alma, too. She was another student from the same school who'd gone missing, but five years before. She was last seen in a popular bar right off campus. She was talking about going to California. No one saw her or heard from her after that."

"When was the article written?" I ask.

"1973," Dean tells me.

"So she went missing around '68. And she was going to California." It takes a fraction of a second for the thoughts to come together. "Manson Family?"

Dean nods solemnly. "It isn't mentioned in the article. The writer was obviously trying to angle that something happened to her that was linked to the disappearance of those three girls, but there's nothing really connecting them except for the fact that they were all female, around the same age, and went to the same college. They didn't have any of the same acquaintances, were studying different things, had different hobbies, worked different jobs."

"And didn't those three girls go missing after visiting the beach?" I ask. Sometimes when we're dealing with multiple cases it can be hazy which details go with which situation. "They were at a concert or something?"

"Right. They'd gone to Myrtle Beach for a show with some friends. Those friends told police they went to the concert just like they planned on, seemed to enjoy it, then when the others said they were going to go to an all-night diner for some food, the girls said they needed to get back to campus. And that was it. So, there really wasn't a connection," Dean says. "Which is actually what inspired me to look into it. If there's any chance any of this really ties together with the rest of the investigation, I need to cover all the bases. And her case just fascinated me."

"So you looked into Alma to see what might have happened to her," I say.

He nods. "There isn't much. Like most of the people who were lured out there. She got it in her mind that there was something bigger and better for her, was caught up in the romance and pseudo-religion, and that was it. I was able to find a couple of news articles and the transcript from a news broadcast from her hometown with her mother talking about Alma's disappearance. She said she'd heard from her twice after she left home, but would never tell her exactly where she was and couldn't be convinced to come home."

"If she disappeared in 1968, that was at the beginning of his cult. He was still just on the edge of psychopathy at that point. Calling himself a guru and leading around a group of women he treated like servants," I say. "That was before any of the killing started, so the mother might have just let it be."

"And that's what it sounded like. She said she was upset that Alma left school and went off to California without leaving an address or making sure anyone knew her plans, but she believed she was going on a spiritual journey. She said in the couple of times she'd talked to her, Alma mentioned a 'Charlie' and how amazing he was. So connected to God, brilliant, kind, generous, talented, an amazing singer," Dean says. "She was completely devoted."

Knowing what came of that devotion in the more than one hundred people who became members of the charismatic leader's "family," the gushing praise makes my stomach turn. But at that time, people didn't know who he really was. They couldn't look ahead and see the incomprehensibly horrible things he would cause. The world is still reeling now.

"That sounds like she was living with him at the Wilson house," I say, referencing the brief period when Manson managed to beguile Charles Wilson of the Beach Boys and lived in his home with an assortment of the women caught in his web.

"Before he even heard 'Helter Skelter,'" Dean mutters.

It's incredible how in this life one thing, something so seemingly innocuous, can completely change everything. How one choice can fracture reality and send pieces of it careening like shrapnel into such a dark and twisted place.

"And she still hasn't been found?" I ask.

"No. I did some research and was able to connect her to the Family even during the trial. I don't have any absolute proof, but enough that it's pretty difficult to argue. There's even a couple of pictures of the women outside the courthouse and one of them looks very much like Alma. They aren't direct pictures of her face, just profiles. But I'm positive it's her," Dean says. "Only after that, there's nothing. Her mother still considers her missing. She believes she is alive, based on what she calls her mother's intuition. She says she can just feel that her child is living, and if she wasn't, she would be able to feel that."

That makes me shudder. I can appreciate the deep, impossible-to-explain connection between parents and their children, particularly mothers. I've seen firsthand the incredible feats that can happen because of that bond and the love that it fosters. And I know that bond can manifest in inexplicable moments of knowledge, of the mother simply knowing her child is in danger, sick, or has been hurt even without there being any indication of it around her. It's a phenomenon that has literally saved lives.

But it's not foolproof. It doesn't always exist. Sometimes a mother feeling like her child is still alive is just her clinging to a desperate hope that she won't have to truly face that indescribable loss. Sometimes feeling that someone is still alive isn't really feeling that they are still living; it's feeling the life that they once had still existing within them.

That kind of hope is what keeps many people breathing when going through these excruciating times, but it's that same hope that makes it even more painful when time stretches on with no answers, or when the answer comes and it's not what they wanted to hear. Hearing that Alma's mother still believes her daughter is alive, out there somewhere, is both inspiring and painful. Too many parents gave up on their children when they left home and ventured out to find themselves or join something they so deeply believed in already, only for those children to end up ensnared in darkness. With nowhere to turn, they had even less of a chance to get out.

But this mother didn't do that. She continued to love her daughter, to think about her and worry about her, to wonder where she was and wish she was home. She loved her enough to keep telling herself Alma was alive and she would one day find her.

It fills me with my own hope to be reminded of that kind of love. And at the same time, it gives me fear for that mother. I hate to think of what she goes through every day and what she will continue to go through until she knows what happened to Alma. Even then, there will be healing to do. What she will be healing from is the question.

"I'm sure this is a ridiculous question, but has anyone really taken the time to go make contact with the remaining members of the Family? I know Manson and the ones who were tried with him have been in prison for, what, fifteen years now?"

"Almost," Dean confirms.

"But there are still plenty of people on the outside who sympathize with him. Alma could be one of them," I say.

"Investigators made contact with as many of them as they could, but that wasn't easy considering how adamantly they try to avoid law enforcement. There are a lot of people who went missing during those years. Some went to Manson, others went to other cults and supposed gurus. It's next to impossible to track them. And there's been some conflict as to who is actually responsible for heading up the investigation. If it should be the police from the area around Conway because she went missing off the college campus there, or if it should be someone from California where she went and there's some information that places her there, or if it should be department from McCutcheon," he says.

"McCutcheon?" I frown.

"Her hometown. It's not too far from the border in Maryland," Dean tells me.

"That sounds familiar. Is it one of the places we're stopping?" I ask.

"The next town over," Dean explains. "McCutcheon isn't exactly a tourist spot. But I wanted to do a quick sweep through there to see if there's anything I can find out about Alma while we're on the road. Then we can make our way through to Baltimore."

"Xavier is very excited about the aquarium," I say. I pause. "He can't…"

"I called. They aren't going to let him snorkel, scuba, or get in a cage with sharks," Dean confirms. "He might get to touch a stingray."

"Okay. I think he can handle that. I know it's a controlled environment with manmade containers and they know everything that's in the water, but I'm not fully confident Xavier isn't going to freak out when we get there. And if he does, I'd prefer he do it when he is not actually in the water or near any large animals," I say.

Xavier does not like water. The couple of beach trips we've had together have primarily consisted of him standing on the sand and staring down the waves or sitting under an umbrella and watching them suspiciously, waiting for something to come out of it and doom humanity. He did run full-force into it one time just to prove to himself he could. A wave caught him and he washed back up to shore like a jellyfish.

He's working on it. But this will be the first time he's been in a large-scale aquarium and I'm not sure how it's going to process in his brain when it looks like he's standing under the ocean. Unfortunately, this is just one of those things we can't really do anything about. We just have to do our best to be mentally prepared and wait and see what happens.

CHAPTER TWELVE

AT THIS RATE OF PACKING, I KNOW I STILL HAVE A COUPLE OF hours before we actually hit the road. It's a perfect opportunity for me to make a stop at the grocery store to stock up on snacks and make sure the emergency kit I keep in the car at all times is bulked up a bit to accommodate the extra days we will be away from home.

I might not share Sam's difficulty trimming down the clothing options I bring with me when traveling, but what I lack in luggage, I more than make up for in emergency preparedness supplies. One thing my father taught me when I was young was that no car should be without at least a basic first aid kit. You never know when you might experience a minor accident, get sick while in traffic, end up with a paper cut. The possibilities are really endless if you listen to Ian Griffin, master of being in the car more on a regular basis than any human being should in their entire life. Having a box with some over-the-counter remedies, antibiotic cream, bandages, tweezers, small scissors, and various little bottles and tubes of other things makes it easy to deal with these inconveniences and keep them from getting worse.

It's basic dad advice for anyone getting on toward adult years, though my father still checks mine each time he's here visiting me. He acts like he isn't, like he's just taking a walk around outside or like he forgot something and needs to go out to the car and get it. Even if he hasn't actually been in my car during that visit. But inevitably if I look out the window I'll see that he's swiped my keys and is prodding around in my trunk examining the kit to make sure I have everything I need and it's in good condition. There have been times when he has suddenly needed a trip to the grocery store and has returned with bags full of first aid supplies and a story about how they were on such a good sale he just couldn't pass them up.

But I take it a step further by having non-perishable food, water, blankets, and towels at the ready. As much as I'd like to think I am always equipped with the highest quality vehicles that can get me through any situation I might encounter, that's not really the case. I have a bad tendency of getting used to my cars and not wanting to replace them, even when they've encountered less than dignified incidents in the course of investigations.

It's not a matter of sentimentality. I'm not the kind to name my cars or buy special accessories to give my car more personality. It's just a matter of liking to know how things work and being able to do what I need to do at a second's notice without having to fumble around with knobs and buttons. When I'm working, I don't want to have to dedicate any thought processes to figuring out how to work something new in my car.

Unfortunately that has resulted in my car recently getting to the end of its life and deciding it was finished while I was out on the road. I've spent my fair share of time spent by the side of the road waiting for roadside assistance to swing by and get me going again, and I'd rather not end up stuck somewhere and wish I had the very simple necessities that could get me through the situation.

Going to the store is only part of why I toss my bag into the passenger seat and drive out of the sleepy neighborhood where I moved in with Sam in his childhood home a couple of streets down from my grandparents' house. I also want to stop by the library for a little bit of research.

The three missing college students Dean was hired to look into came up in my investigation of Vincent Broddeus. As our investigation into his crimes revealed a convoluted, tangled web built over decades living in the shadows, suspicious details bubbled to the surface. Incidents that seemed at first glance to have nothing to do with his network of organized crime exist on the periphery, showing up several times at different points in our investigation to the point where it's impossible to just pretend there's no connection, even if we can't figure out what that connection is.

The case of these three girls is one example. They disappeared nearly twelve years ago and there hasn't been a single hint since then of what might have happened to them. Most often, even in cases that go unsolved for years, decades, or even seemingly forever, some things are known. There are paths to follow, leads that didn't pan out but still seem relevant, or clues that give investigators a sketch of what occurred when those people vanished. Not with these three. There's nothing.

That's why I recommended bringing in Dean. When the three girls showed up several times during the investigation into Broddeus' criminal syndicate, never in any direct way but skirting the edges, I couldn't ignore them. But I also couldn't show for sure that Broddeus did anything to them. Dean is an incredible private investigator, with skills that go far beyond anything I've encountered outside of the Bureau. He will always be my choice to work with whenever possible because of my level of trust in him. Our family bond along with watching him prove himself time and time again gives me absolute confidence not just in his abilities but in his dedication. He will push himself to his limit and then try to find new ones to make sure he gets the job done. I know I can depend on him, and that speaks volumes.

From the beginning, the case of the three missing girls has been a challenge. I've done my best to help in his investigation as much as I can while also leading the team focused on taking down Broddeus. There's been little to go on and there have been plenty of times when it seems like both of us are just spinning our wheels trying to figure out where to go next. But he hasn't given up and I know he won't.

And neither will I, which is why I'm heading into the library and making my way right for the research desk. The librarian there looks up at me with a smile.

"Hey there, Emma," Marianne Pullman says.

She makes no move to cover up the glossy magazine she has spread out on the desk in front of her. She might for other patrons who don't frequent the library quite as often as I do, but I'm here enough that she doesn't feel she needs to put up an image by pretending she hasn't sunk herself into celebrity gossip and dubious home decorating projects on the slick, color-saturated pages rather than venturing into the stacks surrounding her.

"Hey, Marianne. How've you been?"

"Doing good. Thinking about doing a home refresh. You know, embrace the new year and transform my space to transform myself," she says, sweeping her hand over the magazine to indicate her own form of research.

Her words and the sparkle in her eyes belie her age. I smile at her.

"That sounds like quite the undertaking," I note.

"But it will be so worth it," she says. "More research today?"

The sudden pivot in the conversation makes me smile again. "Yes. Just a little. I can't be here long."

"Oh?"

"Got a big road trip planned. We're supposed to be leaving in a couple of hours, but there's something I've got stuck in my head and I need to try to figure it out."

"I'm sure you will," she says. "Come on, I'll get you set up."

At this point I should probably just have my own personal access to the library's media research room. I'm here a couple of times a week at least digging through old records, microfilm, and archives to support my investigations. Each time I come I have to have Marianne unlock the room, give me access to the machines, and bring me any archives or records that are stored in the large basement of the old library building. Some of the more complicated or sensitive information I need to find is only housed in the courthouse archives or hospital record morgues, but I get a tremendous amount of use out of this room and the wealth of information found in the old papers and the slides clicking past on the microfilm machine.

Usually I have some idea of what I'm trying to find when I come. This time, I feel like I'm just throwing out a net and waiting to see what I can pull in. I can't push the name McCutcheon out of my mind. It's stuck there and I can't figure out why. Dean's explanation that it's near one of the places where we're stopping on our road trip makes sense. I would have seen the name while going over the map. But it's something more than that. I know I've come across it before.

It's entirely possible it came up in my own investigation into Broddeus, but I can't remember it. I hadn't heard about Alma Mulroney until today, though I knew about the three other missing students who brought her disappearance to Dean's attention. Though he says there aren't strong connections between the two incidents, the fact that he's latched onto Alma as much as the other three tells me he suspects something more than is immediately obvious.

The two events happened five years apart and seem to have no similarities with the exception of them all going to the same school, but it's something. It's enough to look further.

CHAPTER THIRTEEN

"**T**HERE YOU ARE," DEAN SAYS WHEN I WALK BACK INTO THE house a couple of hours later. "Was the store really busy?"

I have mastered the art of not taking longer than one trip from the car after going to the grocery store, but it comes at the price of fingers squeezed into tightly twisted bag handles. I cringe as I set the armful of supplies I hauled in on the couch. There's no point in bringing them to the kitchen. They are getting loaded right into the cooler and the backseat so we can get on the road.

"No, I ended up taking a detour," I tell him.

"Where?" he asks.

"The library. Ever since you mentioned McCutcheon, I just can't stop thinking about it. I know I've heard that name before, and not just because it's somewhere we're going on a road trip. I came across it at some point. During an investigation or hearing the news. I read about it. Something," I say.

"Did you find anything?"

"Yes and no," I tell him. "No because I still don't know what it was that sounded so familiar. I looked into the three missing girls, I tried to link them to the town or something having to do with Vincent Broddeus. There were a couple things that were tangentially related to him, but not distinctly enough for me to consider it evidence or anything like that. Yes because I found a really interesting story that I got completely sucked into and had to read everything I could find about it."

Dean smirks. "A news story or a fiction story?"

I don't even need to dignify that with an answer. "It's about a missing girl," I tell him.

Dean's eyebrows raise slightly. "Recent?"

"No. Very much not. This girl went missing almost thirty years ago. From McCutcheon. She was really young. Some of the articles I read said she was nine, some said 10. She went to a school that was up in that area called the Dawn Day School. Have you ever heard of it?" I ask.

"I actually have. It came up when I was looking into Alma Mulroney's disappearance. It was a private school that had classes from kindergarten all the way through high school. It was kind of tucked back in the woods. The area around it was turned into an unofficial state park, but the whole place has been pretty much abandoned since," he says.

"Like the school," I say. "It closed back in the late fifties, right after this little girl went missing. Apparently she was at school one day, just like every other day. After school all the parents came and picked their kids up because there wasn't any bus service or anything. A lot of the students ended up spending extra time in the schoolyard every afternoon.

"This little girl had a single father and he had to finish work before coming to get her, so she was always staying late. He always tried to get there, but from what I read she was usually one of the last ones to be picked up."

"What happened to her mother?" Dean asks.

"Everything I read just said that she had died when the girl was very young. I want to look into the school more, its history and everything. There were some veiled statements about past iterations of the school, but nothing that gave any real details. I didn't have the time to look any deeper into it, but I really want to."

"What happened to the little girl?" Dean asks. "You said she went missing. Did they ever find her?"

"No. She was staying after school one day like she did every day and was playing with her friends. All the other students saw her, teachers, other staff. Even some parents talked about seeing her running around on the schoolyard playing hide and seek with some of the other girls.

Then none of the girls could find her. They searched and searched, thinking she had just found a really good hiding spot, but there aren't that many places to hide. It's a walled-in schoolyard with a simple swing set and other play equipment. It wasn't like she had access to the open woods or anything.

"So, after a little while of the girls searching, they decided that her father must have come and picked her up. She adored her father and every day as soon as she saw him, she would run to greet him. It didn't matter what she was doing or if she was in the middle of playing a game. She would run right over to him.

"Apparently she had a pink strap she wrapped around her books and always had a little white sweater with her, even during the summer. If her father saw those things sitting at the side of the schoolyard, he would know they were her books and would pick them up. If she saw him holding them, she would just run off with him. Sometimes they didn't even realize she was gone until they didn't see the books."

"And that's what happened that day," Dean says.

I nod. "They just figured he'd come and they would see her the next day. Only, the caretaker found her books after everybody was gone for the day. They were behind a tree like she'd been sitting behind it reading and no one noticed them when they left. That was the first moment they realized something was wrong."

"Where was her father? Didn't he come to pick her up?"

"He was late. It happened sometimes. Not often, but sometimes. It had never been a problem before. Most of the time other parents would just let their children stay and play with her until he got there. If they had to leave, one of the staff would stay with her.

"He just assumed she'd still be there that day. That he would show up at the school and she would be playing. But when he got there, the schoolyard was deserted. He couldn't find anybody, so he went into the school and looked for her in the clinic. But she wasn't there and neither was the nurse. The only person he could find was a receptionist in the front office who told him that everyone was gone.

"They immediately contacted the police and reported her missing. They did a search of the entire building and the grounds but couldn't find a trace of her. She was never found. The school closed before the next year began. It was devastating for everybody and the parents of the other students started worrying about their children. To this day, there hasn't been a single sign of that girl."

"Were there ever any leads? Anything?" Dean asks.

"That's the thing. There was. Only, it didn't exactly pan out the way anybody expected. There'd been some rumors about her teacher, some people gossiping about his abnormal proclivities and the inappropriate level of attention he seemed to give that little girl in particular."

"But he worked at the school?"

"Well, he'd never been convicted of anything. He'd never even been charged with anything. As far as I've been able to find out, there were never even any formal complaints lodged against him to the school, the police, or anyone else. It was just some people spreading rumors. Only, after she went missing, everything blew up. He became the focus of the community's informal investigation when they decided the police weren't doing enough," I say. "They said he had taken her after school and run off with her. Only, there was never any actual sign of that happening. They even searched his house and found nothing."

"Searched?" Dean frowns. "Does that mean a mob stormed in and ransacked it?"

"I have a feeling it does. Only, newspapers thirty years ago were too polite to say something like that about a teacher, especially one catering to wealthy families. And they definitely wouldn't say it about those wealthy families doing anything to a teacher. And essentially they ended the story about him by saying he left. I also have a feeling that means he was run out of town."

"Wouldn't be the first time we encountered something like that," Dean says.

"No. And unfortunately, it probably won't be the last. People have a really awful tendency to be…"

"Awful?"

I can't help but let out a short laugh. "Pretty much. They can't stand when there isn't a neat and tidy answer to all their questions. When something terrible happens, they think it should be solved immediately. Like police have super powers that will let them instantly know what happened and how to prove it. And if it doesn't happen, then everybody else in the community can take it upon themselves to figure it out. Even if that means choosing somebody to be a scapegoat. It makes them feel better."

"Answers make questions tolerable," Dean says. "There will always be questions. It's just part of life, but the reassurance that there are answers to them within reach makes it possible to get through tough times."

"I know. I only wish people wouldn't make up answers when they didn't have the real ones yet," I say.

"C."

I turn and see Xavier standing at the doorway to the living room. He is eating his way through a sandwich with one hand and holding his luggage in the other.

"C?"

"It's the most commonly guessed answer on multiple choice tests. If someone doesn't know the actual answer, they are extremely unlikely to just leave it blank. Leaving something blank is admitting you don't know, that you are lacking in that bit of knowledge or the ability to come to a reasonable guess as to the answer. Very few people are confident enough to do that. So, they guess," he says.

"Maybe it's that they don't want to just give up," I say.

"No. They don't want to leave any unclosed parentheses. No trailing thoughts. They would rather be wrong and have the closure of something being complete than leave room for questions to still exist."

"Unclosed parentheses?" I ask. He puts the sandwich in his mouth and forms a curved shape with the now-available hand. He turns it toward himself and then the other direction. I nod. "Got it."

"The teacher was their answer C," Dean says. "Complete even if wrong."

"Exactly," Xavier says.

I look at his luggage. "We aren't leaving quite yet. I still need to get some things in the car."

"I've been very lackadaisical about keeping with the schedule and meeting our projected leaving time, but I'm concerned any more flexibility could seriously derail our progress. Off we go," he says.

He heads for the door, putting the sandwich back in his mouth to turn the doorknob. I turn to Dean.

"We didn't have a projected leaving time," I say.

"He did," Dean tells me.

"How far past it are we?"

"Seventeen minutes."

"Well, damn. We're just throwing caution to the wind now," I say. "I guess I should go get Sam and let him know if we don't get it together we're going to end up not making it to our first hotel before Xavier turns back into a pumpkin."

Dean grabs his bag and heads for the door. He turns dramatically to me at the last moment.

"Emma…"

"Yeah?"

"May your parentheses always be open," he says solemnly.

The door pops open, pushing him back a step.

"That is a terrible thing to say to her," Xavier says. He looks at me. "Emma, may your bubbles always be filled without ambiguity, your options be without contradiction, and your Cs always come with full awareness and confidence." His head nods forward slowly as his eyes drift closed.

"Thank you, Xavier," I say.

His head pops back up. "Off we go."

CHAPTER FOURTEEN

ONE OF THESE DAYS, I'M GOING TO BEAT XAVIER AT ONE OF HIS car games during a road trip. Today is not that day. We've already had to take his word for the existence of three of the animals he named during the alphabet game and now he's explaining a complex set of rules for spotting license plates that involves both math and rapid recall of alphanumeric coding. I should be more on top of it considering his pager communication style, but I just don't have it in me to try to calculate all that as cars zip past us on the highway.

"We always just tried to find the states," I say.

"My family did numbers in order," Sam says. "And then the alphabet."

I glance over at Dean and he stares back at me blankly.

"I didn't do a whole lot of road tripping growing up," he admits.

"We did those, too," Xavier says. "There weren't this many cars on the road all the time then, so it didn't go as fast. One time it took us the entire trip both ways just to get to the end of the alphabet. We almost didn't make it. My sister was so worried we were going to have to go home without finding all the letters she made our father drive around town for another half an hour until we found them."

My eyes snap over to Dean, then meet Sam's in the rearview mirror. "Xavier… you have a sister?" Dean asks.

He nods, still staring out the window in search of whatever the next thing is that he needs to continue his pattern. I think it's a Pennsylvania license plate with a two in it, but I'm still not entirely clear on the process.

"Yeah," he responds without significance or emotion. "Maribel. Ah! There it is. Pennsylvania and a six. Twelve points."

And that's it. Just like that, another piece of Xavier.

With ticking off the tourist spots on Xavier's carefully planned itinerary and non-negotiable stops at vending machines along the way, it takes us nearly seven hours to get to the town of Gordon just a few miles away from McCutcheon. It's dark and bitterly cold when we pull into the parking lot and stop under the hazy yellow halo of one of the few lights positioned around the perimeter.

I'm relieved when the engine stops running beneath me and I know I'm going to be able to unfold myself from the car and not have to buckle back in until after I've gotten a night of sleep. Even with as tired as I am and how cold it is, I'm happy. This is my favorite way to travel. I don't really know why, but any time I think of a road trip, my mind immediately goes to cold weather and driving through the dark. It doesn't exactly correspond to the amount of time I spent in Florida when I was young, but maybe there are some question marks about me, too.

We gather what we need to have in the room with us and hustle across the parking lot into the lobby of the hotel. Sam goes to the desk to check in while I make a beeline for the coffeemaker sitting on a small table to the side of the lobby. I fill one of the Styrofoam cups from a stack at the back of the table and wrap my hands around it to absorb its warmth. Dean and Xavier are flipping through a binder of flyers and paper menus from local restaurants, looking for a pizzeria that will deliver to the hotel this late.

By the time Sam comes back to us with the keys to our rooms, Dean has used a courtesy phone to order pizzas and Xavier has wandered down the nearest hallway in search of another vending machine to get us drinks. We still have a cooler full of bottles of water and cans of soda in the car, but I know the road trip rules. The contents of coolers are for when the vehicle is actually in motion, with the sole exception being picnic food that can be eaten at a rest stop or park along the way for especially long daytime stretches of driving. All other food must be derived from a restaurant or a vending machine.

There's a big part of me that wants to blame this philosophy entirely on the fact that I'm traveling with three men, but it wouldn't be true. My college road trips with Bellamy always featured abundant junk food and we wouldn't leave without a baggie of change sitting in the glove compartment waiting for rest stop vending machines to make themselves known. My parents raised me with a great devotion to martial arts practice and physical activity, and I still greet most mornings with a long jog and make good use of the gym Sam built first in the empty bedroom at the back of my grandparents' house and then in what was called the rumpus room when we were teenagers at our current home. But I'm not going to be the one to turn down salt and vinegar potato chips or a plate of fresh, hot cinnamon rolls.

We decide to bring our luggage up to our rooms and settle in a bit while we wait for the pizza, then Dean is going to go back down to the lobby and pick it up. The hotel managed to get us rooms directly across the hall from each other and we agree to meet up in my room to eat. Dean and Xavier go into the room they're sharing and Sam carries the luggage into ours. He puts it onto one of the beds and lets out a breath.

"They didn't have any rooms with just one big bed available," he says.

"Oh, no," I say sarcastically. "I'm going to have to sleep closer to you."

I grin and walk up to him for a kiss. Sam wraps his arms around my waist and obliges, then looks into my face.

"You know, that would be a lot cuter if I wasn't familiar with how closely your preferred sleeping position resembles a starfish," he says. "Or that you steal blankets during the winter like you're bringing balance to the universe after putting all those thieves behind bars."

"Well, you're stuck with me now," I say. "I roped you right into marriage."

"I know. We really rushed into things. We only waited two decades," he replies.

I kiss him again before heading for my luggage and taking out my toiletry pack.

"I'm going to grab a shower. Let me know if the pizza gets here before I'm out," I say.

"Something tells me we're not going to be getting a thirty-minute guarantee out here," he says. "But I'll let you know."

Nothing takes off a chill like a hot shower and I let myself stand under the pleasantly hard stream for as long as I figure I can afford. Sam has the TV on when I walk out in my pajamas and favorite extra-thick socks, drying my hair with a towel.

"No pizza?" I ask.

He shakes his head. "Not yet."

The news is on and he's starting to change the channel when I hear something familiar.

"We have a special segment tonight on the past and future of the Dawn Day School in McCutcheon," the anchor says.

I sit on the edge of the bed next to Sam and press down on the remote with one hand to stop him from changing the channel.

"Hold on. I want to watch this for a second," I tell him.

"What is it?" he asks.

"Dawn Day School. It's not far from here. I was looking into the missing person's case and ended up reading about the school."

There's a brief block of commercials before the news comes back. The anchor immediately tosses the show over to the correspondent on the ground. He's bundled in a thick jacket and black ski hat as he stares straight ahead at the camera waiting for the signal. It apparently comes and he gives a nod of acknowledgement before launching into his spiel.

"Good evening, this is Gavin Christy and I am coming to you from the former site of Dawn Day School in McCutcheon. It's dark, but you can probably see behind me that this was once a truly impressive building. Now closed for nearly thirty years, the school is showing signs of neglect and the unfortunate effect of vandalism over the years. This building has gone through several different eras, starting as a private home, transitioning into a residential school, and most recently housing a private kindergarten through twelfth grade school. It has seen the growth and education of hundreds of local students and many families still mourn its closure."

There's a light knock on the door and Sam opens it to let Dean and Xavier in. I gesture for them to be quiet and come listen.

"But for others, this building is a reminder of tragedy and a mystery that has hung over the town of McCutcheon and surrounding communities for decades. Many don't know that Dawn Day School opened after the former boarding school was closed following years of rumors of mistreatment and even death among the students. After that school was shuttered, the entire staff was replaced and a more familiar day school opened in its place, quickly becoming known as one of the area's finest schools.

"It operated with tremendous success for many years until the tragic and still-unresolved disappearance of nine-year-old Linda Carmine in the late spring of 1957. According to witnesses at the time…"

I look over at Dean. "Linda Carmine. That's her. That's the little girl I was telling you about."

"The one you found in your research?" he asks.

"Yes. That is Dawn Day School. They're doing some sort of segment on it. They're talking about her disappearance," I say.

We listen to the reporter recount much the same information that I was able to find for a few moments before Dean suddenly gets a thoughtful expression on his face and walks out of the room. He knocks a couple seconds later and Sam lets him in again. He's carrying a manila envelope.

"What's that?" I ask.

"You said the name Linda Carmine. It immediately sounded familiar. It took me a couple of seconds to think about it, but then I realized why. Look at this."

He opens the manila envelope and pulls out a stack of papers and pictures. Sifting through them, he selects one and holds it out to me. At first, I'm not sure what I'm looking at. The image is in black and white, two little girls in dresses standing with their arms wrapped around each other in front of what looks like the school. Then I realize one of the faces looks somewhat familiar. I feel like I might have seen her before, but it's not familiar enough for me to place immediately.

"Who is this?" I ask.

"Linda Carmine," he replies. "With Alma Mulroney."

CHAPTER FIFTEEN

I'M SHOCKED BY THE ANSWER, BUT BEFORE I CAN ASK ANYTHING else, Sam touches my leg to get my attention.

"Emma, I think you're going to want to listen to this," he says.

I turn my attention back to the broadcast and see a more recent photo filling the screen.

"Connor Burton disappeared during a hike five years ago. Sally Montgomery disappeared a year before that while birdwatching. Two years before that, Mitchell Henderson disappeared during a solo camping trip. He intended to be gone for more than a month, which delayed anyone realizing something happened to him. It's still not fully known when he actually vanished.

"These are just a few of the names of people who mysteriously went missing in the area around Dawn Day School over the last three decades. They join the four people found dead on the grounds or in the immediate area. Though police did not find anything suspicious about these deaths and there's nothing to indicate the school had anything to do with the disappearances, or even that they are linked, locals say there's something eerie about the old building.

"Despite it being closed and legally off-limits, the old school has been a popular spot for visitors since shortly after its closure. Some are intrigued history buffs, others have come to throw parties out of view, others are thrill-seekers wanting to test the local legends about ghosts lurking the halls. Likely the most common visitors are simply campers seeking refuge from the conditions of the surrounding park when weather turns out less than ideal during their visit.

"The park itself is another example of a once-popular spot now closed. Unlike the school, it is widely known that experienced hikers and campers still frequent the park despite the facilities being inaccessible and there no longer being any maintenance done to the trails or former campgrounds. Despite the park being officially closed, former park officials have gone on record as stating that any visits are strictly at their own risk.

"Two such visitors who say they went from campers to inadvertent thrill-seekers at Dawn Day School are Sasha and Mark Berkeley. This young couple frequently hikes, camps, climbs mountains, white water rafts, and more. So it wasn't unusual when they set out in January three years ago for a spontaneous camping trip in Brecken Run Park. Mark grew up in the area and came to the park often with his family. Foregoing any of the cabins that are still standing, though reportedly in rundown condition, the couple decided to park at the far end of the park and hike in for a more primitive experience.

At approximately twenty square miles, Brecken Run Park is relatively small compared to state and National Parks, but still at one time boasted more than one hundred miles of running, hiking, biking, and horse trails. These trails have been left unmaintained since the park closed, causing them to become overgrown and many of them inaccessible. This is what Mark and Sasha say made their winter visit even more difficult.

"Hiking ten miles into the woods wasn't intended to be a challenging journey for them, clocking in at a fraction of what they are accustomed to doing on their more intensive trips, but they weren't expecting a massive snowstorm to hit the park when they had nothing but their tent and some supplies."

The screen fills with a pre-recorded video of a young couple sitting on a couch next to a fire. Both are wearing brightly patterned sweaters with white turtlenecks and look more appropriate for a promotional video about a mountain resort than any actual outdoor activities.

"We had our emergency radio with us, so we knew a storm was coming," the man I'm assuming is Mark says to the camera. "But the reports didn't sound terribly urgent and we had camped in bad weather conditions before, so we weren't too concerned about it."

"Besides, it was already late by the time we found out the storm was coming and we were so far from our car, it wasn't feasible to pack everything again and head back. We decided to hunker down and weather the storm right where we were," Sasha adds. "Unfortunately, the storm ended up hitting harder and faster than we expected."

"We woke up to a tree falling on our tent. Fortunately, we weren't hurt, but most of our supplies, including our tent itself, were destroyed. We had no choice but to leave the campsite and find somewhere else for the night. Growing up around here, I knew the park well and I also knew Dawn Day School. I had heard all the stories about it and had even visited it several times, so I felt like it was the best option for us to get to quickly and stay warm and safe through the night until we were able to make our way back to our car or to the town to get help."

"How did you feel about this idea?" someone asks from behind the camera.

He doesn't say Sasha's name but seems to be looking at her because she lets out a soft, slightly awkward laugh and looks up at her husband.

"Well, I wasn't so sure about it, to be honest. I don't know the park the way Mark does and I thought it might be better to try to get to town. But he reassured me the school was going to be the fastest choice and would give us the best shelter for the night. I've always been one for an adventure, so I wasn't afraid."

"What about the school? How did you feel about that?"

"Well, it did sound strange, and it wasn't helpful that Mark decided to regale me with the creepiest version of the building's backstory that he could possibly come up with. I've always been a skeptic, so I wasn't buying into the ghost stories, but there was still something unsettling about the building almost as soon as we went inside," Sasha says. "And then things started happening."

The couple looks at each other, the humor gone from their eyes. That shared look speaks more than either of them have said throughout the interview. They're carrying something between them only they understand. They can talk about it. They can share it. But they can't set it down and only the other one can truly appreciate the weight.

The footage returns to Gavin Christy, who describes the couple's terrifying experience locked in the school and apparently tormented by some unseen force.

"The police responded promptly and searched the building thoroughly, though there was no sign of a body or any other indication that any of these events actually happened. Although the official determination of investigators was that Mark and Sasha had fallen victim to delirium due to cold and exhaustion, the couple steadfastly stands behind what they both say they know they experienced."

"I can't explain it," Sasha's voice cuts in. "But I know what I heard and what I saw. I wasn't hallucinating and I certainly didn't make it up."

"We can understand why people might have a hard time believing us," Mark adds in a voice over. "But there have been others who have reported hearing or seeing strange things inside that building. And even though the police say the disappearances and deaths don't have anything to do with each other or with the building, my wife and I aren't embarrassed to say we feel lucky to have made it through the night and gotten out alive."

"Chilling words from a couple who say their experience trying to find shelter at Dawn Day School has left them far more cautious about their adventures and thinking twice about discounting other people's stories. Like Mark said, these aren't the only people who have reported strange happenings around Dawn Day School or Brecken Run Park, and officials say it's the public wariness of the building and the negative reputation of it and its history that have all contributed to the decision to demolish the existing building as part of a plan to revitalize the area and reopen Brecken Run to visitors in the coming years.

"While they understand some will be saddened by the removal of the building and others may be curious about it, it's important to understand that Dawn Day School is still off-limits to any and all visitors. Please remember the building is on private property and going onto it is trespassing. As the area is prepared for demolition, law enforcement will be regularly patrolling."

We turn off the TV as the segment turns to promoting the plans for the future of the park, including a grassy area and playground where the school is now standing.

"That's why it sounded familiar," I say. "The disappearances. They're saying that the police don't think of the deaths as suspicious, but there was at least one in the McCutcheon area that was most definitely a murder and still isn't solved. A team was sent to help because it looked like they might be a victim of a serial killer who was active in West Virginia right around the time when the guy was killed, but they haven't been able to prove that."

"What about the disappearances?" Sam asks.

"They didn't fit the pattern. They were investigated, but it was obvious pretty quickly that they likely aren't linked." I look back to Dean. "That picture of Alma Mulroney with Linda Carmine. What do you know about it?"

"Just that it's the two of them in front of the school. I didn't know what school it was, so it didn't register when you were talking about it. Alma's mother gave it to police a while ago when she first reported her daughter missing and they did a little profile on her for the local newspaper. They showed pictures of her from when she was young all the way up until right before she disappeared. When I went to ask about her case, they gave it to me. They said they tried to give it back to her years ago, but she didn't want to take it. She wanted the investigators to have them so they would remember that she isn't just another name or statistic, she is a whole person with a life and a family."

He takes a breath as he looks down at the smiling little girls. "They didn't tell me her best friend disappeared, too."

CHAPTER SIXTEEN

'M INTRIGUED BY THE WHOLE SITUATION, AND THE MORE I LEARN about it, the more I want to know.

"Maybe there's more to Alma walking away from her life than just getting swept up," I muse. "We haven't been able to find the connection between Broddeus and the three students, but I know he has had dealings near here. Is it possible that Alma's the connection? I still don't know enough about either case to even begin to guess, but from what you've told me, it doesn't seem like these four missing women are connected beyond just the fact that they were students at the same college.

"But now, there's this. Your investigations into the three missing students led you to Alma Mulroney. The reason you were brought in to do that investigation was because those three students from Conway kept coming up on the periphery when we were looking into Broddeus and his criminal network. Right?"

"Yeah," Dean says, not sounding like he's entirely on the same path as me, but I continue on.

THE GIRL AND THE WINTER BONES

"So, that's what brings the two cases together. There hasn't been anything that has directly linked Broddeus to the girls or even to the Conway area. But they are linked to Alma Mulroney because they went to the same college. Even though it was five years separated, with such a small school, there is statistical significance to both sets of disappearances.

"Alma is from McCutcheon, which is a place we've already established as a part of Broddeus' larger criminal network. Alma disappeared eleven years after the disappearance of her best friend, Linda Carmine." I felt like I was on a roll, but the thoughts start to sputter at this point and I pause, pursing my lips together and shaking my head at myself. "No. No, it doesn't make sense."

"What's wrong with it?" Sam asks.

"Well, Dean said he's already been able to trace Alma's movements to California and link her directly to the Manson family. Some of that evidence comes right from her mother, letters and things she's gotten from Alma. So she *was* heard from after her initial disappearance. The question is whether that disappearance was because she was somehow victimized by Broddeus while in South Carolina, and left after that."

"That would fit the narrative of a young girl up and abandoning her life in search of something else," Xavier says. "That's how all those movements grew back in those days. *On the Road*, the Hippie movement, the Manson Family, counterculture in general. Sometimes it really is a sense of adventure and a desire to see more of what the world has to offer. But far more often than that, it's pain and dissatisfaction with the life they are leading that pushes people toward something else. They want to reject everything about their old lives, right down to how they think society should be, and they walk right into the arms of people offering easy, simple answers."

"But it's not that simple," I piggyback off him with a nod. "They think they're taking control of their own lives when really, they're just handing over control to someone else."

"It's control through the illusion of self-actualization and freedom. That is more powerful, and terrifying, than even the most forceful of control. If a person feels like they are living their true selves and have finally been given the freedom to do that, they will feel extreme loyalty toward whomever they perceive as giving those things to them. They will be willing to do nearly anything to defend that person and protect what they've been given."

"She could have left because she went through something with Broddeus or his guys and it compounded what happened to Linda when they were little," I suggest. "Losing her best friend would be extremely difficult to deal with at that age."

"Something like that is extremely difficult to deal with at any age," Dean chimes in. "Look at Ava. She was much older than Alma when Molly disappeared. And it still affects her. She's still looking for her."

"I know," I say, letting out a slightly frustrated breath. "And I get that. I understand there's a lot of turmoil that goes into the decision to leave behind the entire world they've ever known and discover a whole new version of life. That makes sense. But it doesn't offer any new explanation for Linda Carmine. There were so many years between the two disappearances, and Broddeus wasn't criminally active yet at that time. He was so young. I can't really think of any reason he would have to go after her. As far as I could tell, there was never a ransom demand or anything. And her father was wealthy."

"Did they ever look into her father?" Sam asks. "I know that's not exactly something that people love to consider, especially when he had a reputation of being so dedicated to her. But it definitely wouldn't be the first time that someone who everybody thought was such a good parent ended up being the one responsible for their child going missing."

"No, it wouldn't be," I say, my mind immediately going to a particularly complex case I worked a few years ago involving a mother and her daughters. "I didn't see anything that mentioned him as a person of interest, but several articles talked about him being questioned and he did press conferences on the big anniversaries of her disappearance for a long time. It's possible, people do strange things after committing horrific crimes, but it doesn't seem he would do things to purposely bring attention back to her case for years after if he wasn't even being looked at. There would be no point to it. I don't know why, but Linda's disappearance really stuck with me. Since I read about it, I can't stop thinking about it."

"Because nine-year-old girls aren't supposed to go missing while playing a game after school with their friends," Sam says. "They're supposed to be safe at school. And more than that, everybody wants to believe if their children are at school and watched over by adults, there's no way something bad can happen to them. But for Linda Carmine, even a schoolyard full of teachers, parents, and other students wasn't enough to protect her."

"Someone has to know something," I say. "She can't have just vanished into mid-air. Someone saw something or heard something. Or they know something about her that could be a lead. I know they said that they weren't able to find any evidence that the rumors about the teacher were actually true, but just because they couldn't find evidence doesn't mean it didn't happen. What if Alma knew more and was afraid to say anything?"

"I'm meeting with Alma's mother tomorrow," Dean tells me. "You can come and we can see if we can find out more about Linda."

We are all exhausted from the trip and it's late, so as soon as we finish eating, we all go to bed. But by the time the sun comes up, I am awake, making a cup of terrible coffee in the small machine plugged into the hotel room wall. When it has sputtered and coughed its way into the cup, I take it over to the window and move the curtain aside so I can look out over the new morning. Beyond the parking lot and the road around the hotel is a rolling stretch of woods going on toward the horizon. I think of the park surrounding the abandoned school and about Linda Carmine laughing and playing with her friends in the last moments anyone knows about her.

Could all the other moments left empty after those have created ripples that still move today?

The guys get up not too long after me and once we've all had showers, we venture down to the lobby to consult the binder of information to find somewhere for breakfast. The little diner we choose reminds me of Pearl's, but unlike my favorite spot in Sherwood, there's an actual parking lot behind the restaurant rather than us having to drive up and down the road looking for somewhere to park. The differences in the two places become more obvious when we get inside and I'm not immediately confronted with the smell of strong coffee and sausage, but something far sweeter. The case of pastries at the front and heavily flavored coffees aren't a bad fragrance, they just don't make my stomach rumble with hunger the way it does the second I'm in close proximity to Pearl's biscuits and gravy.

"What are you two doing today?" I ask Sam and Xavier while we're waiting for our food to be brought to the table.

Since Dean and I are going to talk to Alma's mother, it's going to leave the two of them on their own for a while. This isn't the most common of situations, and I'm interested to find out what they have in mind.

"Caverns," they say in unison.

My mouth opens and then closes again.

"Caverns?" Dean asks, picking up the thought I apparently dropped.

"We checked out all the brochures in the lobby and that really caught our eye," Sam explains. It's an ancient rock formation. We both thought it sounded like fun."

"We only have one car," I point out.

"We could meet with Alma's mother near the library," Dean suggests. "I'd been thinking about going there anyway and doing some research. It's on the main street of town, close to a couple of restaurants and a coffee shop. We could spend some time at the library and meet her mother for coffee later. Sam can drop us off, they can go to the caverns, and then they can pick us back up this afternoon when they're done."

"And if Xavier discovers a new path through the caverns and we get delayed, the main section of town is only a couple of miles from the hotel. It wouldn't be that hard to do the walk," Sam says.

"You know, when you say things like that I want to think you're joking, but there is that little bit of possibility that you aren't, and that makes it a whole lot less amusing," I say.

"Good thing you trust me," he snickers.

CHAPTER SEVENTEEN

WHEN WE GET BACK TO THE HOTEL, DEAN GOES TO HIS ROOM to call Alma's mother and comes back with confirmation that she will meet us at the coffee shop in a couple of hours. It gives us enough time to get ready for the day and do some research at the library before going over there.

Sam and Xavier are talking about exploring the caves as we walk out to the car, and I'm not sure whether I should be excited about them spending some time together or nervous. This will be the first time they have gone on an outing or adventure with just the two of them, so it's going to be interesting to find out how it goes. It could be fantastic and a chance for them to settle more into the sometimes-awkward relationship that's existed between them since the beginning. They could come out of this with a better understanding of each other and it could bring our little chosen family even closer together.

Or, of course, Xavier could get disoriented, wander off, get lost underground, and Sam won't be able to find him or calm him down even if he does. They get along well, but Sam hasn't yet fully found his footing with Xavier for a situation like that. Dean would be able to think through things he'd said during the day and the names of the caverns or what Xavier ate for breakfast combined with the colors he was wearing and be able to ascertain where he was likely to have gone. He has that level of understanding and connection to Xavier.

Sam would see that he was no longer walking along beside him, panic, and run off in the dark depths of the caverns himself. They'd end up yelling at each other from different chambers like a game of Marco Polo and get banned from all cavern systems immediately after having to be rescued.

But the best I can do is hope for the former scenario and wait to hear otherwise. We follow the directions the clerk at the front desk of the hotel gave us to get to the main part of town and find the library. It's exactly what I think all libraries should look like. Old, stone, resembling a fortress. The steps leading up to the front door are worthy of a brisk jog and tall columns to either side inspire awe in anyone walking inside. It's the kind of entrance that makes you feel like you need to pick up a leather-backed literary tome to go along with the frothy romance you actually went in to borrow just to keep up your library street cred.

Dean and I go inside and head directly for the information desk. The research media room the librarian directs us to is larger than what I'm used to in Sherwood, and she tells us this library is the central location that serves a couple of other towns surrounding Gordon, including McCutcheon. We settle in to find what we can discover and soon I've filled several pages of my notebook with notes about what I've discovered. Dean has a stack of photocopied pages from the resources we were allowed to copy and the smell of the warm paper and fresh ink is almost dizzying.

It doesn't feel like we've been here for nearly as long as we have when Dean checks his watch and realizes we only have a few minutes to get to the coffee shop to meet with Alma's mother. We quickly gather up all of our papers, set the books on the return cart just outside the door, and wave at the librarian, letting her know we will likely be back. She gives a noncommittal nod and returns to the stack of books she is checking back in. The way her hand moves from ink pad to the inside covers of the books, stamping the date, has a rhythm that speaks to the many years she has spent doing that very task.

It doesn't have resentment behind it. She hasn't gotten jaded by doing the same thing over and over. Instead, she seems to approach it with care and seriousness. She is not a volunteer who comes by a few times a week. She went to school for this, studied for this. It's a career she loves and takes tremendous responsibility for. I can completely understand feeling that way about taking care of this beautiful building and its gorgeous collection. I wish Xavier was here to see it. I'll have to try to bring him before we leave town. He'll want to touch all the books, so it will require a time commitment, but we'll figure it out.

The coffee shop is only a couple of blocks from the library, but carrying everything and fighting the sharp, cold wind makes it feel longer. I'm very ready for a hot cup of coffee when we get to the shop. My muscles have that very particular fatigued feeling that comes from cold and wind and I just want to curl up into a pastry.

"Do you know what she looks like?" I ask Dean after we've ordered our drinks.

He looks around. "She's not here yet. Let's get a table."

We sit down and as I sip through the first part of my coffee to thaw myself out, I look back through the notes I took at the library. There are more details and statements I didn't get from my research in Sherwood, but still not enough to give me the connections I'm hoping to find. A few moments later, Dean looks up. I follow his gaze and see a tall, thin woman made even more slight by her oversized coat and dark hair hanging around her narrow face.

He waves at her and she comes over to the table without going to the counter to order anything.

"Dean Steele?" she asks.

Dean nods and stands to shake her hand. "I'm Dean."

"Carla Mulroney," she says.

"It's nice to meet you," he says, gesturing at one of the empty seats at the table as he sits down. "This is my cousin, Emma Griffin."

She nods at me blankly. "Hello."

She sounds like a woman who has been made tired by life but is pressing on. I don't know if this is how she is all the time or if it is just the weight of what she's come to talk about that is wearing on her. Either way, she looks at Dean with deep, emotion-filled eyes that are at once frightened and defiant. She doesn't want to wade any further into the pain, but she is also ready to fight for her daughter in any way she can.

I've seen that look before. I know I'll see it again. It's part of the career I chose, and even if it makes my heart ache every time I see it, I will never regret my path in life. The fact that it's so difficult to see someone going through something like this is the very reason agents and private investigators like Dean and me need to exist. Every time I see it, it hurts, but it reminds me why I'm here.

"Thank you so much for being willing to come talk with me," Dean says.

Carla nods again. "It's been so long since Alma left, I worry that people are going to just forget about her, or stop trying to look for her."

"That's why I'm here. I want to look for her, to find out what happened to her," Dean says. "It's why I got in touch with you. Your daughter's case caught my attention and I wanted to find out more about it."

"I'm sorry, I know we spoke on the phone and you said you're some kind of officer, but you're not from around here. I guess I don't really understand why you would have anything to do with Alma's case," she says.

This is that defiant pain speaking. She's hesitant to put any trust or reliance into this man she doesn't know who is bringing up the worst thing she's ever gone through and making her experience those emotions all over again.

"Not an officer," Dean corrects her quickly. He knows how important it is to differentiate between members of law enforcement and professional investigators like him. Though he is frequently brought in to assist with Bureau cases and some of Sam's investigations, he is still a separate entity. "I'm a private investigator. I'm not affiliated with any kind of law enforcement office."

"Then how did…"

"Emma is with the FBI," he says. He gives a subtle nod toward me, inviting me to continue the explanation.

"I was investigating a large and complex criminal ring and during the course of that investigation, I came across mentions of three girls who went missing from college in Conway about thirteen years ago," I say.

I don't even have to continue the explanation. Carla takes in a sharp breath. She leans back in her seat slightly as if trying to get away from what I'm saying. She pauses for a few seconds, then nods.

"The girls who disappeared from Alma's campus," she says.

"Yes. I wasn't able to find any concrete evidence that their disappearance had anything to do with the criminal I was investigating, but they kept coming up. So I made the recommendation that Dean be brought in as a special consultant for the case. He is an exceptional private investigator and I had confidence he would be able to find any connection, should there actually be one."

I glance over at Dean.

"While I was looking into the disappearances of those three students, I came across an article written for the campus newspaper that mentions Alma. I got intrigued by her story and wanted to look more into it," he explains.

"And I'm here because I was doing my own research after Dean mentioned the town of McCutcheon to me and found the story about Linda Carmine's disappearance. We realized that they knew each other," I say. "While our investigation is still very early, as of right now, Dean and I are investigating the disappearances of all five girls—the three college girls, Alma, and Linda—as possibly connected."

Carla nods slowly. "Alma took Linda's disappearance so hard. It really devastated her."

"How did they know each other?" Dean asks.

"They more than knew each other. They were best friends. They had been since the very first day of kindergarten. I was so worried that Alma wasn't going to fit in at Dawn. A lot of the families already knew each other, but that wasn't the case for us. I didn't know how the other children were going to respond to her or if she would be able to make any friends. But I so wanted her to have the best opportunity she could ever have with that education. So I just had to hope and bring her along.

"And after school on that very first day, I saw her running around on the playground with this precious little girl. I still remember she had two little braids coming down on the side of her head and was wearing a little white sweater. Over the years, I would tease Linda's father that he must have a whole closet with every size of that sweater hanging in it so he could just pull out the next one when she outgrew the last. She always had it with her, even when it was hot. It was almost like a security blanket. She was carrying it the last..." Her breath catches in her throat and there's a hitch in the word. "The last time I saw her."

"Can you tell us about that?" I ask. "Was there anything that stood out to you that last time you saw Linda? Was she playing with anyone you didn't usually see her with? Or acting strangely?"

"No," she says. "She was just walking toward the front door on her way out. She looked happy. Normal. It was like every other day. I was able to take Alma home a little earlier than usual that day and when I found her on the playground, she just said that Linda was already gone. I assumed her father had picked her up. I didn't know anything else about it until much later that evening when he called, frantic, to ask if I knew where Linda was. He thought she might have been in the clinic, or that I might have brought her home with me to play with Alma, but I would never have done that without asking him first. The police came to talk to me the next day, but there wasn't anything else I could tell them. I wish there was."

She looks uneasy, like this isn't the conversation she agreed to have. And it isn't. She's not here to talk about Linda Carmine. She wants to talk about her own daughter, as she should.

"Tell us about Alma," I say.

Carla's eyes soften and she sets her hands on the table in front of her, almost like she thought there was going to be a cup of coffee there and forgot she didn't actually order one. I glance up at the counter and make eye contact with the young man working behind it. I make a subtle gesture toward her and lift up my coffee mug. He nods and turns to the machine.

"Give me just a second. I'll be right back," I say, getting up to go get the coffee for her.

When I come back to the table, she's describing her daughter to Dean, telling him about how smart and beautiful she was. It's the same kinds of things most parents say about their children any time they're asked to describe them. But Carla says them with an extra layer of sincerity, like they aren't expected. She tells us how proud she was when Alma decided to go to college and got into the school in South Carolina. She was worried about her and not exactly thrilled about the idea of her only daughter being so far away from home, but she knew it was good for her. She had spent her entire life in McCutcheon and there was so much more Carla wanted her to see and do.

"If I had known what was going to happen, if I had known the kinds of things she would hear about and the thoughts that would get into her head, I never would have let her go," Carla continues as I sit back down. "It was a small school and when we visited it, I saw so many girls her age. They looked so happy, healthy, and successful. It was exactly what I wanted for her. I thought she would be safe. She would be like them. And she was, at first."

"How often did you talk to her?" he asks.

"We talked on the phone every week and she came home for holidays and breaks for that first year. She always sounded happy and excited. There was always something new she wanted to share with me. Things started to change some in her second year. She talked to me about wild ideas and things I'd never even heard of. Spirituality and different religions, self-enlightenment. Things that were so beyond what I'd always known and what I'd taught her.

"She told me she wanted more out of life. She felt like she was being held back and wasn't getting what she needed, or wasn't doing what she was supposed to be doing. She felt like there was something for her out there. A calling of some kind. Like she was meant to be a part of something so much bigger and more amazing than what she could do at home or even on that college campus."

"Did she mention California to you?" Dean asks.

Carla notices the coffee sitting beside her and looks at me. "Thank you." She reaches for the container of little pink packets sitting in the middle of the table and grabs out several. "Not at first. It wasn't until right before her third year in college that I heard her say anything about California. She had decided not to come home for that summer break and had gotten an apartment down there. I missed her, but I understood. It seemed like she was really settling into her adult life and finding her way.

"As a mother, that's what I wanted for her. But at the same time it was so hard. She kept calling, not as often as before, but I noticed she started mentioning California. We had never even talked about traveling there. I didn't know she had any interest in it. But she said she had a couple of friends who had gone out there and they were asking her to join them and telling her about this incredible man they were with. She didn't give me a name then or tell me what it was all about, just that they had joined a religious group and were doing amazing things. I went down to visit her one weekend and she just kept going on and on about what was going on in California and all the amazing things that were going to happen soon. 'You'll see,' she said over and over. 'When it all starts happening, you'll see. You'll know I was right. And I'll be a part of it.'"

Dean offers a sympathetic grunt, and Carla nods.

"I tried to discourage her, but there was no changing her mind. A few months later, she was gone. I didn't even know until the manager of her apartment called to tell me she hadn't paid rent and they were going to evict her. By then I was so used to not hearing from her for a few weeks at a time that I didn't know what was going on. I went down there and found out she'd been in that bar talking about going to California. I was terrified. I didn't know what I was supposed to do. She didn't leave a forwarding address or a phone number where she could be reached. Anything.

"I was able to go into her apartment and found a letter she'd apparently started writing to me but never sent. I don't know why. It said she was so excited to be starting on her adventure and didn't want me to worry about her. She was being drawn into something beautiful and powerful, something she was so energized by and in awe of. I won't ever forget those words. She was completely taken in. Wherever she was going and whatever she was going to do, she was so intensely invested. It was like she believed she was walking into God's arms."

Dean and I look at each other across the table. Carla had no way of knowing then what we do now. That is exactly what Alma believed.

CHAPTER EIGHTEEN

"ARE YOU SURE THIS IS A GOOD IDEA?" WILL ASKS AS THE group steps out of the dense trees separating the park trails from the old, abandoned road.

It was more of a struggle to hike through the park to the back portion that led them to the road, especially while hauling their bags of supplies and equipment. He's glad they parked up at one of the old parking lots and made their way to a cabin yesterday rather than carrying all of this from the car today. The cabin was not in great condition, and he didn't get too much sleep with cold air seeping through gaps in the walls and door and the sound of mice skittering along the floor all night. He tells himself it's his low energy levels that are making him more hesitant than usual, but the feeling is getting worse as they approach the stone wall around the school grounds.

"What do you mean? We've been talking about coming here for years," David replies, not bothering to look in his direction but still staring ahead at the looming obstacle of the wall.

"I know. But you heard what they were saying on the news. They're cracking down majorly on trespassing and there will be police officers patrolling the area. We didn't get permission to go in there," Will says.

"They've been saying that about trespassing for as long as I can remember. The place is closed. Of course, they don't want people just going in whenever they feel like it for no reason. But that's not what we're doing. We have a purpose being here. And I asked for permission, by the way," David tells him. "No one would ever get back to me. And if they are going to be that dismissive of us, then I don't understand why we should be expected to follow everything that they say."

Will knows his logic doesn't stand up to scrutiny. After all, it doesn't matter how many people get in touch with the owners of the former Dawn Day School. They allowed it to be abandoned for this long, and now will let it be demolished and replaced in just a few months. They don't care what a group of supposed paranormal investigators could possibly find at the place.

And that's why they are here. He's not going to argue with David. There wouldn't be any point. Once David has something in his mind that he wants to do, or that he thinks is the right thing, there is no convincing him otherwise. He has his own very distinct definition of fairness that he adheres to unwaveringly. He expects others to do the same, even the ones who have already directly disagreed with his terms or don't have any reason to know about them.

Not for the first time, Will wonders why he's here. He remembers the early days, when he agreed to be a part of this with David at the beginning. He was excited then, filled with the same curiosity and dedication to the unknown as the rest of them. That was before the attention David started to get. He thinks he is far better known and more important than he actually is, but Will is the only one of the group who seems to notice. The others are just as wrapped up in David as he is in himself. They think he is far more than just a paranormal investigator. They think he has a gift.

It didn't used to be that way. From the very beginning, they were all just people who were fascinated by the concept of life after death, the possibility of something beyond this plane of existence. They wanted to know more about it and find ways to prove that people don't just cease to exist. That they truly can continue on even after dying. They venture into destinations supposedly haunted by souls of the departed with historic research and test the latest scientific advances in the field of paranormal investigation. It's not a joke or a gimmick, but something taken seriously, an academic exercise designed to give more credence to an otherwise criticized and discredited scientific field.

But somewhere along the line, the word got out. The videos and recordings they gathered as evidence were shared like party tricks and David started thinking of himself as the group's de facto leader. He garnered a following, people fascinated by their investigations and also by the charismatic figure himself. They were drawn to him—his good looks and his confident personality. He stopped thinking of what they were doing as academic and everything shifted. Now, everything was far too close to entertainment for Will's comfort.

That wasn't what he had set out to do. He didn't want followers or fans. He didn't want people clamoring for the next opportunity to see one of the videos that they took or read the insufferably dramatic accounts David distributed in hastily-put-together booklets or pamphlets on the bulletin boards all over campus.

All he wanted was to continue looking deeper into the three possibilities of further existence, of something more than what we all experience from day-to-day. It was that dedication and undying curiosity that made him finally agree to join this investigation.

It took some convincing on David's part. Will hadn't wanted to come at first. But the more the rest of the group talked about the investigation and the more Will thought about the reality that the building would no longer be there, that there would no longer be the opportunity to investigate the Dawn Day School, the more he realized this was a chance he couldn't just throw away. Like everybody else, he had heard the stories of the school. He knew about its tragic origins, the couple who designed and built the house to be a home for their future family, the family they were never able to have, and who ended up dying there at the house like all the children taken from them before birth or as tiny infants.

It wasn't a new story. It was like countless other locations where people suffered unimaginable pain and heartache simply because they were victims of their time. He ventured to think pretty much any building with as many years behind it as one like this would know its fair share of tragedy. But the story didn't just stop with the deaths of that couple. It continued on with new chapters. And they didn't necessarily go smoothly.

That was what made this destination so fascinating. So many different types of people had passed through these halls and rooms, experiencing the whole spectrum of emotions as they lived their lives. Will believes it's those emotions that still tie them to this place. Their energy made a mark on this place, and he believes he can somehow make contact with them.

That possibility has never stopped being thrilling to Will. He still gets excited at the thought of engaging with someone who lived generations ago and being able to use those experiences to collect scientific data to support not only the concept of life after death, but of how those entities function within their world and ours.

David no longer seems to have that same kind of fascination. He doesn't want measurable evidence or things that can be compared with existing data to show what they experienced had a completely reasonable explanation. There used to be a very clear set of ethics regarding the evidence they collected. Especially when one of the others in the group, Lila, recommended they start using a video camera to record their investigations so they could look back on them later. They agreed they would never fabricate any evidence in the form of sounds, objects moving, light, shadows, voices, or anything else. They would record things as the camera saw them, give clear, timely markers for if they made a sound or moved out of frame, causing a shadow, and then when they were done, they would carefully go over everything the camera captured.

Those sessions weren't just about sifting through to try to find strange sounds or moving shadows, or the holy grail of a voice. They were also about finding things that could be misinterpreted and noting them so they could either be removed from the footage later or clearly explained prior to anyone seeing them.

It took only a few months for David to get intensely attached to the video footage taken of him during the investigations and the fawning attention he got from it. People believed they really had ventured into the unknown and come back with inarguable evidence. Soon the editing sessions became less frequent and less comprehensive. Things that were clearly just incidental sounds or movements in the environment, or were created by a member of the team either purposely or accidentally, weren't so quickly dismissed, and many started finding their way into the final cuts.

David developed a persona that was loud and dramatic, making far more out of every little thing that happened than was warranted. He started hanging out with fans of their work, who'd tell him he had some sort of special connection to the spirits he was communicating with and that was why he was getting so much good evidence. This changed him even more. He believes now that he has some sort of supernatural power, a sensitivity that enables him to sense when there are spirits around and connect with them on a level beyond that of the rest of the team.

He's become insufferable, and it's obvious at this point that he no longer shares the philosophies and goals they had at the beginning. But Will couldn't give up the opportunity to come here. It's something he wouldn't do on his own and he knows there is very little time left. He wants to see the school, to wander the grounds and go inside in search of some validation for all the stories. There are some locations that simply seem more suited to maintaining spirit life, and this building has it all. Age, pain, death, mystery. Everything that makes up a good ghost story.

He has to see it. Even if it means dealing with David. At least this will be his last time. Will doesn't plan on continuing on with David after this and plans on telling him once their investigation is over. He hopes that at least some of the team will be true to their original vision and agree to work with him on investigations the way they used to be, but he can't be sure. He knows they may well have all gotten sucked into David's ego as much as he has and would prefer to keep soaking in the small-time fame and attention for as long as it's available to them.

"Are you scared?" David asks plainly.

Will darkens his brow. "No."

He isn't scared of the prospect of venturing into an old, abandoned building like this. Most of their investigations involve abandoned buildings just like this one. What concerns him is the stern warning on the news broadcast.

While the grounds and building have always been closed and technically off-limits, there was little to no security or police presence until now, which means if they are caught they could be facing trespassing charges. Will fought through the uncertainty to get all the way here, but now it's pressing down on him more as he actually looks at the grounds.

Additional security measures have been put into place over the last couple of years after the experience of the Berkeley couple. Before, they'd seen pictures and heard accounts of there being a large metal gate across the front of the driveway leading up to the school itself, but it was never actually secured closed. People could just walk right in. Now, the gate is not only firmly closed with two padlocks securing it into place, there's a metal bar across the two halves from the inside, preventing it from moving at all.

"Look," David says as they walk across the street, "if you're scared, you don't have to do this. The others know how to use the equipment and collect all the evidence. You can go back to the cabin and wait for us. It's no big deal."

Will wishes he was the type of person who didn't prickle when dismissed. He wants something like that to not bother him, or even to aggravate him enough to just walk away. Instead, his cheeks burn with a surge of anger. He can't believe David would be so unfazed that the guy who used to be his best friend and partner in this would be hesitant. He wants the glory for himself. Even if it's not authentic. He wants to be able to create a narrative that he can send out into the world, telling anyone who will listen about his harrowing experience and how successful he was at casting away the dark forces within the building while also compassionately freeing the trapped souls of the innocent and good.

Without Will there to contest his account of their experience, David could basically say anything. If anyone else on the team was to question it, David would just say that they weren't in the room at the time and point to the others who would stand up for him. Will is the only one who will no longer take what he says at face value.

David is going to take every opportunity he can to turn visiting this place into his own moment of glory. He knows full well the demolition is coming soon and few people, if any, would have the chance to come and compare their own experiences to what he reports. Without someone to check him, he would have free rein to concoct any story he wanted.

Will can't let that happen. Not just because he doesn't want to see David relishing more ill-gotten fame and adoration, but also because he can't stand the disrespect it shows. If there truly is life after death, if there really are spirits of the dead continuing to inhabit these spaces, they don't deserve to be lied about and treated like sideshows.

Even if his theories don't pan out and there is nothing behind his field of research, real people once lived within these walls. Even if they aren't here anymore, they lived, loved, suffered, triumphed, and died. They made an impact on the world. It isn't right to make up stories about their spirits or about things they have "communicated" from beyond the grave. Will is determined to stop David from doing that. Even if it means going against his better judgment and entering the abandoned site.

Lila, Jonathan, Charlotte, and Daniel follow David across the street and gather close to the wall. Will takes another few seconds just to look at the space, taking it in. This is the only time he'll ever see it this way. He has envisioned coming here for so long and now it is actually happening, but he knows there can never be a return trip. This is his one chance before it is all destroyed. One that happens, the stories will start to fade. The memories of what this place once was will disappear. Not too long from now, no one will even remember the wealthy man who loved his bride so dearly he built this gorgeous home for her. Or the school that went so wrong. Or the child who never went home.

CHAPTER NINETEEN

"THE GATE'S PRETTY SECURED, SO GOING THROUGH IT ISN'T A possibility," David says while everyone gathers around him. "Which leaves us with a couple of options. Either we can go over the wall right here, or we can walk around to the back of the property to find out if the access road has been closed off. I wasn't able to find anything about that road recently, so I don't know if it has been gated off or not. I think the best plan would be to just go over the wall here rather than waste time going around just in case it is blocked off."

That essentially means the decision has already been made, but he wanted to seem magnanimous by positing it to the rest of the crew as if their opinions truly mattered. In all probability, if one of them was to disagree with the idea of going over the stone wall, he would have done it anyway and invited them to make the trek around the property on their own. Considering the speed at which the temperature is dropping and the ominous cloud cover crushing down on them, none is particularly keen to be the one to take up that challenge. He knows that about them.

"Will, why don't you take your camera and go on over there first so you can record me coming over the wall?" David suggests.

He knows there's more to David asking him to go over first then just the chance for another dramatic moment of footage. Just in case there is something on the other side of the wall, David doesn't want to be the first to encounter it. It's been that way since the beginning. When it was just the two of them lurking around old houses they found in the countryside or going to cemeteries in the middle of the night. If ever there was even the slightest chance that there could be danger or negative consequences, David wasn't going to be the one to find out.

Of course, all the footage ever taken only shows him plowing ahead, leading the group without a trace of fear, and always being the one to confront the unknown headlong. Will doesn't care. He doesn't want or need esteem or recognition. He wants the evidence. He wants the answers to the questions he's had ever since he was a little boy, when his great-grandmother told him that the human spirit isn't an idea, it is a tangible thing. That we are more than dust and bone. He'd heard spooky stories and seen creepy Halloween decorations and TV shows supposedly about ghosts, but they were always presented as a gruesome fairy tale, just a silly concept to give people chills.

The way she spoke about them, though, was completely different. She talked about spirits as if they were a normal part of daily life, as if they shared the same space with her at all times. It wasn't a question for her. Heaven is home, she would tell him. There's a journey to get there. And sometimes people take that same journey back and forth many times, just like we do when we travel. We always mean to go back home, but sometimes we linger.

It took away the mystical element, that thing that makes people talk about ghosts and spirits in hushed tones, and made it no different than understanding other mysteries of science and the universe. That stayed with him throughout his life, and when his great-grandmother died, he found himself wondering where she was. Had she gone home? Was she lingering here? Or was she somewhere on the journey?

Will adjusts the strap on the bag containing his camera so it is held closer to his body, and approaches the wall. It's not very tall, but sheer on the front, giving him no foothold to use to launch himself up. Instead, he takes a step back, then runs forward and plants the ball of his foot into the middle of the wall, pressing against it and jumping at the same time so he ends up on his belly over the top. He swings his leg over, pushes back, and drops. It's not a difficult drop and he lands on grass that hasn't been tended to in many years. It's a naturally short stalk, so it isn't overwhelmingly long or tangled, but it gives a softer landing spot.

He stands and turns around to take in the grounds behind him. For a moment, he just appreciates standing here, looking out over the quiet, sleeping space. He can feel the energy crawling on his skin. So much has happened right here. Things that have never been explained. Things that no one even knows. He feels like he could close his eyes and hear the laughter. But it might also mean hearing the screams.

The wind touches his face, sending a chill along the side of his neck. It's carrying ice and snow, threatening a storm that could hit at any moment. He hopes it holds off.

"Are you ready?" David asks.

Will looks around the grounds for another second, hesitating briefly on the small building off to the side. It looks like a supply shed, but the size is slightly off and the window along with a chimney tells him it's actually something else.

"Come on," he calls over to David, getting his camera out and propping it up on his shoulder to focus on the wall.

It takes a few seconds before David comes into view. The way his body is lifting and pauses to hover suggests he didn't get to the top of the wall under his own power. Will imagines Jonathan is crouched down on the other side of the wall, boosting him up. David swings his leg over and crouches for a moment like a cat perched on the top before leaping down. Will steps back to get out of the way, turning the recording off and glaring at David.

"Did it look good?" he asks, looking at Will with the expectation not of a real opinion but of gushing praise. "Did it look like I was coming down from something really high?"

"You looked like you were coming off a wall," Will tells him. "I mean, the camera showed how tall the wall was and you climbing on top of it."

"I'll edit it." He turns around to yell over the wall. "Come on, everybody."

One by one the other members of the team make their way over the wall until the pieces of equipment and everyone is over and ready to go up to the school itself. There's a heavy, wet chill in the air, making everything seem intensely still and quiet. Each of the members of the team looks around themselves as they walk, taking in the empty, darkening yard and the silhouette of the school building coming into view against the white sky.

"What's that?" Lila asks, nodding toward the shed.

"The caretaker's house," David tells her. "He maintained the grounds and did basic handyman type stuff around the school."

"And he lived in that?" she asks, clearly put off by the small size of the building.

"I guess he didn't need much. That was probably part of the appeal of the position on both ends."

"You said that there was some little girl who went missing around here, right?" Charlotte asks.

She's the newest member of the group and doesn't show as much interest in the history of each location as she does the experience she personally has when she gets there. She considers it a purer approach to the research to know little about the destination and what happened there before going into it and starting an investigation. To an extent, Will agrees with her. He understands not wanting unfair influence on what she hears, feels, or sees. But on the other hand, knowing the history of a place provides valuable context that can make seemingly minor occurrences more meaningful.

He likens it to reading the lyrics of a song while listening to it being sung. Having the words right there can take away some of the experience of listening to the song until it becomes clear, but it also ensures the song isn't misunderstood.

In preparation for this visit, they gave Charlotte a little bit of background about the building, but she didn't watch the news special and wasn't a part of any of Will's research into the looming structure. One thing they didn't mention to her was the disappearance of Linda Carmine. A vital piece of local history and a mystery that has been tossed around over as many glasses of whiskey as cups of coffee, that little girl going missing is at the heart of many of the legends and dark, twisted tales about this spot.

Even though arguably the most gut wrenching of events happened well before she was even born, the cheerful face and sweet smile of the nine-year-old captured the popular imagination. Suddenly, she was everyone's child. She represented the innocence of the world disappearing. Parents saw her and hugged their own children a little closer. They thought twice about just leaving them on their own to play or walk around. They applied more rules but also gave more love and more hugs.

"Linda Carmine," David says. "She was nine. She disappeared while she was at recess."

"After school," Will corrects. "She wasn't at recess. She was playing with her friends and when she didn't show back up after a round of hide and go seek, they just assumed her dad picked her up. But he arrived after that, and they realized she was gone."

"Did anybody ever check with the caretaker?" Charlotte asks. "Maybe he snatched her and hid her away in that shack."

David's eyes light up and he turns, making his way over toward the caretaker's house rather than continuing on towards the school.

"That's perfect. Let's try to make contact with her here," he says.

Will shakes his head. "She wasn't here. The caretaker was mowing the lawn the whole time. He helped with the search and they went through his house and didn't find anything."

"How many people know that?" David asks.

"Anyone who does thorough enough research of the case," Will says. "It's in the interviews and news reports."

"So, it's not common knowledge."

Will knows where this is going. He decides to just suck it up and not question or push back against David. It'll make the night easier if he just goes with it and tries to influence the editing later. He has already given up on the idea of using any of the video footage that involves the rest of the team as any form of true evidence. Instead, he continues to collect his own notes and observations to include in his files.

They get through a dramatic session of David walking around the caretaker's house, talking to the cameras wielded by Will and Jonathan about the missing little girl and the mystery still surrounding what happened to her. He makes heavy implications that something horrible could have happened to her right here and then starts talking to her, attempting to reach out to her so she can tell her own story.

When it's finally over, and Will is unsurprised in any way that they got nothing in the form of voices, temperature changes, electromagnetic spikes, or anything else, they continue to the school. The storm is rolling in fast, making the hairs on the back of his neck stand up, and he's glad at least for the shelter they'll have for the night.

CHAPTER TWENTY

"IT FEELS SPOOKY OUT HERE," LILA SAYS, RUBBING HER ARMS looking around.

"It's the storm coming," Charlotte tells her. "Just like the night Mark and Sasha Berkeley came here. It was storming then, too. That's what brought them here."

"You're right," David nods. "They did come here because of the storm. It drew them in. The weather lured them here to the school. It's like the atmosphere changes because of the supernatural forces embedded in the walls and soaked into the grounds around this place. And tonight, the same is happening to us."

Will glances beside and confirms Jonathan is recording as David stands with his arms open as if offering himself up to the supposed forces crafting the storm to draw them into the building. He tries to remain open-minded during these investigations just as any scientist would try to approach their experiments without preconceived notions and a willingness to accept unexpected results. But he stops short at any belief that a supposedly haunted building could control the weather for several surrounding towns.

Considering it is early January in Maryland, it's not a huge leap to expect some snow. But he has to admit the storm is adding to the intense atmosphere. The white of the sky has given way to darkness as the sun sets, but there's still the energy in the air, that tingling feeling of potential that builds until it finally breaks when the first snowflakes fall.

There's a slightly hushed sense of awe as the group approaches the school. Even the signs of obvious neglect don't diminish how magnificent the building clearly was and in so many ways still is. It feels like a tremendous loss that the beautiful structure is going to be demolished rather than preserved in some way. Even if the building can't be used as a school anymore, it seems like there has to be some use it could be put to. Even as a boutique hotel or historic site.

"Is everyone ready?" David asks.

With cameras ready, they climb the front steps. It looks like someone tried to secure the front door with the same kind of additional security as was added to the gate, but it is much more difficult to prevent people from opening a wooden door than it is an iron gate. The wooden board that had been nailed across the front doors has been pried away from one side and then neatly cut to grant access. Someone came very prepared. Will can only imagine that it will be difficult for authorities to actually keep people from coming here. It's been a destination for so long and now that it's being taken away, it will draw in the most committed even more. Right up until the building is taken down, the police will have a challenge on their hands.

Will just hopes they aren't too vigilant tonight. The more layers of security they break through to get inside, the worse the consequences if they are caught. That isn't going to look good for the grant committee when he seeks additional funding for the future research he plans on doing independently rather than with any association with David.

But at the same time, now that they are so close, Will knows the risk is worth it. There's so much potential here, and if there are spirits, he feels like he owes it to them not just to give them back their voices in whatever way he can so they can tell their stories, but also to reassure them as they prepare for the destruction to come.

Will opens the door and takes his first step inside. He feels the significance of the space. He can feel its history, even without there being a supernatural element. A person coming here doesn't have to believe in spirits to feel the years and the lingering memories of everything that's happened here. He has often wondered if that is all ghosts really are. That his great-grandmother might have been wrong and instead of spirits being true continuations of the person after their death, that the feeling is one of collective memory. Similar to instincts and inherent skill, maybe that feeling derives from the human experience itself and is passed on to the next generations. They aren't actually sensing the presence of a spirit but rather remembering that person.

"Let's go ahead and do a sweep to establish baseline parameters for the meters," he says.

Much of the evidence he collects is based off changes in temperature and electromagnetic fields thought to relate to the composition of spirits. Sudden cold temperatures in an area occur with hauntings not because the spirit emits cold, but because they remove the heat from the environment around them in order to supply themselves with energy. Will has heard of other teams experimenting with providing supplemental heat sources during investigations to draw spirits and give them additional energy so they can better manifest and communicate.

He hasn't attempted such an experiment yet but can see the merit in the theory. It's something he plans to try once his funding goes through and he's able to embark on more intensive independent research away from the pageantry and cult of personality that has taken over this team.

They take out their meters and take a few moments to establish the basic temperature of the building and the baseline electromagnetic reading. Will records each of these results so they could be used for comparison later if there are any significant changes. There's always the expectation that there will be some changes throughout a building. Temperatures can vary somewhat and many different influences in the environment can alter the electromagnetic fields within those spaces. Establishing baseline readings before starting the investigation of an area helps to identify and quantify those changes, potentially validating them as evidence.

"I think we should start in the areas of the building that have been least modified since it was originally built," Will says. "This area, the kitchens and staff quarters to the back. They had to overhaul pretty much the entire building over the years, but these areas are the closest to the original layout."

"Good idea. Start with the old and move our way up."

They spend the next twenty minutes walking through this half of the bottom floor of the building. Many of the doors to rooms that were once servants' quarters or staff quarters are locked, but they make their way into the kitchen and then through to the smaller ancillary kitchen at the back of the building.

"This is where the Berkeley couple spent the night," Lila says.

Charlotte shudders. "I can feel something. There's something here."

"Is there someone with us?" David asks the small room. "Are you a servant from when this was a house? Or a staff member from school? A student? Are we speaking with Linda?"

"Give them a second to respond," Will says. "It's not going to do any good if you just rattle off questions like that. If we do get a response, we're not going to know which question they're responding to."

In the glow of his flashlight, Will can see David glaring at him. He doesn't like to be questioned about his techniques. But Will has to take this opportunity seriously. He already plans to investigate on his own during the night, but every moment there within this building is important. Once it's gone, they won't have the chance again. The pressing urgency of the investigation brings up another set of questions that forms the basis of his research.

Are some spirits essentially chained to a specific building or area and can't leave it? Can others choose, as his great-grandmother told him, to go back and forth between whatever plane they exist on here on Earth and Heaven?

And what happens if the building where they have been existing is demolished and something else put in its place?

There have been reports of hauntings that seem to be spirits from past eras continuing to inhabit the area that was once their home or somewhere significant in their lives even though that place is no longer standing. New homes or stores have the lingering spirits of people who once lived, worked, or went to battle in that spot. Will is eager to find out what these spirits see around them. If they truly are intelligent entities or just impressions of energy that have stayed and occasionally become evident to living humans, like static electricity in laundry that turns to sparks when moved in just the right way.

Do they see what they did when they were alive? Or can they perceive what the space has become? There is evidence to support both. Reports of spirits walking through walls where there were once doors or behaving in remodeled rooms the way they would have when the room was still being used for its intended purpose, such as ghostly couples dancing through what once was a ballroom but is no longer. But then also reports of spirits playing pianos that were not there when they were alive, or moving objects that weren't there.

"Will? Did you hear me?"

He realizes he's been so lost in his thoughts he hasn't been paying attention to the rest of the crew. They're staring at him with expectation, as if he's supposed to come up with an answer or a suggestion.

"What's going on?" he asks.

"Charlotte was saying she feels a very heavy, dark presence here and wants to know if this area of the building was ever used for any type of sinister activity. As the team's researcher, I thought you might know."

Will doesn't appreciate his role being reduced so dismissively, but he stops himself from saying anything. It won't matter to David, anyway. In his mind, he is the main event. Everyone else is just support.

"No," Will says. "Nothing I've ever read has given any indication that bad things happened here. Beyond, I suppose, the basic risks of a kitchen. I'm sure someone at some point got a burn or maybe cut themselves while chopping something. But I would hardly say that's sinister."

Charlotte shakes her head again. "No. There's more than that. There's something you don't know. Can't you feel it, David? Can't you sense the fear and agony here?"

David draws himself up, closing his eyes and pulling in a breath as if he's attuning himself to the space around him. He stays that way for a few seconds, then nods.

"I do. You're right. Something happened here. Something horrible. And maybe it doesn't show up in research because nobody knows what happened. At that time, servants could go missing and no one would say anything about it because they didn't mean anything. One of the servants could've been murdered right here and no one would know."

"Servants didn't just go missing without people noticing," Will says. "The staff was extremely important to how this home was run, and by all accounts, the couple who lived here were pretty prominent in the community. It would have been a big deal if one of their servants just disappeared."

David shrugs. "Maybe you're right. But that would only apply if it was one of their servants, now wouldn't it? Someone else could have met their end here without it being questioned because they didn't belong here to begin with. That could have been the beginning of the negativity that has plagued this building. A murderous servant taking advantage of the kindness of their employer and using their home to dispatch their victims would certainly impact the energy of a space."

Will notices Jonathan has been recording this entire conversation and holds up his hand to block the camera lens.

"Stop," he says. "David, I need to talk to you for a second."

David looks at the others gathered in the room. "I think Will wants to share some information with me that is too sensitive to be recorded. While we're gone, why don't the rest of you do an EVP session? Charlotte, see if you can contact the entity you are sensing. They are clearly reaching out to you. Open yourself to them and allow them to communicate. Remember what we've been working on during our sessions."

Will can't help but roll his eyes as he walks out of the small room and into the larger main kitchen. As soon as they are far enough away that he's confident the others can't hear him, he turns on David.

"Your sessions?" he asks.

David smirks. "Yeah. Charlotte is impressed by my spirituality and skill at connecting with the dead. She wants to hone her own abilities and has been meeting with me to learn at my feet."

Disgust ripples through Will's stomach and he makes a distasteful face. "How do you just manipulate people like that and think it's okay?"

David's face drops. "I'm not manipulating anybody. She came to me."

"Because you convinced her, along with all the other people you've bamboozled, that you have some sort of special power. She thinks you're a damn supernatural telephone operator."

"I am," he says.

"Bullshit. You started doing this because you cared about the science of it. Now it's a fucking dog and pony show and you're screwing with people," Will fires back. "Frankly, you can do whatever you want with Charlotte, with Lila, with every girl who throws herself at you because she thinks you can transcend the plane of life or whatever other line of shit you've been feeding them. Doesn't matter to me. What does matter to me is you compromising my research and discrediting me. You can't just make up stories like that and present them as truth."

"Why not? It's what people want to hear," David says.

"It doesn't matter what people want to hear. That's not the point of this. We're supposed to be objectively investigating locations and collecting actual potential evidence. Not concocting cockamamie stories just to sound creepy. It damages the reputation of the building and everyone who has ever interacted with it, it brings up questions about actual crimes that did occur, possibly misleading investigations, and it puts my credibility and the potential for future funding at risk. You need to stop."

Will doesn't care about playing nice anymore. He came into tonight's investigation intending to be civil and calm, and just ignore David's antics as much as possible, but that has already gone by the wayside. It's less than an hour into what could prove to be an extremely long night and things have already gone off the deep end.

David squares off, his hands planting on his hips as his chest puffs toward Will.

"I don't think I need your permission to do anything. And I certainly don't need you telling me how to do my job," he says.

"This isn't your job," Will argues. "It's not a career path. You're not going to get famous by making up stories and faking jump scares."

"I already am," he says.

"You have a cluster of people who buy your idiotic booklets. I really don't think that qualifies as fame. But you know what? After this, you can do whatever you want to do. Pursue all the fame you want. Do any kind of investigation you want and tell any kind of asinine story you think is going to get you the attention that you so desperately crave. But don't attach my name to it. As long as I am here with you, you're going to at least *pretend* like you still have some sort of ethics. You're not going to humiliate me in front of my colleagues in the field."

David lets out a laugh. "Colleagues in the field? Are you serious right now? Do you still actually think of yourself as a scientist? You really believe that you're going to make some sort of groundbreaking discovery that will prove something people have been talking about since the beginning of time but have never actually proven? It's not science, Will."

"The fact that people have been talking about it since human existence only supports the validity of the pursuit," Will argues. "People have always wondered about life after death and have tried to find ways to communicate with their dead loved ones. This field has been around for over a century. The top scientists of the time devoted time and resources to the research of the paranormal."

David laughs again. "Parlor tricks, Will. It was all parlor tricks. Then and now. They used Ouija boards and mirrors. This whole serious approach used to seem cool, but it's gotten tired. Just get with it. Enjoy the notoriety. There are groups that lead tours like this and make a lot of money doing it. Or we could offer our services identifying and removing ghosts from buildings."

"I'm not a fucking Ghostbuster."

"There are worse things you could be," he says.

"Count me out," Will says. "After this, I'm not a part of the team anymore. I'm applying for grant funding and going back to investigating the correct way."

"You're not just going to walk away from me," David says. "You do the research and know how to work the equipment."

"Then learn how to do it yourself," Will tells him. "Go to the library, pick up a book, and research. Get your own equipment and find out how to use it. I'm not going to keep trailing around after you doing this."

Will turns away and starts back toward the small kitchen.

"Don't you realize I hold your reputation in the palm of my hand?" David asks, his voice dropping from his high-pitched protest to something smooth and threatening. "I could make sure that funding never materializes and everything you ever touch turns to shit. You're as much of a fraud as I am. The only difference is I'm willing to admit it and take advantage of it."

Will turns back to him. "Go to hell."

David smirks. "Maybe. Then you can investigate me."

The tension is building between the two of them but breaks with the sound of a scream.

CHAPTER TWENTY-ONE

THE GUYS RUN BACK INTO THE SMALLER KITCHEN AND FIND Jonathan, Lila, and Charlotte running around as a large black bird flutters frantically around the space.

"Where did that come from?" David asks.

"The chimney," Jonathan says. "It just fell down into the fireplace and started fluttering around."

Will goes over to the fireplace and looks in. "That means the flue is open. They didn't seal it off."

"Mark and Sasha talked about that," Lila says. "Remember? They said they spent the night in the kitchen and had a fire going to keep them warm."

"Yeah, but that was three years ago. With everything that they've done to add extra security to the building, I would think that they would make sure the fireplaces are inoperable. That would take away a lot of the appeal of breaking in here for campers," Will says.

"Maybe it's a safety thing," Jonathan offers. "They probably know that even with the security measures put into place, people are going to try to break into the building. Look at us. We're here. And if campers are going to continue to come in here, they're probably going to try to make fires. If they blocked off the chimney, wouldn't that be really dangerous?"

"Yeah, it would be," Will says. "Maybe you're right."

"Jonathan," David calls over. "Get this." He stands on one of the heavy wooden tables up against the wall and holds his flashlight steady on the bird. As soon as Jonathan has his camera focused on him, David's persona returns. "I want all of you to witness this. We are inside the exceptionally haunted Dawn Day School. Since the minute we arrived on these grounds, I've noticed just how active this place is. I wish I could tell you all the feelings going through me. I can sense so many people around us. And we've got extraordinary evidence of the dark forces at work here.

"This black bird came down the chimney while we were investigating a small kitchen I believe to be the site of at least one undiscovered murder. Possibly several. This is clearly the work of a dark entity, possibly a demon possession. The question is whether that demon possession is the cause of the rampant abuse and murder that occurred throughout the history of this building, or if the horrific acts of the people who once lived here beckoned the dark forces and welcomed them to call this home."

"There has never been a documented murder at this school," Will cuts in. "You can't say that."

"What about the bodies found out on the grounds?" Charlotte asks, obviously challenging him in defense of David.

"They were vagrants and lost campers for the most part," Will says. "Cause of death wasn't determined for a couple of them and others died of exposure or drug overdose. There's nothing mystical or paranormal about that. Just people making bad decisions and suffering unfortunate consequences because of it."

"What about the body that the Berkeleys found in that classroom?" Lila presses.

"The police got here within minutes of that call and searched the entire building, up and down. There was no body anywhere."

"You think they made it up?" Charlotte asks.

"It certainly wouldn't be the first time somebody made something up," Will replies with a shrug. "But I don't necessarily think they meant to make it up. They were trapped after getting caught up in a very intense snowstorm. At that point, delirium could hit quickly and cause all kinds of hallucinations."

"They said they weren't hallucinating," Jonathan says.

"People who are hallucinating generally don't have the awareness that they are hallucinating, Jonathan," Will gripes in irritation. "That's what makes it so terrifying. They thought it was real."

The bird has stopped flying around frantically and is perched on the stone outcropping above the fireplace.

"Are we just going to leave it?" Lila asked.

"No," Will says. "We have to get it out. It won't be able to fly back up the chimney most likely."

"Then you wrangle it," David says. "I'm not touching that thing."

It takes a few minutes, but Will is finally able to get his hands on the bird and hold tightly onto it so it doesn't flutter away from him. The last thing he wants is for it to get out of his grasp and get loose in the rest of the building. With only the light from his flashlight hanging down from his hip Illuminating his way, he rushes back through the bottom floor of the building to the front door. It hadn't closed all the way when they first came inside, stopped by a piece of the board blocking it. He is able to catch the side of the door with the toe of his shoe and pull it open.

He remains mostly inside but leans out across the wide front porch to release the bird. It leaves his hands in a burst, flying up toward the sky and into a circle, like it's relieved to be out of the building and in the fresh air again. As Will is watching the bird soar away, the first snow-flakes start to fall. Within seconds, the slow fluttering turns into a sheet of white coming down from the sky. The wind blows up, swirling the snow until it is almost impossible to see anything beyond the door. It settles down within a few seconds, but that brief moment of intensity spoke to what this storm is capable of.

Will steps back inside and shuts the heavy door, giving it a hard shove to ensure it's securely in place. He finds the rest of the group standing in the hallway among the closed doors of the staff quarters. David is trying to open one of them, but it's locked.

"Can any of you pick locks?" he asks.

"There probably isn't anything in there. When they closed the boarding school, didn't have any need for staff quarters anymore. The day school likely used these as offices or storage. Which means they were probably emptied out when the school was closed," Will says.

"Not if they're anything like the classrooms Mark and Sasha described," Lila counters. "They said that the classrooms they went into had desks and chairs, the front office still had office supplies. Even the clinic had things in it. They didn't fully empty out this place when they closed it down. They just left most of it."

"Which means, for all we know, it could be left untouched just past this door," David adds. "What better way to reach out to someone still lingering here than to actually visit them in their own private room?"

"It's locked," Will says. "I don't know about the rest of you, but I didn't come with a toolbox handy. Why don't we go upstairs? There's a lot more of this place to explore and we can't even get started on our real investigation until we've done all the baseline checks. It's getting late."

David steps up to another of the doors and tries it. It is just as securely locked and he shakes it with aggravation.

"Fine," he grumbles. "We'll come back to this later. Let's see what's upstairs."

They go back into the front of the building and up the impressive stairwell toward the second floor. This floor, like the entryway, front parlor, and hallways leading into the kitchens, looks very much like it must have when this was still a home. Part of the appeal of the boarding school was the beauty and opulence of the building and the luxurious home environment it offered the students enrolled there. It gave the image of quality and exclusivity, reinforcing to the parents who paid exorbitant tuition and fees for their children to attend the school that they were going to receive the best quality education and opportunities other people wouldn't be given.

The beauty that was designed to please a beloved wife and create a sumptuous home meant for welcoming friends, family, and the eventual children they desired so dearly became a disguise in the years following their deaths. What was once meant for pleasure turned into a veil that covered up the horrible things that were happening within those walls. It's so much harder for a parent to believe that something bad could be happening to their child in a place so beautiful.

They roam through the upper floor, dipping into some of the rooms and finding them empty or with only a handful of school furniture and equipment. One has an old bed and a dresser, as if this was the one residential room that remained after the transition from a boarding school to a day school. Will wonders who slept in this room, if it was their primary residence or just somewhere they stayed occasionally.

David is visibly excited by finding this room. He hurries them through taking the initial readings so he can start the investigation right there. As he starts talking to whatever entity he has decided is hovering around the room, Will walks over to the window to look out at the snow. After the first aggressive rush, the storm has slowed so now flakes are just falling lightly to the ground. It creates a serene image that reminds Will of a snow globe illuminated by the bright moon and a thick blanket of stars that appeared when the white sky dissipated.

Something catches his attention out of the corner of his eye. The reflection of the moon and stars against the snow gives enough light in the schoolyard to see something dark moving. Will shifts his position to get a better look and sees the dark silhouette of a person swinging slowly back and forth on the old, rusty metal swing set at the side of the yard.

He recognizes it from pictures of the school when it was still in operation and delighted children played on it in the afternoons. Beside it is the old-fashioned Merry-Go-Round, essentially a large metal disc designed to spin around a static center beam and with only metal handlebars in place around the edges to provide any sort of safety for the children twirling around. Now the disc is still, frozen in time as the weather gradually reduces it to rust.

But he's focused on the figure on the swing. It moves back and forth slowly, seemingly unbothered by the snow or the wind. He watches it for a few seconds, an eerie feeling creeping up the back of his neck. He can't tell anything about the person. What looks like a heavy coat, thick pants and boots, and possibly a scarf pulled up around their face makes it impossible to determine their size or if they are male or female, much less any identifiable features.

The figure holds onto the chains to either side of them with gloved hands, their legs swinging languidly to keep them moving. Will turns away from the window.

"Hey," he says. "Come here for a second."

The rest of the group is gathered in the center of the room and David is carrying on half of a conversation, asking questions and requesting the spirit he's supposedly communicating with to give him a sign if it doesn't want him to sit on the bed. They ignore Will and he takes a step closer to them.

"Guys," he says with a little more force. "You need to see this. Someone is here."

David's head lifts and his eyes narrow. "What do you mean someone's here?"

"Look."

Will guides them back to the window and points toward the swing set, but when he looks at it, he sees the figure is gone. The swing is still moving slowly back and forth, twisting slightly.

"What are we looking at?" Jonathan asks.

"It's a swing set," Lila says. "For recess."

Will glares at her. "I know what it is." He looks through the window again. "There was someone on it."

"Someone?" Charlotte asks.

"They were in a coat and scarf and everything. I couldn't actually see their face. But they were there. Somebody was swinging on that swing set."

Jonathan chuckles. "Someone out having fun in a snowstorm?"

"I don't know what they were doing, but they were there," Will insists. "Look, the swing is still moving."

"There's wind," Lila points out. "Your eyes are playing tricks on you."

"Maybe not," David says. "I know Will has never been one of us that has had the gift of sensitivity. He hasn't been able to detect the spirits and communicate with them the way I have. But this is such an active location. There's so much going on here. So much turmoil. Maybe there's a spirit reaching out to him specifically. We already know they are able to detect our feelings and our thoughts. They know more about us than we know about ourselves sometimes, including when we are the right person to help them with something specific."

Will rolls his eyes, but David is undeterred.

"A spirit attached to this place or to the grounds could have chosen Will. They could be trying to connect with him and compelled him to go to that window so he could see them. We need to be sensitive to that connection and to the presence of that spirit. The fact that the spirit manifested enough for him to be able to see them is exceptional. We need to show that we are open to them communicating with Will, and with all of us, and try to find out who they are. If we can, we might be able to help them."

Of course, the camera is rolling as David says this, his hand resting lightly on Lila's arm as Charlotte's eyes flash.

The smooth, easy way those words flowed out of David doesn't sit well with Will. They feel too convenient, like they were right there at the edge of his mind waiting to be said. The unsettling feeling that came over him when he saw the person on the swing is still creeping along his spine, but now there's a hint of suspicion in the pit of his belly.

He stands back as they finish their investigation of the room and then move to the next floor. More former bedrooms take up half of this floor while the other half is attic space. Various belongings still line the walls and pile up in corners. It's not as crammed full as the attic in his parents' home when he was growing up, or the storage space in his own small apartment, but the variety of things cast aside up here tell a long, sprawling story of the history of the building. Some of the items are antique and even archaic, while others are more contemporary to his mother's time. It's a mix of the different uses and eras of the school, tangible reminders of the people who were here. It's the kind of thing that gives him a thrill and sparks his interest, making his investigations even more important.

David walks up to a wardrobe pushed up against one wall and pulls it open. Clothes are still hanging inside, and he pulls out what looks like an old-fashioned nightdress. He examines it, looking closely at the details of the fabric and commenting on its size before spreading it out across a pile of boxes so he can step back and look at it. Will doesn't like where this is going.

"Whose nightgown is this?" he asks. "Does it belong to the lady of the house? Mrs. Boudreaux? Is this your gown? Did you used to wear it when you were sleeping?"

"If that does belong to her and she is here, she's not going to answer you," Will says. "You can't just talk to her like she comes from the same time you do. When she was alive, no man other than her husband and her doctor would ever see her nightclothes. It would be horrifying to her for a man, especially a stranger, to just start digging through her clothes and asking her about her sleeping habits. She would be mortified and there's no way she'd communicate with you."

Almost as soon as the words are out of his mouth, the door to the attic space swings closed.

CHAPTER TWENTY-TWO

LILA LETS OUT A FRIGHTENED CRY AND JUMPS BACKWARD, COL-
liding with Jonathan, who scrambles to keep himself on his feet and
stop himself from dropping the camera.

"How did that happen?" Charlotte asks. "That door was standing open."

"Maybe the Mrs. isn't as demure as Will thought," David muses. He
takes a step closer to the door. "Is that you, Mrs. Boudreaux? Did I upset
you by taking your nightgown out and looking at it?"

There's collective silence, everyone in the room holding their
breaths. A few seconds later, a knock somewhere beyond the door
draws a startled gasp from the group.

"Thank you," David says, his lips twitching into a smile. "Thank you
for that response. I'm sorry if I upset you. I'll put it back."

He goes back over to the wardrobe and puts the garment back
inside, closing the door. There's another knock followed by three more,

seeming to come from the hallway outside the door, but moving away from it.

"Oh, my god," Lila whispers. "She actually is here."

The suspicious feeling gnaws at Will's stomach. He watches David's movements carefully, gauging if he is as surprised by the sounds as everyone else or if he seems to be anticipating something happening.

"If this is Mrs. Boudreaux, please let us know," he says. "Make another sound."

They wait, but nothing happens. Lila's eyes dart between Charlotte and David. She reaches out for David's arm and clings to him. He pats her arm.

"Don't be afraid. Remember, whoever this spirit is can't hurt you. All they can do is frighten you. Don't let them."

"What if it's not a normal spirit?" Lila asks. "What if it's a demon?"

"Is that what this is?" David asks. "Are you a demon? If you are, show yourself. Come to us now." After another few seconds of silence, he smiles down at her. "Everything is fine. Don't let yourself be afraid. That's when you are vulnerable. You have to remind yourself that you, as the living, are the one with the power. You don't have to give in to the feelings that these spirits try to force on you." He looks up again. "Do you mean to be scaring us? Are you trying to get us to leave?"

A louder crash makes Will jump.

"David," Lila hisses.

"We're not going to be afraid of you. There's nothing you can do to us. We're here to communicate with you. We want to tell your story. If you want to communicate with us, we can make sure people know who you were and what happened to you. Is that something you'd like?" David asks.

Will rolls his eyes and stalks across the room. "This is ridiculous. I'm done."

He grabs the handle on the door and tries to open it, but it won't move. He tries again, but the doorknob stays firm.

"What's going on?" Charlotte asks.

"It won't open," Will says.

"Stop messing around and trying to get attention," Jonathan says.

Will presses a hand to the door and firms his grip on the doorknob with the other, looking around the perimeter of the door to make sure there isn't something that fell against it or a visible lock that might have accidentally engaged.

"I'm not," Will says. "Trust me, I don't need any of your attention. This thing will not open. The doorknob won't even move."

Jonathan sets down his camera and for a fleeting moment, Will envisions the frame now, the image the camera is capturing skewed by the camera lying on its side, sitting at an angle to where they are standing. It's probably catching mostly their legs and a good portion of the floor.

"Let me try it," Jonathan says, approaching the door.

Will steps aside and gestures at the door with the sweep of one hand. "Be my guest."

Jonathan takes hold of the doorknob and tries to turn it. The frustrated expression on his face drops and he looks down at his hand wrapped around the knob. In the glow of the headlamp Jonathan wears in lieu of carrying a flashlight around, Will can see his grip tighten and release a few times like the larger man is testing his own sense of touch and gauging the strength in his grasp. He tries to tug the door again and it shifts in place in its frame but doesn't open.

"It's locked or something," he finally relents.

"No!" Lila gasps. "We're locked in here? Nobody knows we're even here. What's going to happen to us?"

"We're going to be fine," David says. "Calm down. Everything is going to be alright. Charlotte, do you feel something right now?"

Anger is starting to build up in the pit of Will's stomach. He's not afraid. There isn't a single fiber of his being that believes there's any kind of entity causing the door not to open. The explanation seems far more human—and infuriating. Charlotte gets that look on her face and reaches up to press her fingertips to her temples. Drawing in a deep breath through her nose, she pauses at the peak of the breath, holding it for just too long until it seems like she could topple over, then lets it out in a burst.

"Yes. Oh, yes. There's a strong presence here. Yes, I can feel you. I know you're here with us. There's so much pain and sadness. But also anger. This entity wants us to know something. It's very important."

Her hand comes up to cover her eyes and she starts to sway. Will wonders if she has yet realized that the camera isn't focused on her. The recording is going to pick up the words, but the theatrical performance is lost on just the team. Though, by the way Lila is still cowering and staring at her with widened eyes, now completely wrapped up in this narrative that she would believe the entire team has been ghosts all along if that's what David told her, maybe it's having more than enough effect.

"Who is it?" David asks, coming away from the door to get closer to Charlotte. "Can you get any impression of whether it's a man or a woman? Or what age?"

"It's hard," Charlotte tells him, her eyes closed and her fingertips still pressed to her head. "They don't want to come through. They don't want to connect."

Will walks over to the door and takes hold of the doorknob. Just like he expected, it turns easily this time and opens. He stalks out of the room without bothering to wait for the rest of the team. They run after him, each emerging into the hallway with looks on their faces like they've been trapped in that attic for days.

"You were right, David!" Lila gushes. "The spirit helped Will. It must have forced the other entity away and unlocked the door for us. Will, you need to connect with it. You need to talk to it and find out what it wants you to know and why it chose you."

"We should go back downstairs and set up our command center," David says. "It's time to really start this investigation. Things are getting exciting and active already and I don't want to waste any time."

He gestures down the hallway with the same expectation as usual for Will to go ahead, but he doesn't move. After a beat, David looks at Jonathan, who follows the unspoken instruction without hesitation. The girls go along after him, but before David can fall in line, ensuring he is not only not the first of the group, but also not the one at the back, Will steps in front of him.

"What the hell is wrong with you?" he hisses.

"What are you talking about?" David asks.

"I already told you that you can't do this kind of crap. You might think it's fun to get the girls all worked up and get really dramatic footage you can convince other people is real, but I'm not falling for it. I know you set all this up."

David's eyes narrow at him.

"Set what up? What are you implying?"

"I'm not implying anything. I'm saying straight out that you orchestrated everything that has happened," Will clarifies. "Maybe the bird coming down the chimney wasn't you, but I wouldn't put it past you. The sounds, the door getting stuck, probably the person I saw on the swing set. That was all you. Tell me, David, who did you manage to convince to go along with your lies for you? Is it some theater student thinking they've gotten a role in an experimental performance piece? Or are you taking advantage of some desperate fan who thinks they are going to be part of your inner circle now?"

"I didn't do any of this. That's actually what you think of me? That I would hire somebody to come out in a snowstorm and pretend to be a ghost?" David asks.

"Absolutely," Will says without missing a beat. "Maybe you didn't know there was going to be a storm when you first set it up. But I don't doubt for a second you would stoop to something like this. You've been faking evidence and pretending things have significance when they don't for months. You admitted it yourself. You don't think any of this is real. So why wouldn't you take it another step further and actually script one of these investigations? It's a nice touch that you didn't let Lila and Jonathan at least in on it. I'm still going back and forth about Charlotte. It would make sense for you to tell her so she could practice her little clairvoyant medium routine. But, if she wasn't surprised by what was happening in the attic, she's a far better actor than you are."

"You seriously have some nerve," David scoffs. "I made you. Without me and the effort I've put into turning this into something worthwhile you would still just be a nobody fake scientist running around all the places you got permission to be in and writing articles no one wants for their journals."

"You haven't done anything for me but piss me off. Your antics diminish the validity of anything I put forward. I'm not like Charlotte thinking I can sway back and forth for a while and then have friendly chats with Casper. I'm here to do actual experiments and collect actual data I can analyze. You are under some kind of delusion that I need you, but let me make myself extremely clear. I *don't* need you. I *never* needed you. I started all of this well before you and I'll continue on after you're gone." He stops, taking a breath. "In fact, consider me gone now. You do whatever you want to do, but I'm not a part of it."

"What are you doing?" David asks as Will adjusts his camera over his shoulder and starts to walk away. "You're just going to leave in the middle of a snowstorm? You're suddenly an outdoorsman now and can hike your way back to camp through the snow?"

"No. I'm going to take my equipment and use it for what it's actually intended for rather than letting it be used as a prop for whatever the hell you're doing. This place is big enough that we don't have to cross paths. Just stay out of my way," he says.

David's face darkens. "You're going to be sorry. No one walks away from me. I warned you before. I'll make sure no one ever looks twice at a single thing you do. Everyone will see you as the fraud and I'll come out of this looking even better than I already do. I hope you have a backup plan in place, buddy, because you can kiss that grant goodbye. Maybe you should start practicing driving faster so you can make sure the pizzas you'll be delivering for the rest of your life get to the customers in thirty minutes or less."

Will turns slowly to face David. The smirk on his face makes Will's hands clench, but he stays steady. Before he can say anything, the rest of the group comes back around the corner.

"What's going on?" Lila asks. "We've been waiting downstairs."

"Nothing," David says. "Will was just talking about his plans for the rest of the investigation. He suggested we do some solo investigating to cover more ground and I think that's a great idea. He'll be able to get in tune with the spirits better if he's off on his own."

"What do the rest of us do?" Jonathan asks.

"Stay together and explore. Record everything. We'll piece it all together later. Lila, you've talked to Will about the history of this place, right?"

"Some," she says.

"Use that to guide you. I'm going to get the command center set up and head toward the opposite side of the building. We'll meet up later," he says. "Do you have your walkie?"

Jonathan pats the device on his hip and David nods, meeting Will's eyes.

"Let's go, then."

CHAPTER TWENTY-THREE

AVID FOCUSES ON KEEPING THE ANGER OFF HIS FACE AS HE walks down the hall with the rest of the group. Beneath the confident veneer and calm smile, he's seething. He can't believe Will is doing this. He can't believe he's disrespecting him this way. They started with nothing. They met at college and soon learned they shared a fascination for the paranormal.

Yes, Will was always the more dedicated of the two. He took it far more seriously. When other people talked about spirits and hauntings, it was easy to not take them seriously or think that they were a little bit crazy. But not Will. He talks about the possibility of a spirit world existing around ours just like researchers talk about any other science. It was never something he was one hundred percent positive of, but he always said that as soon as a scientist is unwaveringly positive that everything they believe is true, they are no longer a scientist. Those who are truly dedicated to science question everything. They don't hold beliefs, they hold theories. They have ideas. They wonder.

Their friendship was built on the very concept of finding out what it really meant for a place to be haunted. They researched locations together. Listened to ghost stories and legends from locals. They went on ghost walks and guided tours, then eventually started on their own.

Most people made fun of them. Some people were fascinated by them. Will didn't care either way. What mattered to him was coming up with every question he could possibly ask about the paranormal and supernatural, then going out and trying to collect the evidence needed to answer those questions. He truly wanted one of two things. To either find abundant, reliable facts and information he could write up into papers to be submitted to scientific journals that would sway the greater public toward the understanding that ghosts are real and what natural rules they operated by, or to go through every scientific channel he could come up with and test his theories to the fullest extent to come to the conclusion that what people think of as ghosts are actually something else of far more tangible, earthly composition.

He hesitated to ever say he would be proven right or wrong. Even if he found the most concrete evidence that had ever been collected in favor of ghosts being real, there would always be a shadow of doubt in the very back of his mind. And if all the evidence he gathered showed that the supernatural didn't exist, he would accept it with a glimmer of denial and the quiet determination that maybe one day he would be the one to find the missing piece.

David was the one who figured out they could turn their investigations into something. He's the one who realized that people, even the ones who made fun of them for chasing ghosts around, were intrigued by the idea of trying to contact the other world. He's the one who came up with the idea of not just videotaping their investigation for the sake of having evidence Will could then analyze, but to distribute as a form of entertainment. He's the one who made them into personalities and turned this whole thing into a money-making venture.

Will might be the one who knew the equipment better and who put the time and effort into finding the locations and doing the research. But in the bigger picture, that didn't really matter. They didn't both need to be doing all the research. They didn't both need to buy the equipment and find out how to operate it. They were a team. At least they were supposed to be. And in teams, people delegate. Everybody has a role and fulfilling those roles is what makes things work.

David's role was to be the leader. The face of the group. The one to draw people in and keep them engaged. It was Will's to be his support. He still gives so much credence to what David has long-since decided was a fleeting interest that was discredited a long time ago. He believed it all so much once, and there are times when he really does want to keep believing it. He wants there to be something else. He just never found enough to convince him. Will is supposed to be the one to keep digging into the stories of the past and building the structure David then uses to shape their investigations.

The people watching the videos of the investigations and reading the descriptions David spun don't care about the authenticity. It wouldn't make any true tangible difference to their lives if the stories they get are completely factual, as long as they're thrilling. These are people who want ghosts to be real. They want the chill down their spines when thinking about haunted houses, or the hopeful lift that comes from thinking that there is life after death. Some even want the satisfaction and vengeance of believing people who had done evil things in their lives are now trapped in places they never wanted to be.

Those people aren't going to get that kind of fulfillment from reading scientific analysis and comparison of evidence. It wouldn't matter to them if the sounds the team heard while walking through an abandoned building in the middle of the night could be easily debunked. David's fans want to vicariously experience the excitement of coming into contact with otherworldly forces. He gives them that. He lets them pretend they're coming along for the investigation and venturing into the unknown.

Will and David were supposed to be a team. Until they weren't.

Will wants to leave, to walk away from everything David has built. He wants to ruin him by telling everyone that he fakes evidence and doesn't really believe any part of these investigations. But David isn't going to let him. He'll take him down first.

The group, sans Will, makes their way out down to the front entryway. Lila stops short.

"The door," she says.

"What about it?" Jonathan asks.

"It's open. Will said he made sure it was closed after he released the bird. But look at it. It's open," she says, pointing at the front door.

David looks and notices that the door is, in fact, standing open several inches. Snowflakes drift in from outside and a gust of wind chills his face even more.

"Was it like that when you were waiting for me?" he asks.

"We didn't come out this far," Charlotte explains. "We waited in the hallway just outside the kitchen."

He isn't sure what to think of the door as he walks over to it.

"Did Will go out there?" he asks.

"I don't think so," Jonathan says. "He went past us going down the hall, but I think he went toward the classrooms."

David pushes the door closed. "It's an old door. It's probably just the wind."

Lila's eyes flash back and forth along with the beam from her flashlight. "You don't think it was the spirit Will saw outside? The one that locked us up in the attic?"

"No," David tells her. "I don't think so." He realizes the team is looking to him for more. They want a better explanation, so he comes up with one. "The spirits in this building love this place. They have positive emotions associated with it. It was their home, after all. They would want to protect it, and they follow the social rules of their time. They wouldn't leave the front door standing open."

It doesn't occur to him until after he's already said it that he probably could have just told them that it would take far too much energy for a spirit to summon the strength to open a door that way and would instead just walk through it. Usually something like that would have been the first thing that came to his mind. But he realizes he's questioning what's going on himself.

"Where are you going to set up the command center?" Jonathan asks him.

It snaps David out of his thoughts and he looks down at the pile of gear the team brought with them and left on the entryway floor before they started roaming the halls of the old school.

"The old kitchen," he says. "It's easy to find and only has one access point. Plus, if we decide to extend our investigation into tomorrow or even overnight tomorrow, we know the fireplace works. It will warm us up and let us cook."

"Do you need help bringing everything in there?" Charlotte asks.

David didn't think it through completely when he said he would bring everything into the command center himself. He wanted the control of establishing their home base himself and then to determine where he would go on his individual investigation and how long he would actually investigate. Now he feels like he can't go back on it, so he shakes his head.

"No. I can handle it. You three get started on your investigation. We'll meet up later," he says.

He takes up his first load of equipment and starts to the kitchen before they can say anything else. The kitchen feels colder than even the rest of the building does and he hurries to move everything into it. His eyes linger on the fireplace for a second. He considers starting a fire but thinks better of it. They'll start one later, when they convene here. For now, it isn't a good idea to have one going without anyone there to monitor it. Even though the room is mostly stone, there's always the chance of a jumping ember, and he doesn't trust that the bird that flew into the building isn't one of several who might have been building nests that could easily catch.

He grabs some food out of one of the bags and eats while listening back through the recordings on his handheld recorder, starting to plan how to shape the narrative of the sounds and sights they've captured. He stays as long as he thinks he can get away with and then leaves for his solo investigation. As he walks out into the hallway, the hairs on the back of his neck prick up like he's being watched. Someone's eyes are on him. He listens for breath, for footsteps, something to tell him where the person is, but he doesn't hear anything.

"Is someone there?" he asks. "Jonathan?"

There's no response and he continues. The feeling doesn't leave him as he heads toward the former ballroom. The silence starts to get to him and he turns on his recorder, narrating everything he's doing and the thoughts that are—or should be—going through his mind as he makes his way through the dark and cold. He tries to remember everything Will told him about this area of the building so he can regurgitate it to viewers.

He's almost to the hall that leads into the ballroom when he hears something beside him. It sounds close, within just a few feet, but when he sweeps his flashlight around the area surrounding him, he doesn't see anything. He's in a corridor like the others in the building, the walls on either side of him covered in pictures and abandoned artwork. He wonders if it will all be left when the building is demolished or if someone will come and take it down first.

If they do, what will happen to it? No one cared enough to remove it when the school closed nearly thirty years ago. What would have changed now?

But there is always the power of nostalgia. Knowing the building will be gone and there will no longer be any option at all for revisiting it could make people who previously thought they were done with that part of their lives suddenly eager to hold onto part of it. And then there are the collectors. People who have never even stepped foot in the school and don't know anyone who was ever a teacher, administrator, staff member, or student, but have gotten sucked into the macabre tales of the former school. They crave a tangible piece of it, something they can hold onto and feel like they are a part of the history of that place.

There are collectors like that for all places with a reputation for being haunted, and anyone who can deliver them a genuine piece of the location can charge an exorbitant amount. The thought makes David's heart race a little faster. If he can find out who is handling the demolition, maybe he can convince them to let him come in and remove some of these things. Dealing in these kinds of unique goods could be the next level for his brand.

He's trying to soothe himself with those thoughts to distract himself from the sound of something close by that sounds like footsteps and something scratching. He stops short and listens again. The scratching gets louder, like someone's dragging a giant nail across a giant chalkboard.

Just another quirk of the building, he convinces himself. It's old. It hasn't been maintained in many years and there are things about it that are going to make noise or not work the way they're expected to. The same reason the door to the attic didn't open. Will thinks he brought someone in to scare them, but he didn't. The door must have just gotten stuck with the moisture in the air and needed just the right amount of pressure to open up. It was only a coincidence that it happened when they were in the attic.

A heavier thud somewhere near him makes David whip around. There's still nothing. He shines his light ahead of him and notices the beam is starting to falter. He can't remember if he changed the batteries the way Will always hounded on him to do. It's basic, Will would say. Your flashlight should always have fresh batteries.

His beam is dimming and he knows it will soon go out completely. Not wanting to get caught anywhere in this building alone and with no source of illumination, he decides to go back to the kitchen. He knows there are fresh batteries in the supply packs and he can trade them out.

He moves more quickly back through the building, waiting to find or at least hear other members of the team. He doesn't find any of them and nothing seems out of the ordinary until he walks through the main kitchen to the smaller room beyond. He notices something faintly coming around the edges of the closed door and thinks it might be Will inside with one of the lanterns.

"You couldn't deal with people here alone so you had to…" he starts, taking hold of the latch on the door and pushing it open.

But when it does, he sees that Will isn't in the room. It's empty except for the fire roaring orange in the fireplace.

CHAPTER TWENTY-FOUR

AVID STOPS IN THE DOORWAY, STARING AT THE FLAMES GETTING drawn up into the chimney by the wind outside. Several logs sit in the middle of the fireplace, supporting a fire clearly built by someone who has done it many times before. It wasn't just thrown together but deliberately arranged to ensure the strongest fire that would last as long as possible.

He hasn't been gone that long. Not long enough, he would think, for someone to be able to build that kind of fire and not be seen. He steps backward out of the small room and into the main kitchen. His flashlight is milky and dim now, but he swings it around the space, trying to dissolve away as many of the shadows as he can. Maybe one of the team is hiding there to watch his reaction to the fire. It could be a joke, to see if they could scare him.

Or it could be an idea for a segment. If that's the case, it could be brilliant. His genuine shock would be a great image. Only, no one was in the auxiliary kitchen to record his reaction. And it's not something his team has ever done. They believe the investigations are completely real. They follow his lead when it comes to validating evidence. They don't try to stage it for the cameras.

"Who's here?" he asks into the quiet kitchen. "Jonathan? Did you start that fire? Did you want to see my reaction?" He realizes it could be something different. "Are you doing an experiment? Starting the fire to create heat to see if you can draw the spirits? That's a great idea and it could be really effective, but you need to go over things like this with me before you do them. Something like this could compromise other elements of the investigation."

In truth, there's no concern that this could compromise anything beyond making their equipment smell like smoke. They've dabbled in using heat and the chaotic incitement of fire in luring spirits before. It wouldn't be all that strange for the team to recall that and decide they wanted to attempt it on their own. They've all been very good about staying in the background and doing what David designs, but there are moments when he can see the shimmer of envy in their eyes, the desire for some of the recognition for themselves.

All have been good about it except Will. But Will is confounding. He doesn't want the attention or the fame. At least, he says he doesn't. Maybe that's just him trying to seem better than David. From the beginning there has always been the element of wanting to publish his findings and seek recognition within the scientific community. He craves the accolades other researchers get. But those researchers haven't devoted their careers and their talents to talking with the dead.

"Will?" David asks. "Is that you? Are you doing another one of your experiments? Do whatever the hell you want, but don't get in my way and don't do it near my command center." He keeps swinging the dying light, walking slowly around the room until he's seen every inch of it. "And speaking of the command center, I moved all your shit in here. You need to get it out and find your own place for the night. If you don't want to be a part of the team anymore, so be it. But that means cutting all ties. You don't get to have it both ways."

There's no response. He hears nothing in the room or beyond it. He realizes now he's been talking just to fill the silence. He hasn't seen anything in the kitchen, so he walks out into the hallway.

"Whoever started the fire needs to come put it out," he calls out into the darkness. "You can start it again before we call it a night, but we can't just leave it burning in there alone. We don't know how functional the chimney actually is and an ember could spark something in the room."

He listens to the silence for a second and just before he's about to call them out for trying to spook him, the scratching on the wall returns. It's close again, somewhere to one side. It isn't the sound of a trapped animal who has gotten into the bones of the house and is frantically tearing at the wood to try to get out. Instead, they are long, steady sounds, like something being slowly dragged along a rough surface. As David turns from one side to the other to try to see where it's coming from, his flashlight goes out.

Muttering profanities, he shakes it, slamming the end against the heel of his hand. It sputters on and off a couple of times before turning off and staying that way. There are few windows on the lower floor of the building and in this area, there are none, leaving him in thick, inky darkness. The scraping sound is louder now. It's coming from all sides, closing in around him.

He reaches out one hand to touch the wall beside him. In that fraction of a second before it comes in contact with the old wallpaper, his stomach rolls with worry about what he might find in the darkness. He uses his touch on the wall to guide him back the short distance along the hall to the kitchen. Inside, he finds his way around the industrial counters added when the house became a school.

It isn't until he's made it all the way across and is back at the door of the small kitchen, enough light coming in from the window to show him his surroundings, that he realizes the fire is out.

The smell is heavy in the air and tendrils of steam and smoke rise up from the remnants, but the flames are gone. It burned such a short time that there is none of the acrid smell that comes from wood reduced to ash but it is distinctly thick. It didn't just go out on its own. Someone doused it with water.

David's heart pounds in his chest.

"What the hell is going on? Who's here? Stop screwing with me and come out here," he says. "Will, is this your idea of a sick joke? Do you think you're making some kind of point right now?"

He wants that to be the explanation. He wants his former best friend to be angry enough for the pettiness to have taken over rational adult thought and for him to be doing this just to scare him. Will wanting to generate fear and doubt in him is far preferable than any other explanation David can come up with. But he refuses to give him the satisfaction of it. He won't panic or show that this has gotten to him. Instead, he walks into the room and heads straight for the supply bag sitting up against one of the walls.

"My flashlight is giving me some trouble, so I'm going to put in fresh batteries," he announces in a more level voice. "That won't come as much of a shock to those who have been with me for a while. You might recall from past investigations, particularly the Halloween investigation of Hollywood Cemetery during our road trip to Richmond two years ago, that spirits will frequently drain the energy from batteries. They use that energy to manifest so they can be seen by the living or communicate somehow.

"We start each investigation with brand new batteries in all of our equipment, so I'm sure it's extremely appealing to a tired or hungry spirit when we walk into their space and have all this energy just available for them to take. Of course, we are always eager for them to reach out to us in any way they can, so we always have a large supply of fresh batteries available to keep our equipment going. There we go. I have my new batteries in and my flashlight is back up and running again. Now it's time to make our way back to the ballroom and see if any of the galas Mr. and Mrs. Boudreaux were famous for hosting are still going on all these years later."

Replacing any hesitation or fear with the overt confidence of his video persona, David shines his flashlight beam in front of him and walks through the kitchen, down the hall, and back to the ballroom. He makes it all the way this time and spends a few minutes walking around the open space. It no longer looks like a ballroom. The schools repurposed it for several different things, including a gymnasium, but there are some small details left in place that harken back to those grand evenings and lavish displays of hospitality and wealth.

"Mrs. Boudreaux?" he calls out, standing in the middle of the room and shining his light up at the intricately decorative ceiling overhead. "I've heard that you really loved having people over and throwing big parties for them. What was the best party you ever threw here? What kind of food did you have? Was there a lot of dancing? Are any of your guests still here with you? Was your party so good they literally never wanted it to end?"

A sound behind him makes him stop. It's not the scratching of before but something easier to recognize. Footsteps. They aren't heavy, aren't running. There isn't urgency behind them. Just steady, deliberate footsteps coming toward him. He turns around to see who it is and sees a flicker of movement in the dark part of the room beyond the glow of his flashlight.

"Who is that?" he asks. "I just saw you. Someone is here with me. Come into the light so I can see you better. Or tell me who you are."

David is very aware of the recorder still recording everything. He takes a few steps toward where he saw the movement and hears the steps to the side of him. Whipping around, he slashes through the air with his flashlight to catch whoever is there.

"If there's still a party going on here in the old ballroom, I'd like an invitation. I've been told I'm a pretty good dancer. If there are any single ladies here who have space on their dance card, come up to me and take my hand so I can dance with you." He hopes his voice doesn't sound as shaky on the recording as he hears it in his head. "I'm not feeling a lot of hospitality right now. I don't feel like I'm welcome here. Is that true? Maybe it isn't the lady of the house and her friends who are still spending time in this place. Maybe it's one of the teachers from when this was a boarding school. I've heard that some of the teachers weren't exactly kind to their students. Do you know what I'm talking about? Did you have students you had to be especially hard on while they were in school? How did it feel for them to close the school down after all of your devotion over the years?"

David moves in the direction of the footsteps again and hears breathing. Standing his ground, he lifts his flashlight. The figure he sees is a few feet away, enough that it's still too much in the shadows to be recognized. He takes a step toward him at the same time the figure comes at him. In his last second before the figure surges forward, grabs David's hair, and yanks his head back, he's able to scream one more word before the blade slides through.

"Will!"

CHAPTER TWENTY-FIVE

"DID YOU HEAR THAT?" LILA ASKS, HER HEAD SNAPPING IN the direction of the door.

"Hear what?" Charlotte asks with a heavy sigh.

She's aggravated at Lila stopping her in the middle of attempting to channel any spirits that might be spending their time around the clinic. After going through the front part of the main office and an old art room, Charlotte, Lila, and Jonathan decided to find the clinic the Berkeley couple mentioned when describing the terrifying night they spent at Dawn Day School. Sasha Berkeley had talked about the room feeling strange to her and having a heaviness to it that she couldn't shake.

The three of them wanted to know what that was all about. They wanted to see it for themselves. As soon as they stepped inside the clinic, Charlotte understood what they meant. Anyone would feel the same thing when they went into the small, old-fashioned sick ward. Just standing there looking at the dark green cots and the curtain pulled back to the side sent a bit of a chill down her spine.

It has nothing to do with her belief in her own special gifts, abilities she's had since she was a small child. Her mother has them, too, just like her mother before her and her mother before her. The women in her family all have heightened awareness and the ability to sense and experience things that no one else could. Her mother always knew friends or family members were sick before they mentioned it to anyone. Her grandmother would call people and tell them not to leave the house, warning them that if they did, something terrible would happen to them. The one time someone didn't heed that advice, he got into a car accident and nearly died within ten minutes of leaving home.

It was her birthright. Charlotte's family still talks about waiting after she was born to see when her own sensitivities and abilities would come to the surface. None of them expected hers to appear as the ability to sense and communicate with the dead.

But she didn't even need to tune in with that extra sense to feel the uneasiness that comes with this space inside the school. She's very aware of what could have happened within these walls, both when it was being used as the clinic of a school and before. As they walked toward it, Lila told her that Will's research showed this area of the house was once used as a quarantine ward during breakouts of severe illness through the community as well as a place for convalescing from other ailments, including each time Mrs. Boudreaux miscarried a pregnancy or delivered her baby only for it to die shortly after. She'd lie in this space, her own body struggling to heal and get through the incredible trauma, while her heart gradually broke and her mind spiraled deeper and deeper until she was far removed from reality.

Charlotte felt the ache of those losses, the fear of the horrible illnesses burning through the students, the pain and sadness of childhood injuries when a child couldn't be with their parents but had to rely on a school nurse to reassure and comfort them. This clinic wasn't just a place where children took naps or came to have their temperature taken when they complained of not feeling well. It saw so much more.

She wanted to connect with anyone who might still be here; she'd been trying to reach out and connect with someone when Lila interrupted. They are a team and they are supposed to get along and be happy working together, but there are moments when Charlotte really has trouble feeling that way about Lila. The other woman is younger and more whimsical, but Charlotte doesn't believe she brings any real benefit to the team. She was there before Charlotte and David introduced her with the supporting detail that he and Will met her in college several months after putting together their first paranormal investigation.

THE GIRL AND THE WINTER BONES

This made Charlotte assume Lila would have the same kind of dedication and ability as the guys. But as they started working together, Charlotte realized Lila is far more of the Halloween haunted house kind of person than she is the paranormal haunting kind. There is a distinct difference, though people on the outside might not see that. They might not understand the line between the adrenaline rush that comes from walking into an authentic location that is home to actual spirits and the one that comes from frightening sets and props and jump scares. The difference between being scared of the next loud sound and the imagery, even if that is heightened by a core of belief in the reality of it, and being scared because that reality is right in front of you.

It's not to say Lila doesn't think that what they are doing is real. She does. But her motivation and dedication seems far more surface level. She's driven by the fun and the thrill rather than the true potential to help the people who they contact.

Then again, Lila doesn't have the gift Charlotte and David do. It's different for them. Lila can experience the spirits through their manifestations, the sounds they're able to make, the cold that seeps into your bones when you are near them, the occasional movement of an object or flicker of a shadow. She knows they are there. But that's a world apart from Charlotte feeling their presence and communicating with them. She's been asked countless times before how that works. People learn she is a paranormal investigator and immediately get the mocking, derisive look on their faces, their lips twisting up into the cruel cousin of a smile, and their eyes shifting to each other as if they want private confirmation of how ridiculous the whole concept is. Then come the questions:

"Do you see them standing there in front of you like real people?"

"They are real people. They're just dead."

"So, you do see them."

"I have, but not usually. I can feel them and communicate with them."

"You can hear them talking?"

"Not with my ears, not like I can hear you."

"Not with your ears? What else would you hear with?"

"I sense what they want to say to me. I can feel their emotions and the words come into my mind like someone has already said them and I am just remembering them. Just like I can still hear what you just said to me in my mind."

"So, you might just be making it up."

"Did I make up what you said?"

"No, but I actually said it."

"So did they."

"But how do you know that?"

"I just do. It's something not everyone can do, so I don't expect everyone to understand it."

"Do you really think it makes any difference? Like, why does it matter if you go into some old place and talk to someone who's been dead for a hundred years. What good does that do?"

"I think there are ways I can help them."

"Because you know how to be a ghost better than the ghosts do? You can figure out something about their existence and what they are supposed to do next that they never figured out for themselves?"

And it goes on, the conversation often becoming cyclical as they try to trip her up and find holes in her logic or her conviction. Charlotte doesn't care. She didn't go into paranormal investigating with the thought that it would be embraced and accepted by everyone. She went into it because of the deep, constantly gnawing curiosity that makes it impossible for her to ignore the existence of another world overlapped with our own, right there just beneath a veil. Lifting that veil is her most closely held aspiration.

David shares that with her, along with his own ability to connect with the spiritual world on a deeper, more personal level. He believes in the team and their responsibility to give these people their voices and bring awareness of them to the rest of the living. So Charlotte cooperates. She plays nice with Lila even in moments like this.

"It sounded like someone shouting," Lila says. "I think it was David."

"I didn't hear it," Jonathan says.

"Are you sure?" Charlotte asks.

"Yes. I heard it. I think something's wrong."

"He is probably communicating with a difficult entity," Jonathan offers. "Remember, he said there's darkness here."

Lila shakes her head. "No. It didn't sound like that. I think we need to go find him and make sure he's alright."

"He's doing a solo investigation," Charlotte argues. "He wouldn't like being interrupted."

She's hoping the subtle message sinks in for Lila, though she doubts it will. Lila is still staring at the door, biting into her bottom lip as her eyebrows knit close together. She looks like she's debating with herself.

"I'm going to go," she finally says. "You don't have to come with me if you don't think you should. I'll go alone."

"You don't know where you're going," Jonathan says.

"I can find my way. It's just a building. He sent us this direction because he was planning on doing his investigation on the other side of the school. I'll go there."

She hesitates as if waiting for one of the others to say they'll go with her. When they don't, she heads for the door. Charlotte watches the beam of her flashlight move down the hall until the darkness swallows it.

"Do you think everything's okay?" she asks.

"It's fine. I didn't hear anything. But if she did, like I said, it was probably just David provoking something. You know how he likes to do that."

Charlotte nods. "Yeah. He does." She thinks for a second, then turns back to the cots. "Let's keep going here for a couple more minutes and then I want to go down into the classroom section. I want to go to the classroom where Sasha and Mark Berkeley say they saw the body. The police didn't find anything when they went back to investigate, but that doesn't mean the couple wasn't seeing something manifesting and it just looked very real to them. I want to see if I can sense anything there."

CHAPTER TWENTY-SIX

SECOND THOUGHTS ARE ALREADY RACING THROUGH LILA'S MIND as soon as she is far enough away from the clinic that she can only see the beam of her own flashlight and the sound of her own breath in her ears. The sense of being alone is tangible in the pitch darkness. She is very aware of not having the rest of the team with her and that she is unfamiliar with the building she's walking through.

A lot of times they review the floor plans or sketches of the places they are going to visit, or at least find enough pictures of former uses of the buildings to piece together how their location is laid out. They didn't have that benefit with this investigation. They went into it with a basic understanding of what the building was like when it was a private residence and then when it was a school, but not a full overview.

Their usual walkthrough before starting the investigation was thrown off course by the sudden activity that sprung up, so they didn't even go through several sections. One of those sections being the one David was going into for his solo investigation. He's been talking about the old ballroom since Will told them about it. The grandeur and fantastical lavishness of having a ballroom in a private home and then filling that ballroom with luxurious parties and feasts appeals to David. It's so different than life now it feels almost crafted.

She knows he was looking forward to finding it and the others are probably right in that he would be angry with her if he really is just trying to antagonize a spirit and she interrupts him, breaking the connection he's building. But she knows she heard him yell out. Even if the others didn't hear it, she knows his voice. And she knows it didn't sound normal.

She finds herself feeling the compulsion to talk as she moves through the building. It's ingrained from all the investigations she's done with David and the rest of the team. It's just something they do as they go around a place, asking questions, explaining to whomever might be listening who they are and why they are there. Lila never really put much thought into it before. It was just part of the process. Now she realizes it isn't really that she wants to talk to any spirits that might be around her. She wants the security of the recorder or the camera. Having those there and talking to them somehow makes the eerie chill of places like this less intense. The talking distracts her and knowing she's being recorded makes her feel more secure.

As she walks back through the entryway, she checks the door out of the corner of her eye to make sure it's still closed but tells herself she's not doing it. The door is in place but she still hurries past it. She listens intently to the quiet, waiting to hear David's voice again. She's both relieved and more worried the longer she goes without hearing it. It might mean that he's perfectly fine and has moved on from that part of his investigation, or it might mean that something went wrong when she heard him cry out and now he's not able to call for help again.

Her flashlight beam catches the corner of a plaque on the wall and she reads it. The directions engraved on it indicate the library is down the hallway in front of her. She seems to remember that the original ballroom was located near the home's library, which was repurposed for the school's library later. Lila heads down the hallway, but before she reaches anything that looks like it could have once been part of the ballroom, she hears something crashing with a heavy thud.

The sound makes her jump, causing her heart to race almost painfully in her chest. She turns sharply toward it and sees she's right next to the library. Beyond the doorway she sees a hint of a flashlight beam bouncing somewhere in the darkened stacks. Her shoulders relax and a self-chiding smile comes to her lips. David isn't in the ballroom, he's in the library. Lila wouldn't have expected there to still be any books there, but there must be something since she clearly heard him knock something over. Considering all the items they've found left behind scattered throughout the building, some of the collection might still be there.

"David?" Lila calls out softly as she takes a step into the library. She doesn't want to startle him by being too loud.

She hears a response, but it's muffled like he is further back in the room so his voice isn't getting all the way to her. Her nose wrinkles at the smell of dampness and dust in the thick carpeting on the floor. Shining her flashlight down onto it, she can see that it was once beautiful, the color of wine with interweaving gold and deep blue and green flowers. Now it's dingy and caked with dirt and cobwebs.

Like in some of the other rooms, the library looks largely intact. It's as if they found out that the school was closing and just decided it wasn't worth the effort of trying to move everything out. There are gaps where some of the pieces of furniture were clearly removed and some stacks of cast-offs from other rooms sit in the corners like they're waiting for something, but there are also several green leather armchairs and heavily scrolled wood tables in the open center of the room.

The color of the armchairs strikes her as an odd choice. They look very much like the clinic cots, an association she wouldn't think they would want to make among the students.

"David?" she calls out again. "It's Lila." The flashlight beam is still flickering and swaying ahead of her like he's walking behind one of the shelves and the light is bouncing in between books that are still there. "Am I interrupting you?"

There's no response, but he could be so invested in his work that he might not even hear her. She leaves the sitting area and ventures into the stacks. The room looks like it was left largely as it was when it was a home, with massive wood shelves built into the walls and furniture in the center, but then further shelves were added to accommodate the books that students would need.

Ahead of her she can see the flashlight beam more clearly and walks toward it.

"I was in the clinic with Charlotte and Jonathan and I thought I heard you yell," she says. "I thought something might be wrong so I came to find you. I was going toward the ballroom but then I heard something in here. It scared the hell out of me before I realized it must be you. Did you knock something over?"

She comes around the corner but David isn't there. Instead, his flashlight hangs down from a piece of twine, twisting and swaying as if someone had just walked past and bumped it. She reaches for it, wrapping her hand around it curiously.

"Why would he..."

Another thud behind her makes her jump and Lila whips around. Her heart pounds in her chest and her breath is heavy enough to rattle in her ears as she stares out into the rest of the library, darting her head left and right. The juxtaposition between the newer shelves and the ones clearly from when the building was a house makes the space even stranger and more unsettling, like the two eras have crashed together and are struggling for dominance.

"David?"

A softer sound makes her turn around and she lets out a gasp when a noose drops down inches from her face.

Jonathan feels off-balance being in the clinic with Charlotte alone. They never investigate just the two of them. She's been with the team for a little while, but it still feels like he barely knows her. There's never really been an opportunity for the two of them to spend any time just getting to know each other, which makes it somewhat awkward to be here with her. He's used to the dynamic of the entire team, each doing their own part within the investigation. Now it feels like they have to take on what the other three would do and he doesn't know how to pull that off.

"Are you done here?" he asks after a few minutes of Charlotte silently walking around the clinic, occasionally pausing to lay her hand on something or close her eyes like she's waiting.

"I think so," she says. "I was expecting more activity in here, but I'm not really getting much."

"Maybe they still feel sick or tired," he offers. "They might not want to talk. Or they might think you're a nurse and be afraid of you."

Charlotte seems to contemplate this and nods. "You're probably right. Maybe we can come back later and I'll sit down and talk with them some more and explain everything. But they've probably had enough now."

"Do you want to see if we can find the others?" he asks.

"We don't have to. I don't want to waste any time. There's so much to see here," she says.

"Alright." It's a strange reaction, but he almost feels honored that she said that. "Where do you want to go next?"

"I want to find that classroom," she says.

"Sounds good."

They leave the clinic and head away from the front entryway to move toward the classrooms. They only have the descriptions of what Mark and Sasha said as well as what Will got from reports from other visitors over the years. They have an idea of where to go, but not an exact classroom. Some of the reports have said the second one, others have said the fourth. They'll have to see which ones are open and try to figure it out.

They're nearly at the corner that turns out into the hallway of classrooms when they hear a sound that's familiar but that Jonathan can't exactly place. It isn't until he sees the floor ahead of them in the light from the lamp on his head that he knows what it is.

Thud, pop pop pop.

A blue playground ball bounces lightly a few times then rolls across the floor, coming to a stop a few feet from them.

Jonathan and Charlotte stop, staring at the ball, then turn to each other.

"Where did that come from?" Charlotte asks in a hushed tone.

"It's just like Sasha and Mark Berkeley said. They said they saw two playground balls like that during the time they were here. They bounced and rolled down the hallway, but they never saw where they came from," Jonathan says.

"Then we have to find out," Charlotte says. "Come on."

They go around the corner and move down the hall, sweeping their lights back and forth to fill as much of the space as they can.

"This room is open," Jonathan says, pointing out one of the classrooms to the side.

They go inside and see that the desks and chairs are stacked up against one wall and cartons of books fill the top of a table against another. The chalkboard shows evidence of having been cleaned, but new inscriptions have been made across it in chalk.

"I don't think this is it," Charlotte says.

The next classroom looks much the same, but as they are getting further into the hallway, Jonathan notices something on the floor. He focuses the camera on it, making sure to capture everything he's seeing as they walk toward it.

"Do you see that?" he asks, wanting to document the image but not wanting to alarm Charlotte. "Does that look like blood to you?"

The streaks across the floor are red and glistening, creating a narrow path across the hall that seems to start at one wall. They walk up to it and film several seconds of it before following it to the door. Charlotte takes hold of the doorknob without hesitation, but as soon as she opens the door and steps inside, she screams and stumbles backward, nearly knocking Jonathan down. He rights himself and grabs onto Charlotte.

"What is it? What's wrong?"

Charlotte gestures into the classroom but can't seem to form any words. Jonathan moves her gently aside and goes in. He only makes it a step before he processes the horror he's seeing inside the room. The desks are arranged like a class is underway, oriented to the front of the classroom where a teacher should be standing. There seem to be no more student desks and chairs in here than were in the other classroom, but unlike the ones in those rooms, these aren't empty.

They are full of corpses.

CHAPTER TWENTY-SEVEN

C HARLOTTE'S HEAD IS SPINNING. SHE PRESSES BACK AGAINST THE wall, her hand over her mouth as she tries to steady her heart and stop herself from passing out. Despite her efforts, her knees start to buckle and as she squeezes her eyes closed to try to stay conscious, she slides down the wall onto the floor. Her other hand hits the marble beside her. Most feels cold on the marble, but some of her fingertips touch warmth and she opens her eyes to see it resting in the blood on the floor.

Scrambling away from the gruesome pool, she grabs the flashlight she dropped and gets shakily to her feet.

"Jonathan," she says. "Jonathan, we need to go. We need to get help."

He doesn't respond and her stomach sinks. She doesn't want to go back in. She never wants to see what she saw in that room again. But she also knows it's seared into her mind. She can't escape it. She'll never be able to forget it.

"Jonathan," she says again, a last desperate effort.

THE GIRL AND THE WINTER BONES

She wants to run, but she knows she can't. She can't just leave him alone without knowing what's going on. Charlotte braces herself and walks back into the classroom. More than a dozen desks are arranged facing the front of the room and nearly all of them have a body propped in the seat. Her stomach lurches and she covers her mouth again, fighting to stop herself from getting sick. The smell is overwhelming. She doesn't know how she didn't notice it before. It hits her hard, sitting in the back of her throat and making her feel like it's clinging to her skin.

The bodies are in various states of decomposition. They appear to have been here for differing lengths of time, some degraded down to bone and dried remnants of flesh and others mummified by the elements. Others look far newer. These are the most horrific. The ones that have clearly been dead for years have lost much of their humanity. They are obviously human, but seeing just the skeletons or the structures stretched with dried flesh like leather makes them look almost like props, like Halloween decorations.

She could tell herself it was a prank if she had just seen those. If they'd walked into the room and all of the desks were filled with skeletons, she might have been startled at first, but then she would have dismissed it as a trite joke, closed the room so it didn't confuse their investigation, and moved on.

She can't do that with the fresh bodies. These are impossible to ignore, impossible to dismiss or justify. They maintain so many aspects of the people they were when they were alive. Skin, hair, lips, fingernails. Expressions. Jewelry. All painful, horrifying reminders that these are human beings now decaying in an abandoned school. They have names. They have people who know them, love them, miss them. Wonder where they are and what happened to them.

She tries not to look at them, searching instead for Jonathan. She finds him huddled on the floor, propped up on his toes with his knees to his chest, his head hanging down. His hands are on the desk in front of him and he's bouncing slightly like he's so overcome with the emotions filling him that he can't keep them contained. It isn't until she has walked over to him and crouched down beside him that Charlotte catches a glimpse out of the corner of her eye of the body sitting at the desk in front of Jonathan.

It's not just a body. It's David.

Letting out a strangled cry, she stumbles backward. Blood stains the front of his shirt where it seems to have poured down from his throat. His hands rested on the desk in front of him don't have any indication of cuts or scrapes. He almost looks as though he could lift his head up and start talking to them. But the amount of blood is far too much. He couldn't survive that loss.

And someone did that to him. Someone who could still be in the building with them.

Charlotte forces the fear out of the mind and allows adrenaline to take over. She grabs onto Jonathan and pulls on him, trying to get him to his feet.

"We have to go," she hisses. "We have to find the others and get out of here. We have to find Lila and Will. We have to *leave.*"

Her pleas finally seem to sink in and Jonathan gets to his feet. He lets her drag him out into the hallway and as soon as he's there, he sags over, his hands pressing down onto his thighs and his head dropping down as he gulps for air.

"What the hell is going on?" he finally manages to say.

"I don't know," Charlotte says. "But whoever did that could still be here. We need to find the others and try to find some help."

Jonathan shakes his head. "We can't. We can't get out. The snow. There's no way we can hike through that storm. Oh, my god."

He sounds like he's going to be sick and Charlotte grabs onto his arms to try to steady him.

"Listen to me. We have two options here. We can stay in here, take our chances with someone who collected a classroom full of corpses, and just hope someone finds us before we get added to it. Or we can find the rest of the team and battle the snowstorm to try to survive," she says. "Which one?"

Jonathan nods. "Let's go."

Charlotte nods back at him. "Good. Okay. We need to find Lila and Will. We can't leave them."

"Oh, no," Jonathan says.

"What?"

"Lila. She went to find David. She said she heard him yell. He's in there. Where is she?" he asks.

Charlotte's stomach twists and her heart sinks. They didn't believe Lila when she said she heard David shout while they were in the clinic. They'd dismissed her and it caused her to head out into the school by herself to find him and check to make sure he was alright. He most certainly is not alright. Now they don't know where she is.

"She was going to look for him in what used to be the ballroom," she says. "We need to go there. She might still be there. Or maybe we'll find her on the way."

"How about Will? Wasn't he going to come investigate the class-room area?" Jonathan asks. "Isn't that what David said?"

"He said he was going to a different part of the school. Maybe he went into another wing or back upstairs."

Thud, pop, pop, pop.

The familiar sound stops both of them and they turn to look at the end of the hallway where a red playground ball has just bounced into view. Charlotte takes several steps backward. The beam of her flashlight shakes with the trembling of her hand. She turns around to look down the opposite side of the hall to see where they can go. There's a door and they run for it. It opens out into another hall, this one carpeted and lined with heavier wood doors.

Jonathan and Charlotte run down the hallway without any idea where it leads, just trying to put as much distance between themselves and the end of the other hall as they possibly can while also trying to make their way to the wing with the former ballroom.

"The windows," Jonathan says. "Charlotte, look at the windows."

She glances to one side and sees snow falling heavily outside, reflecting the glow of the moon until it seems almost as bright as day-light. But that's not what he's pointing out. He's showing her the ornate metal cages covering them. Two others have been boarded up from the inside, likely the result of the glass being broken from the outside, but she knows that even if they were to manage to pull the boards away from the walls, the decorative metal bars would be on the other side. They won't be able to climb out through them.

"Here," Charlotte says, tugging him around a corner to a small set of steps leading up to another hallway. It's shorter, containing only two rooms. They scamper up the steps but quickly discover both doors are locked, forcing them to go back down the steps and into the hallway. "Where now? What do we do?"

"I don't know," Jonathan starts, but pauses. Charlotte sees his eyes widen. "Do you hear that?"

"Hear what?" she asks.

He points up, indicating for her to listen. At first, there's nothing, then she hears a low scraping coming from somewhere nearby. It sounds like something scratching against the floor or a wall, but the hallway is empty.

"That. What is that?"

"I don't know." She thinks for a second. "We need to get to the kitchen. The others know that's the command center. They'll go back there," Charlotte says. "And if nothing else, we can barricade ourselves inside it. If we can't get out, we'll just have to make sure that we stay in until one of the officers comes by to patrol," she says. She takes a breath. "You choose."

CHAPTER TWENTY-EIGHT

JONATHAN AND CHARLOTTE PRESS CLOSE TO THE WALL NEXT TO the door they went through to get into the new wing of the building. They listen carefully, trying to detect any indication of someone waiting on the other side.

"I don't hear anything," Jonathan whispers.

Charlotte shakes her head. "Neither do I."

"They still might be there. They could be standing right on the other side of the door waiting for us to come back through," he says.

"He could be," she acknowledges, "but there's nothing we can do. There's nowhere else to go. This wing doesn't lead anywhere else and the windows have bars. The only way to get out is to go back through that hallway. It's our only choice."

She watches his face and the emotions rippling over it. She wishes she could ask for help right now. That she could close her eyes and sense someone there with them who would guide them through and get them out. But there's nothing. Everything she'd been feeling since they first arrived at the school is gone. There are no more tingles down the back of her neck. No more flutters in her chest. No more sensations of whispers in her ears. She had felt like there were so many spirits there with them, people they simply couldn't see surrounding them and trying to have their stories told.

Now, it's just a dark, cavernous old building ready to swallow them.

Each draws in a deep breath and they nod at each other, steadying themselves. Jonathan reaches for the handle on the door and Charlotte sees his hand hesitate. She moves his hand away and in one motion grabs the handle and pushes the door open. They burst into the hallway, both prepared for someone to descend on them, but nothing happens.

They run past the classroom and through the heavy streak of blood across the floor, focused ahead on the corner that will bring them around to the front hallway. They have to find the others. They can't just abandon them without them knowing the kind of danger they're in.

Human compassion and the connection they have, even if none of them would go so far as to call it friendship, tells them they have to do what they can to make sure the rest of them get out of this place alive.

Self-preservation tells them to just run.

As they run for the corner, Charlotte notices the playground ball is gone. It makes her shudder. They are nearly to the end of the hall when a loud sound just around the corner makes them skid to a stop. They clutch each other, gasping for air while trying hard to quiet their breaths. Gripping each other's arms if for no other reason than to feel something solid and warm, as a reminder that beyond the terrifying void of the rest of the building, they aren't alone, Charlotte and Jonathan back up several feet down the hallway.

"Turn off your light," Charlotte says.

"What?" Jonathan asks, sounding shocked by the command. "If I turn off my light, we're not going to be able to see."

"And no one will be able to see us," she points out. "If we don't have our lights on, no one will be able to tell where we are unless they have a light of their own. And that way, we'll be able to see them first. We're going to have to try to navigate this place by memory and moonlight."

He hesitates for a second but finally reaches up and turns his headlamp off, sending them into darkness. For a second, it seems there is no longer anything around them. The dark is tangible, with tiny sparks of electricity flashing through their mind appearing as shimmers just in front of their eyes. But after a few moments, their vision adjusts to the darkness and they are able to detect hints of light coming through the windows in the two open classrooms ahead of them.

It isn't much, but it's enough to give them a vague idea of the direction they are moving and show where the hallway curves. The unbroken halo of light also reminds them with each step that no one else has come into the space with them. For now, they are safe.

That feeling doesn't last long. Seconds later, there's another startling sound, only this one comes from behind them. They break into a frantic run and in the chaos of that immediate fear, they get separated. Charlotte doesn't realize Jonathan is no longer beside her until she has run around the corner and deep into the school. When she pauses, she notices she no longer hears him breathing, and then it settles in that she doesn't know where she is. The darkness combined with her blind terror sends her running through other hallways until she doesn't recognize where she has ended up.

Turning around, disoriented, she tries to figure out where she is. She tries to remember how far she came, where she turned, but none of it will come to mind. She only remembers hearing the sounds behind them and running. Somewhere in the dark, far enough away that the distance masks the sound and yet makes it more sickening, she hears a gut-wrenching, desperate scream—and then a crash.

Her hand flies up to cover her mouth and stop the sound of her own scream as she presses back against a wall. Wherever she is, there are no windows. It feels as if she has been submerged in ink. Her flashlight feels heavy in her hand, but she can't bring herself to push the button to turn it on. As much as she craves the light, she fears it as well.

She doesn't know how long she sits there, crouching against the wall, her body shaking, before she forces herself to stand. She doesn't know this place well. But there's someone who does. Someone is stalking the halls very aware of where they are and how to get around. She's a target, isolated and at a disadvantage. She's been dropped down into a maze and left to thrash around until she finds a way out. Or until someone finds it for her.

Muttering reassurances to herself, she keeps her hands pressed to the wall behind her and slides gradually sideways along it. If she can continue to feel the wall behind her, she knows that at least her back is safe. She continues that way until she feels her fingertips go around the curved edge of a corner. She stops and listens. She can't hear anything. No breaths. No footsteps. Nothing to tell her that someone else is anywhere close.

She slides herself around the corner and notices a pool of moonlight on the floor a few yards ahead of her. Maybe she managed to turn herself around and get back to the main entryway. She moves toward it at a faster pace now and she is already within a few feet of the corner when she realizes it isn't moonlight. Someone is coming toward her with a light.

Charlotte stifles a scream and turns around, running for her life. She can hear the footsteps coming behind her. She tries to turn into a hallway and smashes into a wall. Blood pours down her mouth and she crumples to the ground. Dizzy, she stumbles trying to get up, already knowing that her pursuer is swooping down on her.

"Hey!" she hears a voice hiss.

She turns away, covering her head with her arm, and tries to crawl away, but she feels a hand clamp down on her back. Everything goes dark.

When her awareness returns, it is of someone holding her and saying her name over and over. The voice sounds like it's coming through water, she can't recognize it. She tries to pull away from the grip but can't move.

"Charlotte, stop. It's me. It's Will."

She opens her eyes and sees Will's face in the glow of a small camping lantern set on the floor beside her.

"Will? Where did you come from?"

"I was upstairs. I decided to go back up to the attic to investigate it again," he says. "I was trying to figure out how that door would have gotten stuck if David didn't hire somebody to come pretend to be a spirit and they were holding it closed."

Charlotte shakes her head frantically. "No. No, he didn't hire anybody. That was real. There really was somebody outside. They came in."

Will nods. "I know. I've been trying to find the rest of you. I found Lila."

She blinks a few times. "What do you mean? What do you mean you found her?"

"She's dead," Will says.

Charlotte's chest lurches. "Where? Where is she?"

"I found her in the library," he says.

"The library? You said you were upstairs in the attic."

Questions and suspicions start to roll through Charlotte's head. He just told her he was up in the attic investigating and now says he found Lila in the library. That's on the bottom floor of the building. How could he have found her?

"I was," he says. "But I didn't figure anything out, so I came back down. I thought I heard something, so I went to the library. That's when I found Lila. I knew I had to find you and Jonathan, too."

The words resonate with Charlotte. Not so much what he said but what he didn't. She wriggles herself out of his arms and gets her feet. She feels shaky and not completely in control of her body, but she can't let herself be weak right now. Shaking her head, she takes a step back.

"You needed to find me and Jonathan?" she asks.

"Yes," Will says. "I was worried about you. Something happened to Lila. I needed to find you."

"What about David?" she asks.

"David?" he replies with a frown.

"You know this building," she says, realization settling in. "You know more about it than any of the rest of us. You know where the rooms are. You know how to get around it. You did this."

"What are you talking about?" Will asks. "Did what?"

"David and the others. Where is Jonathan?" she asks.

"The others? Charlotte," he starts, taking a step toward her, but she pulls back, her heart beating so fast it feels like it's vibrating. "Charlotte, what is going on? We need to get out of here."

"Just us?" she asks. "Oh, my god. What did you do to him? The same thing that you did to David? What did you do to Lila?"

"What?"

Her eyes flash to the walls on either side of them and something clicks.

"Servants' passages. There are servants' passages behind the walls. That's how you got around without anyone seeing you."

"I don't know what you're talking about. What about David?"

"You didn't mention him. You said you needed to find me and Jonathan. You didn't mention David. That's because you already knew he's dead in that classroom."

He reaches for her and Charlotte ducks under his arm, swinging her elbow backward to hit him in the back of the head. She gets past him and runs. She turns on her flashlight as she goes, no longer caring if she's seen. She doesn't have to hide from something she knows.

She realizes she ran down into the area near the ballroom and the library and runs down the hall until she sees the ballroom. Running into it, she looks around for access to the patio. On the outside of the school, a large, gracious porch still sits just beyond what was once the ballroom, nostalgic for the couples who used to step outside to get fresh air and a few moments alone during the parties thrown there.

If she can get out onto the patio, she can climb over the stone wall around its edges and run. It makes her sick to think of leaving without knowing where Jonathan is, but she has no choice. She can't go look for him. This is her only chance.

Her flashlight shows the inside of the space has been changed drastically since it was a ballroom, and the further she goes, the more the tiny glimmer of hope she had been feeling fades away. She can't find a door that leads outside. She saw it when they were looking at the outside of the building, but she can't find it now. She realizes it was likely walled off, blocked off to convert the space, but left on the outside for the aesthetic. She can't get out.

Charlotte turns and watches light come into the room and start moving toward her.

CHAPTER TWENTY-NINE

WILL'S EARS ARE STILL BUZZING FROM THE IMPACT OF Charlotte's elbow as he makes his way down the hall. He has to find her. She mentioned the servants' hallways. He wants to know how she knows about them. They were something he'd kept to himself when telling them about the building. He wanted to see if they could find out about them on their own. Years ago, when the team was still new, he never would have even thought of doing something like that. He wouldn't have used the other investigators as part of his experiments.

But there are a lot of things he wouldn't have done years ago. Things have changed now.

Her hitting him in the back of the head made him stumble slightly and felt like it shook up his thoughts, but when his brain settled, he could hear Charlotte's footsteps heading away. He knows she's in the ballroom. There's only one way in and one way out of that space, which means if he can get to it while she is still inside, she will have much less of a chance of running away from him again.

He gets just outside what used to be the lavish entertainment space in time to see a light moving through the door and inside. It isn't Charlotte. Whoever it is isn't carrying a flashlight like Charlotte is—and is moving without urgency. They seem to just be roaming the hallway. His stomach tightens and for an instant, he wants to call out but he stops himself.

Instead, he holds his own light down by his thigh to dampen the glow slightly, keeping enough of it to illuminate his path but not enough to call attention to himself. He presses back against the wall and moves along it sideways. Just before he gets to the door to the ballroom wing, he hears a cry. Tossing aside all attempts at being stealthy, Will runs inside. A beam of light shines across the dark room from where Charlotte's flashlight is lying on the ground, and nearby, a lantern provides a halo of light.

It's enough for him to see a figure holding onto Charlotte by her neck. It looks very much like the figure he saw sitting on the swing set.

"Hey!" he shouts, running toward them.

The figure doesn't respond. They don't care that Will is there or that he's coming. In the handful of running paces it takes him to get to within a few yards of them, the figure has released Charlotte's neck with one hand and taken something out of their pocket. Before Will can process what he's seeing, the figure smashes a hammer into the side of Charlotte's head. She instantly crumbles to the ground and her attacker crouches down beside her, hitting her three more times in rapid succession.

Will's instinct is to run forward and try to pull the person off of Charlotte. He wants to try to save her. But she's not making any noise. She hasn't moved. And even in the small amount of light, he can see the blood spreading across the floor around Charlotte. There's nothing he can do for her. She can't be saved. The only thing he can do is try to find Jonathan and get out alive.

He needs to be able to tell somebody what he saw. About Charlotte. About Lila.

He turns and runs, knowing the killer is going to pursue him. He didn't do anything to conceal his presence in the room and now they know he saw them. As he runs, he can't help but think about what Charlotte had told him about David. She said he's dead. In a classroom.

He immediately knows what that means.

Will runs through the hall and into the next. Listening for footsteps following him, he detours around a corner and feels for the movable panel in the wall. When he finds it, he opens the access point to the servants' hallway behind the wall.

Passages like this were not unusual during the time when this building was originally constructed. It was simply thought to be proper for the staff of a home to move around as undetected as possible. They used these passages to get to different parts of the home to bring food, to clean, to do anything that they needed to do without any members of the family or any guests seeing them. It would have taken away from the opulent atmosphere of one of their elaborate parties to see the staff carrying away dirty dishes or refilling trays. It's more effective to simply feel like those happen by magic.

There's nothing magic about what Will is using these passages for now. He needs to stay out of sight and get to the classroom wing as quickly as he can. If he is to believe what Charlotte told him, it's likely the killer knows about these passages as well and has been using them to move around the building while they have been investigating. But if it gets him to safety quicker, it will have been worth the risk.

Trying to keep his thoughts clear so he's able to navigate the narrow halls, he makes his way across the building and to the piano he knows will open out into the classroom hallway. It had surprised him when he found out that these passages had been left intact when the home was converted into a school. It'd taken much deeper digging for him to find out that when the home was converted, the decision had been made to leave the passages as a security measure. With threats of war constantly hovering over them, administrators believed it was important to have somewhere inside the building where the children could be gathered and protected. The internal hallways were strong and had no windows, making them better to withstand any type of attack. The fact that they were virtually impossible to detect for someone who didn't already know about them would keep them out of sight and safer if there was some type of invasion.

It is a horrifying and saddening thought, but Will is thankful for it.

He bursts out of the hidden door and immediately notices the blood across the floor. It leads directly where he expected it to. He knew when Charlotte mentioned the classroom that she was talking about the same one the Berkeley couple talked about after their night in the school, the same one where Linda Carmine sat before she went missing. He doesn't know the significance. He doesn't understand why anyone would choose that particular classroom except as a cruel joke.

Not letting the blood on the floor dissuade him, he walks into the classroom. Seconds later, he runs out. He fights the sickness rushing up his throat as he runs for the entrance to the school. He doesn't have time to look for anybody else. He doesn't have time to try to make any sort of difference. At this point, the chances that Johnathan has survived are next to nothing. He would have seen him or heard something.

Will gets to the front of the school and goes for the front door. He tries to open it, but it won't move. No matter how much strength he puts into it, it doesn't even shift. It's locked. As he's trying to decide what to do next, he smells something strange. Fire.

Panic rushes through him. He doesn't know where to go or how to escape. The front door is inaccessible. The windows are barred. A sudden thought flashes into his mind and he runs for the staff quarters near the kitchen. Flames are already shooting out of the small kitchen and he knows it's only a matter of time before the rest of the building catches. The amount of stone used for the construction will help to slow the spread, but there is more than enough wood, wallpaper, and other combustible materials for the entire place to go up.

He runs past the doors to the staff rooms and finds the final one in the hallway. It is small and unassuming, but to Will, it represents the possibility of salvation. The door is locked, but a hard kick splinters the wood enough for him to pull it away and push through. He falls down the first few steps but regains his footing and runs down into the basement. It smells musty and damp. Much like many of the rooms upstairs, the basement is stacked with crates and discarded belongings. There are plenty of places to hide, but that isn't an option. With the flames moving through the school, Will needs to get out.

There's only one option and he doesn't know if it's going to work. The basement has no traditional back door, but he does remember a cellar door in pictures. He tries to orient himself and figure out where he is in the context of the entire building. Overhead, he hears muffled sounds that could be doors slamming and footsteps. He holds his lantern high to spread the light around as much as he can and finally catches sight of the angled door positioned at the top of three steps. It reminds him of *The Wizard of Oz*. It sends a wild, fleeting memory of being a small child and hiding from the flying monkeys shooting through his head.

Will pushes on the door and it shifts just slightly. He flings the inside latch open and pushes again but it still doesn't open. It must be latched on the outside. Will forces all his weight against the doors with his shoulder, then goes down the steps and backs up several feet before running up and slamming himself against the door. Pain shoots through him, but he doesn't care. The wood has splintered. He does it again and on the third try, the old latch gives way and he feels the rush of cold air and snowflakes coming in from outside.

He drags in breaths of the clean air as he scrambles out of the door. But he can't go far. He's disoriented and weak, and the cold cuts into him. He isn't wearing enough gear to protect him from the low temperature. He glances over his shoulder and sees the flames and dark smoke billowing around the back of the building. He runs as hard as he can through the already deep snow, trying to get to the wall at the back of the grounds. If he can get over that wall, he can get to the road and head for help.

Several few yards from the cellar door, his vision starts to go black. A few steps later, he collapses, his body sprawled out in the snow.

CHAPTER THIRTY

WE ARE JUST GETTING BACK INTO THE CAR AFTER A QUICK STOP for gas and a couple more road snacks when my pager goes off on my hip. I take it off and look at the screen.

"Who is it?" Sam asks.

My eyebrows furrow. "It's Eric. I need to call him back. He says it's urgent." I put my drink and snacks in the car. "Just give me a second. I'm going to run and call him from the pay phone. I'll be right back."

I grab some change from the glass jar I keep in the door of the car and head for the payphone positioned at the edge of the parking lot. Eric answers on the first ring.

"Hey, what's going on?" I ask.

"Are you still in McCutcheon?" he asks.

"No," I say. "I left yesterday. Why?"

"I need you to go back."

"Why? What happened?" I ask.

"A few hours ago an officer patrolling the area around the Dawn Day School saw smoke. He called for help and they investigated. They found one person lying out in the snow. When they were able to get the fire under control and go inside, they discovered more bodies inside. A lot of bodies. You just need to get there."

By late afternoon, I'm in a meeting room at the homicide division in the McCutcheon police department. The table in front of me is laden with images and written reports from the responding officers. What I'm seeing is dizzying. I couldn't get many details out of Eric when I talked to him. He just wanted me to get back to the area as fast as I could so I could be a part of the investigation from the beginning.

He has already determined this case should be handled by the Bureau. I was surprised he would have made that determination so early, but now that I see the scope of what we're dealing with, I understand. It's not just the number of bodies found in the school. It's the massive range of victims, death dates, and causes of death.

This doesn't just look like a serial killer. It looks like a collection. Some of the bodies are so badly decomposed it's impossible to even tell whether they are male or female and what age. It will take extensive work by the medical examiner to identify all of these victims and find out what happened to them. By the time I arrived, only one has been identified. A man named Timothy Sterling had his ID card in his pocket when he was murdered. It doesn't provide any further details, but by the expiration date listed on that card, I can assume he has been dead for many years. He is also from New Jersey, making this an inter-state crime, further cementing the place of the FBI in the investigation.

Not that I have stormed in to take over. That isn't how this works. It's a common misconception that the FBI just sweeps into homicide or other cases and just pushes out any other agencies or departments. That isn't the case. I prefer to work in conjunction with the local police and state departments as much as possible. My mindset is that it's always better to have more boots on the ground and minds in the game when it comes to unraveling cases, particularly ones as immediately complex as this one.

Fortunately, there is no resistance from the Gordon or McCutcheon departments when I arrive. They were the ones who'd gotten in contact with Eric and asked for our assistance. They knew from the moment the body count started adding up that this was more than they were going to be able to handle on their own. Violent crime of any kind, much less murder, is extremely uncommon in this area. A couple a year, maybe, and the vast majority of the time those are domestic in nature.

They've never seen anything like this.

"You said you have some recording devices?" I ask one of the officers who responded to the scene and helped supervise the initial processing of the scene.

"Yes," Officer Chappell confirms. "Some cameras and a couple of voice recorders. It looks like there was some other equipment in the room where the fire started but it was all destroyed."

"Why did they have all that equipment?" I ask. "Were they with the media?"

I just watched the news special on the school and everything that had happened there a couple days ago. It would make sense for there to be another group there doing a more in-depth documentary on the building, especially considering the plans for it to be demolished in just a couple of months.

"I don't think so," he says. "We haven't gone through much of what's on the recorders yet, but from what we have listened to, it seems like this was a paranormal investigation team."

"Oh, jeez," I say, rolling my eyes so hard I feel like the connective tissue on the back might twist and snap. "Are you serious?"

"Yeah. Looks like it. The recording I listened to had them talking about the history of the building and why that means there must be spirits present. Talking about telling their stories before the building was destroyed and they lost their only chance," he says.

I prop my elbow on the desk and put my forehead in my hand, rubbing the sides with my middle finger and thumb. This is not my first brush with people immersing themselves in the concept of the paranormal. It isn't even my first case involving a paranormal team. But that doesn't make it any less unbelievable.

"There are four people dead and another one partially frozen with massive blood loss in the hospital fighting to stay alive because they broke into a decrepit old building looking for ghosts?" I clarify.

"Looks like it," Officer Chappell says.

"Perfect," I say with a heavy exhale. "And what about the other bodies? They were found in a classroom?"

"Yes."

He pulls out a picture of the bodies propped in the desks of one of the classrooms and points to one of them.

"He's fresh," he says. I cringe slightly at the choice of description but don't say anything. "But he didn't have any ID on him."

"Did any of them?" I ask.

"The victim out in the snow. Will Baylor. He's unconscious so we can't ask him anything. We're trying to use his personal contacts to make more identifications."

"And some of the bodies are old," I note.

"Yes. Some to the point of mummification or full skeletal condition. They've been there for years."

"How could nobody have noticed this before now? There have been other people in that school. That couple that was on the news. They were there. They reported a body," I say.

He nods, the expression on his face looking like he'd been hoping I wasn't going to bring that up.

"When the police investigated, they didn't find anything like that. Every classroom in that school was searched. There wasn't anything."

"Or there was and it was just missed. This isn't the work of three years," I say, pointing to the picture. "These people have been dead for a long time, and that means they were kept somewhere. We need to find out where. And I need all the footage from the cameras and the audio from the recorders."

"You got it," he nods.

"How about the rest of the school? How much damage was done by the fire?" I ask.

"The room where the fire started is destroyed. Some of the back of the building was also fairly damaged. But the rest of the building was saved."

"Good. The team needs to start collecting everything they can find that might have anything to do with these crimes. Past and present," I say.

"Everything?" he asks.

I look him directly in the eye, my expression steady. "Everything."

⌐

"Believe it or not, these people had something of a following," I tell Sam later when I get to the hotel room he'd booked for us in the same hotel we'd just checked out of a couple days before. "Primarily the victim found in the classroom with the older bodies. David Casey. I guess you'd call him the leader of the group. Remember the team from the Arrow Lake case?"

"How could I forget that?"

I nod, unbuttoning my jeans and shaking them off my legs so I can pull on a pair of comfortable sweats and relax.

"True. I guess I mean remember the way the team was structured? There was a very clear hierarchy and they followed the instructions, and the word, of the leader. David was that leader for this group. And he was building up quite a fanbase."

"Through what?" Sam asks.

"The officer who talked to his mother said that he wrote booklets about his investigations and sold them as well as video and audio footage, and they even had a newsletter they distributed. People were really invested in his personality and his evidence. She said that he'd gotten a lot more into the business and marketing of the whole thing recently, but it used to be really serious," I say.

"Serious? How can this be serious?"

I nod. "Apparently he actually studied paranormal science in college. And the surviving victim, Will Baylor, is an actual researcher in the field. He gets funding from various organizations to conduct experiments and collect evidence about the existence of the paranormal and the better understanding thereof," I say, trying to accurately repeat what David's mother had told me.

"Wow," Sam remarks. "That's not what I was expecting."

"Yeah," I say, flopping down on the bed. "Neither did I."

"You said the Will guy was a victim, too. How did he manage to get away from his attacker?"

"Well, it doesn't look like he was actually attacked. The other victims show various signs of trauma. David's throat was slit, one of the female victims was strangled and hanged, the other female victim was bludgeoned to death and a bloody hammer was found nearby. The fourth of the contemporary victims was found in another of the classrooms under a large pile of furniture. It's going to take some piecing together by the medical examiner to determine if he was killed by those things falling on him, or if he was already dead when they were piled on top of him.

All of them have signs of tremendous violence. But Will doesn't. He was unconscious, suffering from hypothermia, and bleeding heavily when the officers found him. But after the doctors at the hospital examined him, they found that all of his injuries seem to have come from when he broke out of a cellar door. The police confirmed the door was broken open and there was blood, hair, and torn clothing on some of the wood. It looks like he slammed himself against the door until it broke and cut his head, face, neck, and shoulder on the wood and metal pieces in the process," I explain.

"Four other people went through that much, but he wasn't even touched?" Sam asks. "That doesn't strike anybody else as suspicious?"

"Oh, it definitely does. But right now, the whole thing is suspicious. Especially when you think about the other dozen bodies in that room as well as the disappearances and deaths that have been linked to that area over the last several years," I say.

"I thought none of the bodies found around the school were considered criminal," Sam says.

"They weren't. But clearly that is going to have to be reconsidered," I say. "People don't just happen to die right next to a building later found to be playing host to almost twenty bodies. I can't guarantee that any of the missing people are among those dead or that any of them have anything to do with it, but they need to be looked into."

My eyes catch one of the flowers on the hotel bedspread and I stare at it, my mind churning.

"What is it?" Sam asks.

"Hmm?" I ask, looking up at him.

"You've got that look on your face. What are you thinking about?"

"Linda Carmine and Alma Mulroney," I say.

"Do you think either of them are linked to this?" he asks.

"I don't know. But, again …"

He nods. "I know."

CHAPTER THIRTY-ONE

"IT WAS THE FOURTH-GRADE CLASSROOM?" I ASK, WALKING through the medical examiner's office.

"Yes," she says. "And by the description from Sasha and Mark Berkeley, it was the same room where they say they found the body three years ago. It seems they might have actually been right."

"But then where did the body go?" I ask.

She shrugs. "Fortunately, that's not my job to find out. That one's on you."

"Great. Well, if it was the fourth-grade classroom, that means it was the classroom Linda Carmine attended before she disappeared," I say.

She gets a regretful look on her face and nods. "Yeah. I knew you were going to ask about that. That occurred to me as soon as I found out what classroom it was. But just from my initial examination of all the bodies, there aren't any young girls. The youngest victim is most likely a mid-teenager. And male. None of these victims could be Linda Carmine."

"How about Alma Mulroney?"

"I'm not familiar with her."

"Linda's best friend. She went missing eleven years after Linda did. She'd have been college-age."

"There are a couple of victims who might fit that profile, but I can't say anything conclusively right now. But I can tell you that some of these victims have been dead for many years. And others are more recent. I have noticed a couple of stab wounds, bludgeoning. There isn't any consistent cause of death. I haven't found identification in any more of their belongings. It's going to take quite a bit of time to ID them all and find out what happened to them. You're going to have to be patient."

I'm not feeling patient. With this many people dead and possible links to several other cases, there isn't time for me to sit around and wait. It might take the medical examiner a long time to figure out what she can about those bodies, but like she said, finding out what happened isn't her job. That's mine. She can do what needs to be done on her end, but I'm not going to wait around for it.

I go back to the police department for just long enough to fill in the rest of the team about what the medical examiner said.

"That was the fourth-grade classroom, the one Linda Carmine was in. I need somebody to search out every person who was in that class and find out where they are right now. So far, it's very obvious that some of those bodies could not possibly be anybody who was in the class. But there are others who could be. I want confirmation of every one of those students' current status and location, whether dead or alive. I'm going to talk with Alma Mulroney's mother. Have something for me when I get back."

While Dean, Xavier, and I head for Carla Mulroney's house, Sam goes to meet with Sasha and Mark Berkeley. They shared a lot during their interview we watched on the news segment, but I don't feel like I got all the information they could offer. I want him to get their entire story and ask them a few specific questions. They might be able to provide us with some context that could help direct the investigation.

Carla is visibly resistant when we arrive at her house. She stands on the other side of the door, holding it open just enough so that part of her face is visible through the gap.

"Yes?" she asks as if she is surprised by our arrival even though we called ahead of time.

"Carla?" I say. "It's Emma. Emma Griffin. Remember?"

"And Dean Steele," Dean adds, leaning slightly so that she can see him better.

"And Xavier Renton," Xavier introduces with just as much familiarity.

"You said you would be willing to talk to us for a few minutes. Can we come in?" I ask.

She hesitates, then nods and steps back. For a second, I think she might just shut the door in our faces, but she opens it the rest of the way and gestures for us to come in.

"I told you everything," Carla says when we sit down in her small, cozy living room. It's decorated with an old-fashioned taste, reminding me of the way my grandmother's living room looked when I was a teenager. "I don't know what else I can do to help you." Her eyes widen just slightly and there's a faint shimmer of hope in them. "Unless... did you find her? Did you find Alma?"

My heart sinks. I really didn't want her to think that.

"No. We didn't find her. But something did happen and we don't know for sure, but it could have some link to Linda, and possibly to Alma," Dean says.

Carla's eyes flick back and forth between Dean and me. "What? What happened?"

The rest of the investigative team and I had agreed on a list of details I would share with Carla in the course of this discussion. It's important for portions of Investigations to be kept confidential, particularly in the very early stages of the investigation, to protect their integrity. But sometimes it's critical to share some of that information with people who could have further information. Knowing what is to be shared and what can't be is vital to making sure everyone in the investigation is on the same page. Too many cases have been compromised by people leaking information or accidentally confirming things that were supposed to be kept confidential. With as many threads as are appearing in these cases, I'm going to have to tread very lightly.

I carefully explain what happened at the school, giving the same story as we shared with the local media to put on the news and in the papers. It is a general overview with smoothed edges and rounded corners. No specific numbers. No specific causes of death. Leaving out the detail about the fourth-grade classroom. That is one detail that I give Carla after asking for her discretion.

When I'm finished, she's staring at the coffee table between us as if lost in her own thoughts. We sit silently, giving her time. Finally, she lifts her head to look at me.

"None of them are Linda?"

"No. The medical examiner says that none of them are of the right age."

"But what if he kept her for a while? She would be older now," Carla points out.

"She doesn't think that any of the ages of the people and the degree of decomposition line up enough for any of them to be Linda," I tell her as gently as I can.

"How about Alma?"

It's a question I knew was coming even if I didn't want it to.

"At this time, we really don't know. I gave her a description of the timeline and her age, and she says that there are a couple of the victims that could line up, but she will need far more time to examine them to get any concrete information."

Carla nods sadly. "She never got over it. Linda disappearing. The two of them were so close. I've never seen a friendship like that. It didn't matter how much time they spent together at school or outside of school, as soon as they had to be apart, Alma was broken-hearted. It was like there was a part of her missing when Linda wasn't around. Angelo said Linda used to be the same way. He would find little notes in her room of things she wrote down that she wanted to tell Alma the next time she saw her. He said that she would constantly talk about her and come up with plans of all the things they were going to do together. Sometimes it was as simple as going to the zoo to see the new babies born in the spring. Then it would be that they were going to join the Navy together and go down on submarines.

"He never discouraged her. That was something I admired about him so much. There was never anything he told her that she couldn't do. If she wanted to do it, he believed in her. I think that was his wife coming through. He loved her so much and he wanted to make sure that her daughter had everything she possibly could. He wanted her to live such a big life."

Emotion fills her voice and she looks down, drawing in a breath. A second later, she looks back up.

"I was always afraid something like that was going to happen," she whispers.

I'm surprised by the declaration.

"You were always afraid one of them was going to go missing?" I ask.

"Yes," she says without hesitation. "One of them or one of the other girls in the school. As long as that teacher was there, none of the girls in the school were safe."

I look over at Dean.

"That teacher… you mean Linda and Alma's teacher?"

"Richard Smith," she says, the words coming out of her mouth with a heavy bitterness like she's spitting out something rolled in dirt. "I said from the start there shouldn't have been a man teaching those little children."

"There are plenty of male teachers," I point out.

"Not then," she says. "Maybe now, but not then. It was strange and I didn't like it. If I hadn't wanted so much for Alma to have access to that school, I would have prevented her from being in his class. It wasn't right. And he proved me right."

"What do you mean by that?" Dean asks.

"Everybody knew he had a fixation on little girls. He got way too friendly with his students. Way too close. Especially Linda. His relationship with her was completely inappropriate. I always told Alma never to go anywhere alone with him and if she saw anyone alone with him, she was to make sure she told me."

"Did you ever witness anything inappropriate?" I ask.

"No. Not myself. But I heard plenty about it. Everybody did. But the school wouldn't do anything about it. They said there was no actual proof and they couldn't take a man's job away just because people didn't like how it looked to have him teaching children," Carla says.

"If you never saw anything and the school didn't think that there was enough merit to the accusation to fire him, how did you know there was any type of inappropriate conduct happening?" I ask.

"Do you have any children, Agent Griffin?" she asks.

I take a second to make sure I can hold back the sigh that wants to come out in response to the question. It's not the first time I've heard it or some variation of it. It's difficult for some people to understand why Sam and I haven't had children. They can't seem to grasp that it is our choice and one that I am more than comfortable with. I get the same feeling from that question that I do from people questioning how a woman became a successful FBI agent or who is in charge of an investigation because clearly I couldn't be. They ask if I want a family, not seeming to understand that I already have one.

"No," I tell her. "I don't."

"A mother knows."

I walk away from the conversation with Carla with the thought of the teacher sitting heavily in the center of my chest. I want to think if Richard Smith had done something as horrible as Carla was accusing, law enforcement wouldn't have gotten it wrong, but I know there's no guarantee of that. Everyone in law enforcement is human. No matter how devoted they are, no matter how much they put of themselves into every case, there are times when mistakes are made. When criminals manage to get past them. Even to the point of the crimes themselves going unacknowledged.

I know what happened to Richard Smith after Linda's disappearance. I know how the town turned on him and he was driven away, punished without charge, arrest, or trial. It gives me sympathy for him. But I can't entirely discount the rumors against him. If nothing else, that kind of treatment only underscores potential motive to lash out against the community that ostracized him. It's worth looking into.

CHAPTER THIRTY-TWO

"**W**HERE ARE DEAN AND XAVIER?" SAM ASKS WHEN I MEET him for lunch after talking with Alma.

"They went to do some research for me. And I think Dean is going to bring Xavier to a miniature golf place they saw up the road. He said something about the obstacles looking really fun and there being three different courses."

"Wow," Sam says. "That should take Xavier upwards of ten minutes to finish."

I chuckle as I look over the menu. "Yeah, something like that. His math skills could really let him run a good hustle."

"Emma Johnson," Sam scolds playfully. "Did I just hear you suggest somebody should willfully break the law with a financial fraud scheme?"

"I didn't say anything about a financial fraud scheme. I meant he could play professional mini golf," I protest.

Sam laughs. "That's definitely not what you meant."

I settle on what I want to order and put the menu down.

"The world will never know. Anyway, what did you find out from Sasha and Mark Berkeley? Anything new?"

"They basically told the same story that we heard on the news, but they added a few more details that I thought you might think were interesting."

The waitress walks up and we make our orders. She sets glasses of water down in front of us and I take a sip as she walks away.

"What kind of details?"

"They went into quite a few rooms while they were there. One of them was the main office. They said that there were still office supplies and things in the receptionist's desk and some books in the principal's office. They also found what Sasha is completely convinced is a real human tongue in one of the drawers."

"A human tongue?" I ask.

"Yes. Apparently it was in the bottom of one of the drawers when they found a scrapbook. Mark says he thought it was fake because some group did a Halloween haunted house attraction through there one time. He thought it was just a prop that got forgotten about and the police never found it."

"They also weren't able to find an entire body," I point out. "I'll mention it to the medical examiner and see if any of her new friends are missing a tongue. What about the scrapbook?"

"It was just some book with a bunch of pictures and documents from the history of the school. It was inscribed thanking somebody for their service to the school. They assumed it was the principal, but they couldn't read the name. Both of them pointed out how strange they thought it was that somebody would just leave something like that at the school after it closed. It seems like a pretty sentimental gift and they would think the recipient would want to take it with them."

"I'd think so," I note.

"They also went into the clinic and said there were a bunch of records still in the filing cabinet. They thought that was strange, too."

I nod. "It is. We're going to need to go back to the school and get those things. I don't know what kind of significance they might have, but I want to go over them."

We eat and as we are getting up to leave, my pager goes off. I see that it's Officer Chappell and I flag down the waitress to find out if there's a phone I can use. She directs me to the manager's office and I call in to the department.

"It's Agent Griffin," I say when he answers. "Everything okay?"

"We've been watching the videos and listening to the recorders like you asked. There's something I think you should hear."

"I'm on my way."

"What am I listening to?"

Officer Chappell sits down across from me with a legal pad and pen. I notice the paper seems full of scribbled notes and bullet points.

"This is from the recorder found in a recreational room. It used to be the school's gym, but it was also used for other activities. When it was a house originally, it was the ballroom. So you will hear David talking about the ballroom. That's what he's discussing."

"This is a recorder from David Casey, the victim?"

"Yes. He was doing what he describes as a solo investigation. I'm going to skip ahead quite a bit because there's a lot of him talking about what they've already seen and everything, but none of it seems particularly relevant. What I want you to hear comes toward the end," he tells me.

"Just to be clear, I don't need you to tell me what's relevant. I am going to need to review every one of these videos and recordings," I say.

He looks sheepish but nods. "Of course. I'm sorry. I didn't mean to… I just thought this part was important for you to hear."

"Okay. Go ahead."

He starts the recorder and I listen to a few seconds of David talking about the spirits and their presence. His voice sounds a little shaky as he talks about not feeling welcome in the space and wondering if he's communicating with the woman who used to throw parties there or some of her guests. When his voice stops, I hear something faint in the background.

"What's that?" I ask. "Is that footsteps?"

"That's what it sounds like," Chappell says.

A few seconds later, I hear shuffling and a gasp, then one more word. This time, he screamed.

"Did he just say 'Will?'" I ask.

Chappell nods. "That's what it sounded like to me. I think that's the moment when he was attacked. If you keep listening, there are several minutes of sounds, but no other words. Then the recorder is turned off."

"What kinds of sounds?" I ask.

Almost as soon as I have asked the question, I hear the wet, unmistakable sound of a blade through flesh. Then a couple of groans and grunts like someone is putting tremendous energy into something, followed by a soft scraping sound.

"We think that's the sound of his body being moved."

"Was there blood leading to the classroom?" I ask.

"No. There's blood in the ballroom and then some in the hall near the classroom, but none in other areas of the school."

"How is that possible?" I ask.

"We don't know yet," he says.

"Let me listen to it again."

He rewinds the tape and plays it for me. When it's over, I have no doubt about what I heard. In his last moments, David screamed out Will's name.

"Do you think he could have seen his attacker?" Chappell asks.

"That's what it sounds like. But we need Will's side. How is his condition?" I ask.

"I haven't heard any updates," he says.

"Alright. I'll give them a call. Thanks for bringing this to my attention. I'm going to bring everything with me when I go back to my hotel tonight and go over it."

I'm getting up to leave when the door to the meeting room opens. Another officer sticks his head in.

"There's a bunch of people out here that watched the news," he says. "They want to know if their loved ones could be among the victims."

"Shit," I mutter. "I thought they weren't going to release the story until tonight."

"I guess they changed their mind and went with it as a midday breaking story," Officer Grace says.

Chappell and I hurry out of the meeting room and follow Grace to the front of the precinct. Several people have gathered inside and are hurling questions at the receptionist. So many words overlapping makes it impossible to understand everything that any one of them is saying, but I can catch snippets and they all want to know the same thing.

Could the loved one missing from their life be among those bodies?

It's heart-wrenching to see so many people with desperation in their eyes asking about their siblings, parents, children, neighbors, and friends. It's obvious some of them don't actually have any true hope. They are only there because they feel like they have to be. That if they don't ask, they are giving up on the person. As I look out over the group, a face stands out to me. It doesn't look exactly the same, but I know I've seen it. It's Linda Carmine's father.

I whistle to make everyone quiet down and hold up my hands to get their attention.

"Everyone, please listen to me. I'm sure the news about what happened at the school has been extremely upsetting to all of you. And I know you want to find out if any of the victims could be related to the cases of your missing loved ones. I assure you we are working as quickly as we possibly can to identify the victims and find out what happened to them. This is a process that will take time and I'm asking for your understanding and your patience.

"As of right now, very few identifications have been made, and the majority of those were the four victims killed the night before last. I promise you I will make sure each and every one of you will get all of the information we can share as soon as we are able. Until then, we will need to be allowed to do our jobs. Please go home and we will get in touch with you when we can. Thank you."

The crowd starts to disperse and I push through them to get to Linda's father.

"Angelo Carmine?" I ask.

He turns toward me. "Yes?"

"My name is Agent Emma Griffin. I'm with the FBI and I'm heading up this investigation. Would you have time to talk to me for a few minutes?" I ask.

He nods. "Absolutely. I can't right now. I really have to get back to work. I just came here on my lunch break as soon as I heard what happened. But I can meet up with you another time."

"Of course. Any time that you have available." I take out the small metal clip I keep in my pocket and hand him one of my business cards. "Please, page me when you know you'll have time. Or you can call here and give them a message. Thank you."

He nods, the sadness obvious in his eyes even after all these years. "Can I at least ask…"

"Linda isn't there," I tell him. "I'm sorry."

He gives a weak smile and nods. "I don't know if I should feel frustrated or relieved."

"Both," I tell him. "They both fit right now."

CHAPTER THIRTY-THREE

M Y HEART IS STILL ACHING FOR ANGELO AS I MAKE MY WAY TO the school to check on the progress of the crime scene investigation team. I need to make sure they are collecting anything from the school that might be pertinent. Now that I know about the scrapbook in the principal's office and the records at the clinic, I want to look over them as well. I'm not sure what they could have to do with anything, but when it comes to investigating murder, there is no room to overlook anything.

The police have opened up the closed entrance to the road leading up to the driveway for the school. Several officers stand at the entrance to block access to anyone not involved in the investigation. But as I drive up the old road, I see control of traffic at the entrance hasn't stopped a crowd from forming at the base of the driveway. They must have come through the park after hearing what happened. They move out of the way as I approach the end of the drive so I can go up to the school, but a couple of them swoop in and try to get my attention.

They press their hands to the window and one pounds on the hood. I park and get out to confront the crowd.

"What the hell is going on here?" I demand.

"We want to know the same thing," one of the men who'd pressed his hands to the glass beside my face asks, trying to take another step toward me.

He's forced back by the officer, but his eyes flash angrily at me.

"Back off," I say. "There's no need to cause more trouble."

"And who do you think you are telling me what to do, woman?" he snaps.

The officer tries to pull him away, but I hold up my hand to stop him. I reach into my pocket and pull out my shield.

"Agent Emma Griffin. FBI. I'm leading this investigation."

His face drops and goes pale, then his cheeks redden. His fists clench beside him and he looks like the anger he's forcing to stay locked inside him is making him shake, but he doesn't say anything else.

"We'll open the gate for you," one of the officers tells me. "They're expecting you up there."

"Thank you," I say.

"When are they going to know who was dead in there?" someone calls to me from the crowd.

"I want to see the bodies," someone else says. "I need to know if my nephew is there. He disappeared six months ago."

"He's not there," a man right behind her added. "No one is. I want to see the bodies because I don't think there are any. This is all a hoax. It's fake. Nobody found any corpses. Nobody was murdered."

"Yes, they were. Almost the whole team is gone. You don't understand. David was everything," a young girl adds in a voice that sounds like she is seconds away from bursting into tears. By the look on her face, I would guess this wouldn't be the first bout of sobbing that came from hearing about the deaths.

The derisive man scoffs and shakes his head. "That fake ghost hunter hack? You seriously believed a single word he said? I guarantee you he's going to pop up perfectly fine with a brand-new video for sale in a couple days and some post to go with it proclaiming himself miraculously summoned back from the dead by the spirits. And undoubtedly a new booklet to get the full story, at an added price, of course. Maybe this will be the one that turns into an entire book. This is ridiculous. It's a hoax."

"You sure seem to know a lot about somebody you call a hack," the young girl fires back.

"At work I'm surrounded by idiots who have gotten caught up with all the nonsense. That's why I'm out here. They are basically gnashing their teeth and rending their garments over this guy. I told them it isn't real china, but they won't believe me. This is all just a stunt to make people less angry that they're tearing down this building and he's going to get even more of a boost in his popularity because of it," the man says. "I am here to prove they've all been taken for a ride."

"Why can't we get closer?" another person in the crowd asks. "The public has a right to know what's happening right in our own backyard. We deserve to know what we're dealing with in our community."

A few of the others cheer and I see the officers on either side of the gate shift their weight like they are preparing themselves. They sense the same build-up of tension I do. It doesn't matter that this area is generally extremely low on crime and rarely sees violence. Anybody in law enforcement knows the potential of an angry or frightened mob of people. When they are combined, it's even more dangerous.

Groups like this can whip each other up into a frenzy. What starts as innocent curiosity or a genuine concern that a loved one might have been involved can rapidly degrade into riot conditions. Particularly when the law enforcement officers present are outnumbered, the situation can turn deadly very quickly. Nobody with the desire to protect peace and justice wants to face something like that.

I can't say no one in law enforcement, though. I wish I could. It makes me feel sick to my stomach and creates a tight knot of rage inside me that I can't even describe to think about the agents and officers I've encountered who go against that sense of honor. There was a time in my life when I believed that wasn't possible. I considered anybody who served in an investigative or enforcement capacity to be deserving of the utmost respect. I didn't believe any of them would be capable of doing anything unethical, anything that might hurt someone intentionally rather than helping them.

Unfortunately, I learned. Fortunately, it's still rare enough that I haven't lost my commitment to my field or my belief in the people who share it with me. But the possibility is always there.

"You are not being allowed closer to the school because it is an active crime scene," I announce over the crowd. "The investigation is still very much under way and the only people granted access are those involved in that investigation. I assure you this is a very real situation. I can understand you are all feeling frustrated and concerned about what you heard. You might have encountered conflicting information and don't know what to think. What I can tell you is there are multiple victims and multiple times of death. Anything else will be released at an appropriate time.

"If you would think that you might have information that could help identify any of the victims or assist in the investigation, please step to the side and speak with one of the officers. They can take your statement directly, or can get you in touch with me and I will speak with you when I have the opportunity. For now, the best thing you can do is leave the area. Being here could distract the team and also pose a safety risk."

"We have the right to be here and find out what's going on," someone protests.

"Actually, you don't. This is private property and not accessible by the public. The park itself is also closed and should not be used by anyone without authorization. Local police and other officials have made it clear that no one should be in the area. As of right now, all of you are trespassing and could be arrested. I suggest you leave and wait for any other information to become available." I walk back to my door and open it. Before I get inside, I look directly at the conspiracy theorist still standing at the edge of the crowd and staring at the school. "And never touch an agent's vehicle ever again."

As I drive toward the gate, some of the gathered crowd comply with my instructions to leave while others wait for an officer to approach them. An officer opens the gate for me and I drive through and up to the school, leaving the second brewing mob of my day behind me.

The atmosphere of the school is completely different than when I first came here. When I arrived, it was still deep in the chaos and intensity of the first hours of the investigation. Everyone was still running around trying to figure out exactly what happened, looking for more victims, sifting through the burned damage. It was tense and almost frantic in some moments.

Now the energy has shifted. It is more focused and calmer as the crime scene investigation team methodically works through each area of the school. Everything has to be photographed and documented. Any items inside the building need to be inventoried and a determination made as to whether they might have any application to the situation.

Having watched some of the video recordings taken by the victims gives some extra context to what I'm seeing as I walk through the space. After ensuring the team has my instructions for what to collect and how to document it properly, I walk out and head back down out of the driveway again. Despite my warnings, I'm not surprised to see that some of the crowd is still down at the bottom of the driveway.

THE GIRL AND THE WINTER BONES

They've moved across the street and many have gone home, but others have joined. I'm planning on just driving past without acknowledging them, allowing the local police force to handle it, but then a face at the back of the crowd stops me.

Rolling down my window, I beckon one of the officers over to me. I point out the person who caught my attention, a man named Edgar Brandt, and ask the officer to take him into custody and bring him into the station. I need to find out why one of the known associates of Vincent Broddeus is lurking around here, looking far too curious about what's going on.

CHAPTER THIRTY-FOUR

TWO HOURS LATER, EDGAR BRANDT IS WALKING OUT OF THE police department and I'm standing in the break room, trying to get down a cup of terrible coffee that was probably brewed yesterday. "You look like you're fighting a losing battle with that."

I look up to see Sam coming into the room carrying a large brown paper bag in one hand and a travel cup in the other. I nod and set the tipped white mug I was drinking out of back down on the counter and force the sip down.

"It's awful. I think it's a new technique for keeping the officers from getting complacent. Just give them coffee that tastes like pond sludge but could also qualify for an octane rating."

"Sounds effective. But since you don't need any help in that regard, you're allowed to drink the good coffee that I brought you. I also got you some dinner since I figured you probably didn't stop at any point to eat and aren't planning on it in the foreseeable future," he says.

I let out a breath. "Thank you. I didn't even realize it was getting that late. I just finished talking with Edgar Brandt."

Sam gives me a quizzical look as he walks over to one of the few tables crowded in the back of the break room and puts the bag down. He unfolds the top and reaches inside to start unloading what looks like takeout containers from a Chinese restaurant.

"Edgar Brandt? Why does that name sound so familiar?" he asks.

"Because he is already all tangled up in the Vincent Broddeus investigation. His name came up when I was digging into his contacts and the network of smaller criminals he uses as pawns to make sure things work out smoothly for him. Granted, Brandt isn't as much of a pawn as many of the others are. He had worked his way up in the ranks to learn at least some of Broddeus's trust. But as soon as he caught wind that the Bureau was sniffing around, he basically disappeared."

"I can't imagine that went over terribly well," Sam notes.

"Actually, I think it was orchestrated. He was essentially being treated as a mule. He facilitated communications and is suspected of transporting various pieces of evidence we were never able to uncover. We haven't been able to nail him down enough to even get an arrest warrant. So, imagine my surprise when I saw him standing outside the school when I came out," I say.

"What was he doing there?"

"According to him, he was passing through the area and heard about the murders, so was curious. When he asked around, he found out that some people were gathering at the school to demand transparency in the investigation and he decided to offer moral support," I say. "Which I thought was a really creative way of describing the situation I witnessed out there today. Those people were ready to riot. There wasn't a huge number of them, but it looked like they were about to start looking for something to ram the gate and storm the school. And Brandt was right there with them."

Sam looks at me like he finds the explanation just about as plausible as I did when I heard it come out of Brandt's mouth.

"So you brought him in for questioning?" he asks.

"Of course, I did. I wasn't just going to let him show up like that and then walk away."

"Was he able to tell you anything?"

"I'm sure he's *able* to," I specify, "but—what a surprise—he didn't."

"What a surprise," Sam echoes.

"Just the same explanation over and over. He even did his best to disavow his old criminal life and make it sound like there was just some sort of big misunderstanding that landed him in the middle of so much criminal activity. But I have a feeling he knows something. He wouldn't have come out to the middle of a major investigation like this for no reason. He knows something. I just have to find out what. I already called Eric to ask him for any records about Brandt and what we know about him."

"Is he going to send them to you?" Sam asks.

"He says there's probably too much to fax over, so he's having a couple of researchers look through everything and distill the most important parts. I asked him to make sure I got phone records, letters that were seized, anything that might show links he has with anybody. I want to find out why he came here. I know it wasn't just out of curiosity. Either he heard about the murders and knows something or was sent here, or he already knew what was going to happen and came to watch the aftermath," I say.

"Where is he now?"

I let out a heavy sigh. "I don't know. We had to let him go. He wasn't under arrest for anything and technically there was nothing we could hold him for. If we were able to get an arrest warrant, I could have taken him in, but even that's shaky. He was never brought up on any charges and even though he's been suspected of all kinds of things, there's nothing I can do without proof."

"I'm sorry, babe. I know that has to be frustrating. Come on and eat. You'll feel better when you have some food in you and can think more clearly."

We settle in to eat our food, but I can't turn my brain off. The fact that Brandt showed up at the school with the concerned citizens and rubber-neckers, not to mention the conspiracy theorist, is just picking away at my brain. This is a man who has gone to great lengths to stay out of the grip of the police and the FBI. Agencies all over the country have been looking for him and trying to get him into custody to find out what he knows about Broddeus' crime network. He's managed to avoid all of us for this long, but then he suddenly decided to show up at a crime scene out of curiosity?

He knew full well that place would be crawling with police officers, and had to have at least some suspicion that the Bureau would have been called in as well. He probably wouldn't have thought right off the top of his head that it would have been me. After all, these aren't my usual stomping grounds. So it's possible he decided he would take the risk thinking the agents present might not immediately recognize him. It still strikes me as strange.

Or maybe, somehow, he knew I was in the area. Maybe he knew I'd be there and wanted to watch me. The thought doesn't scare me so much as makes me frustrated. I'm not afraid of him. I've faced worse. I just need to figure out what the hell he's up to.

We haven't finished eating yet when Dean comes into the room. I lift my eyebrows at him in lieu of asking what he found out, not wanting to have to wait until I even finish swallowing the bite in my mouth.

"Teacher's dead," Dean says.

That hits me hard and I shake my head, narrowing my eyes.

"Dead? Richard Smith?"

"Yes. It took me a little while to track him down because he did his best to disappear after leaving here. Not that I can say I blame him. The people around here weren't exactly kind after Linda Carmine's disappearance. He left and started a new life, but several years after that, he was involved in a plane crash. He didn't survive," Dean says.

"Damn," I mutter.

"Does that change what you were thinking about the case?" Sam asks.

"It just eliminates a possible path to follow," I tell him.

I spend another few hours at the department going through the items taken from the school, sifting out the things that I think might be relevant and putting aside those that don't have anything to do with the investigation. I also end up with a small pile of things that have to do with Linda and Alma. Pieces of art from the art room. A couple of textbooks with their names written in them. A little pink hat left over from the cold months before her disappearance with Linda's name label stitched inside.

After documenting these items, I bring them in to Officer Chappell to let him know I think we should return them to the girls' parents. He agrees and I pack the items in individual boxes. They go into the backseat of my rental car. I'll visit them in the morning. It's late by the time I go back to the hotel and stand in a hot shower for several long minutes before climbing into bed for a couple of hours of rest. It barely feels like I've slept when I force myself out of Sam's arms and into clothes the next day. I sweep my hair up into a ponytail, put on a bit of makeup to make myself look at least awake if nothing else, and go down to the desk to ask for a phone book.

Angelo Carmine answers sounding a little confused. That's not unexpected for somebody getting a phone call this early in the morning. Much like calls that come in during the late-night hours, the ones that break the usual quiet of the morning are rarely good. I try to sound optimistic and almost cheerful as soon as he answers to take away the edge. I'm pleasantly surprised when he tells me he was actually planning on calling me later. He has some time today and wanted to talk if I still needed to.

I quickly agree and we make a plan to meet at his house in an hour. It's enough time for me to quickly swing by Carla Mulroney's house to drop off Alma's things before getting to him. He answers the door with a cup of coffee in his hand and holds it up to offer me one.

"That would be great, thank you," I tell him.

Angelo invites me inside and I follow him to the kitchen where he pours my coffee.

"Cream and sugar?" he asks.

"Oh, no, thank you. Just black."

He hands it to me and I take a grateful sip. It's strong and intensely dark, exactly how I like it. This is a man who knows coffee. But I assume he's also a man who has spent many nights of his life sitting up, unable to sleep, and has needed something to fuel him through the days that have followed.

He brings me into the living room and we sit in large, thickly cushioned armchairs to either side of a fireplace. There's a fire glowing inside and the warmth on my skin is comforting after the biting chill of the morning.

"Thank you for coming," he says as he sits across from me.

"Thank you for having me in your home," I reply. "I know this can't be easy for you. Everything being brought up again and having to think about your daughter's disappearance."

"I have never stopped thinking about her," he says. "Not since the moment I found out she was missing."

"I'm sorry," I say.

"It's part of my life. It has been for thirty years and it will be until the day I die. Even if I never find out what happened to her, it's not going to change that she's gone. People have said that she could still be alive. She was such a pretty girl, she could have been taken and sold. Someday somebody could find her and bring her home." He gives a slight, bitter laugh. "They act like somehow she would instantly be nine again if that happened. That they would find her and bring her back here, and as soon as she walked through the door, she would be my little girl again."

"That's not ever going to happen. Even if Linda is alive out there somewhere, I've lost thirty years with her. I didn't get a chance to see her grow up. I didn't get a chance to see her in a prom dress or watch her graduate. I didn't get to find out what she wanted to be as an adult.

Some days she was completely committed to whatever big idea she and Alma had going at the time. And other days she just wanted to be a wife and a mother and not even think about a career. She was nine years old, Agent Griffin. Everything was ahead of her. And I missed every bit of it."

I nod sympathetically. "I know and I am trying with everything in me to find some answers for you. It won't bring her back. It won't give you back any of that time. I'm not saying it will. I know very well that finally getting answers after waiting for them for a long time doesn't give you back anything that was taken from you. But I hope that it will at the very least provide you with some comfort. And I will do everything I possibly can to make sure that happens," I say.

"Thank you, Agent Griffin," Angelo says. "But I don't understand. Does that mean you believe that these deaths have something to do with Linda's disappearance? What could they have in common? She was just a little girl, and it was thirty years ago."

"I know. And to be completely honest with you, I don't know if they are related in any way other than everything happening at the school. But I can't stop thinking about her case. If there is any kind of connection, I want to find it." He nods and I set down my coffee so I can pick up the box I'd put on the floor beside me. "I wanted to bring you this."

"What is it?" he asks.

"A lot of things were left behind when the school was closed. I've been having the crime scene investigation team remove a lot of it so we can determine if it has anything to do with any of the crimes associated with the school. I don't know if you are familiar with the group that was murdered there the other night."

"I heard something about them being a documentary crew of some kind," he says.

"Not exactly." I give him a brief explanation of the paranormal investigator group. "They left behind video and audio recordings and we've been collecting items they referenced or interacted with. While they were going through the school, they found some items that belonged to Linda. They should have been returned to you a long time ago."

I hand him the box and watch as he opens it, his face going soft and tears coming to his eyes as soon as he sees the belongings from his little girl so many years ago. He reaches in and takes out her hat, holding it to his nose and breathing in like he's trying to find any remaining scent of her that could have lingered after the last time she wore it.

"She loved this hat," he tells me. "She loved pink anything. She was growing out of it and I told her she was going to have to get a new one for the next winter. She was so worried she wasn't going to be able to find one in just the right color, so I had asked a neighbor of mine to knit one for her. It was going to be a surprise. I wondered what happened to this one."

I sit with him while he goes through the paintings Linda did and the textbooks with her name in them. He flips through one and a note flutters out of it. He picks it up and a little sob catches in his throat.

"This is her handwriting," he says. "It's asking Alma if she wants to have a sleepover. That must have been from the weekend before she disappeared. Those two were always together."

"Carla told me," I say. "It sounds like they had a really special friendship."

"They did. As much as I hate to say it, somehow it almost seems appropriate that they should end up the way they did," he says.

"Both missing?" I ask.

Angelo nods. "It's like they really did have to do everything together."

I understand what he's saying, but it's a somewhat startling comment.

"Do you know what happened to Alma?" I ask. "Has Carla ever given you any details about it?"

He shakes his head. "Carla and I didn't know each other well and didn't really associate other than chatting a little here and there when the girls wanted to play. We've spoken a few times since Linda's disappearance, but other than the occasional running into each other in town and exchanging a few words, we haven't spoken in years."

"The most reliable information about her disappearance suggests that she left to join the Manson Family," I tell him bluntly.

His mouth falls slightly open and then his jaw hardens.

"I hadn't heard that. It's horrible," he says.

I nod. "She's still missing. Carla believes she's still alive. She says she regrets letting her go off to college."

Angelo sighs as he looks down at the painting still in his hands. "Right after Linda disappeared, there were search parties and everybody put a lot of time and energy into looking for her. Then it just kind of faded away. The police called off the searches and everybody just seemed to stop thinking about her. They stopped saying her name. The pictures of her gradually disappeared from stores and telephone poles. The school closed and there wasn't even mention of her when it did.

"But I never stopped. Every day I thought about her. Every day I thought about what could have happened. I tried to think of anything I could that would make it better or that could give me answers, but nothing ever did. I've never been able to stop thinking about that day and all the little decisions that were made. Which of them would have changed things? Which would have saved her? If I hadn't had that meeting or I rescheduled it, would she have come home?"

"You can't let yourself think that way," I tell him.

"But I do."

The front door opens and a man around my age comes in. He looks back and forth between me and Angelo.

"What's going on?" he asks.

Angelo gestures at him. "This is Gio. My son." He gestures at me. "This is Agent Emma Griffin. She's with the FBI."

"FBI?" Gio frowns. "Why is she here?"

"I'm investigating the murders at the Dawn Day School," I say. "Of course, your sister's disappearance has come up."

Gio's face goes dark and his shoulders tighten and pull back.

"What could my sister have to do with people being murdered there now?" he asks. "She was a little girl thirty years ago."

"I know. But it's critical to look at all possible angles," I say.

"Don't you think my family has gone through enough pain already?" Gio demands. "I hate that it all has to keep being dragged back up so we have to experience it over and over. All of you need to just leave us alone." He looks at Angelo. "I'll call you later."

Gio storms out of the house, slamming the door so hard the house shakes.

"I'm sorry about him," Angelo says. "Linda's disappearance was really hard on him, too. Sometimes I feel like a lot of it is my fault. I put so much energy and attention into trying to find her that I might not have been a very good father to him during those first years. I was thinking so much about myself and what I was going through that I might not have given him what he needed to help him deal with it in his way."

"You don't need to apologize," I say. "Nobody really knows what to do when they face a tragedy like that. Some people think they know how they would react or how other people should react, but you can't actually know until you've waded into the middle of it and it's surrounding you. Like the old timers say, at that point, the only thing to do is go through it."

"I still feel like I'm trying to do that," he says. "I don't know what happened to her. We don't have an explanation. We don't have a ..." He hesitates. "We don't have proof that she's dead or that she's alive. There are some days when it almost feels like she never existed. Like maybe I imagined her and this is all just in my head."

"You didn't imagine her," I assure him. "Linda is your daughter. She always will be, no matter what happened to her. You have every right to still feel anything you feel about her and about the situation."

"What about that teacher?"

CHAPTER THIRTY-FIVE

I'D BEEN TRYING TO COME UP WITH A WAY TO BRING UP RICHARD Smith and the rumors of his involvement in Linda's disappearance, but Angelo did it for me. I take a sip of my coffee to give myself a second to sort through my thoughts and compile the questions I want to ask to guide the conversation, then set the cup down.

"I wanted to ask you about him," I say. "I've heard some things about him and what happened after her disappearance, but I'd like to get it from you as well. I think your perspective on it would be very important. What can you tell me about him? As a person, as Linda's teacher. Anything."

"I didn't know him until he started teaching Linda. He was a new-comer to the area when he got hired to teach at the school, years before Linda started there. That was one of the big boasts of the school. They weren't just going to settle for the teachers who lived in the area the way the public schools did. They wanted to make sure that the children enrolled in Dawn got the very best education available, and that meant more than just high-quality facilities and resources. They wanted the most desirable teachers. So they searched for them and when they found teachers who fit their standards, they brought them to the area. Some moved to Gordon, others to McCutcheon. It just depended on what they were looking for."

"Was it surprising to you that they hired a male teacher?" I ask, remembering Carla Mulroney's intense reaction.

"It was different, sure, and I wasn't expecting it, so I suppose you could say I was surprised, but it didn't bother me. Not right off the bat, anyway. After all, I was a single father raising two young children. I was doing something people didn't expect men to be doing, too. I remember even having that conversation with him the first time we met.

"There was an open house at the school each year for the parents and students to come meet the teachers. I happened to go into the classroom right at the same time a mother was leaving it, tutting and shaking her head, appalled that they would have a *man* teaching such young children. It was going to confuse them and damage their development, she said. Actually said it outright, loud enough for everybody around to hear her," Angelo says.

"Including Richard Smith," I say.

"Yes. He heard her and looked upset, but at the same time like it wasn't the first time he heard things like that. I said something about it. I don't remember what exactly, but something to kind of make him feel better and let him know that not everybody felt that way. He told me he'd gotten a lot of both good and bad when he decided to be a teacher," he tells me. "Some parents saw that he wanted to be a good teacher, and wanted to support him in that. But of course, there were people who thought only women should be teaching and had bad ideas about men who took up the position. A male professor at a university, or even at the high school level, was one thing, but young students needed the tender, nurturing influence of a woman. An extension of their mothers. It was strange and off-putting for a man to want to spend that much time with children, especially a man who had none of his own.

"I told him those were the same kind of people who liked to tell me that I needed to find a woman to be a mother to my children and that it was a shame I was all alone with them. I agreed it was a shame, but only because I so desperately missed my wife, but I very much disagreed I needed to find a woman. They already had a mother. Just because she was no longer living didn't mean she wasn't their mother. And so I got disapproving looks and tongue clicking and wagging heads. People trying to introduce me to their single sisters or cousins or friends. They said it was especially bad that Linda didn't have a woman in her life because she was going to need someone to teach her about all the things women need to know."

"I don't understand why anybody thinks saying things like that is helpful," I remark. "My father raised me from before I was twelve and he was wonderful at it. Of course, I missed my mother and wished she was there with us, but there was never a time when I felt like I was disadvantaged in some way because I was raised by my father, or like he did me a disservice by not going off and getting married again."

"I tried not to let those comments bother me. Particularly when they were said by people who didn't know me or my family. But I have to admit there were times when I wondered if I was doing the wrong thing by not looking for another wife. I didn't want one. I didn't have any interest in getting into a relationship and knew I'd never find anyone to love ever again. Linda's mother Faye was the love of my life. She was everything. There was no point in trying to replicate that because it wasn't ever going to happen. But there were times when I considered looking for someone just so that Linda and Gio would have that other parental figure, someone who could be a part of their lives, without any expectation of great love and romance from me.

"It got worse after Linda disappeared. I questioned myself a thousand times. Maybe it was my fault. Maybe if I had a wife, Linda wouldn't have been at school so late. Maybe she could have picked her up on time instead of waiting for me. Or maybe Linda would have known something I didn't know to teach her and could have avoided whatever happened to her. Or maybe—"

"Again, you can't blame yourself," I cut in, trying to stop him from spiraling. "I hate to say it, but children with two parents and strict households are lost every year. You didn't do anything wrong."

He draws in a breath to steady himself and we fall into silence for a few seconds. I decide to try to get the conversation back on track. "So, you got along with him at first. When did that change? Or did it?"

"I started hearing some rumors about him a few weeks into the school year. Nothing really direct, just a couple of whispers about the way he looked at some of the young mothers and how odd it was that he'd never been married. At that time there was still the definite perception that if a man wasn't married when he was in his thirties, there was clearly something wrong with him. Then there was a banquet to honor teachers and administration who had been with the school for ten years or more. When his name was called, he wasn't in the auditorium. He came rushing in a little while later looking quite sheepish and people noticed he looked disheveled. When school started up again after the weekend, one of the students who had been in his class wasn't there anymore. No one ever heard from her family again. They just up and left town."

"But there was never a whole story about what might have happened? No charges ever brought against him? Anything?" I ask.

"No. Things were different back then. Women gossiped over coffee or while they got their hair done. Men for the most part stayed out of the gossip, but sometimes talked about big things going on over a coffee break at work or while they were golfing on the weekends. But even then, there wasn't a lot of direct accusation. People talked in a lot of innuendo and suggestion. It was just what was done. At that time, there were little hints that those two incidents had something to do with each other, but when nothing came of them, it was put behind us and we moved on.

"Then more rumors started coming up that he was getting too close to the children and had a shifty personality, like he was hiding something. One of the girls said she saw him doing something, but wouldn't say what, because he'd asked her to keep it a secret and she would never tell a secret. Some people tried to compel her parents to force her to talk, but they wouldn't. They said they trusted their daughter and if it was very serious or dangerous, they knew she would tell them."

"What did you think about that?" I ask.

"I think that parents know their children better than anyone else and should listen to their instincts when it comes to them. They should protect them above anything," he says. "But I also think it's important to remember that children don't always understand what they see or hear. That little girl might have known something but didn't even know the significance of it. She might not have realized it was dangerous or urgent in any way."

"I agree with you," I say. "It's important to remember that children are children. It might sound simple and like everyone should know that, but too often adults only consider things the way they see them. They know something could be bad because they've learned it, not because it's innate knowledge. Add that to the idea of teaching children that secrets are something special and should never be shared, and things can quickly get out of control."

"Yes, they can."

"Do you think that he had anything to do with Linda's disappearance?" I ask.

"I don't want to think he did. But I also can't stop thinking about it. Rumors like that don't just come out of nowhere. Something has to be behind them," he says.

"That's not necessarily true. It's easy for one comment or a seemingly small lie to snowball into something completely overwhelming and take over a community without there being any basis in reality. No charges were ever brought against him and he wasn't removed from the school until after Linda disappeared. People want someone to blame when something like this happens. They want to be able to hold someone accountable. It makes them feel better thinking that the person responsible hasn't gotten away with it," I say. "Unfortunately, that doesn't always mean that the right person is accused."

"I just wish I could understand what happened that day and where it went wrong. When did she say the wrong thing or take a wrong turn? When did she smile at the wrong moment or put her trust in the wrong person? Not having Linda anymore is pain like I couldn't ever put into words, but what makes it worse is not knowing. Not just what happened to her to take her away from me but all of it. Any of it.

"Every day, she would tell me about her day at school. We had a special tradition, just the two of us. I would pick her up from school and bring her down to the pharmacy for an ice cream soda. Gio was still in nursery school and went to a nanny in the afternoons, so Linda and I got that special time together. We would sit at the counter and talk about what happened during the day. She'd tell me what she learned and the activities she did. What she played at recess and while she waited for me. Anything that was coming up she was excited about or worried about.

"On Saturdays both Linda and Gio had lessons at the enrichment center. Ballet, music, horse riding, art. They always wanted to do something and I wanted them to do it all. Everything that made them happy. I know it's what their mother would have wanted for them. She had such big dreams for them. I was doing everything I could to make sure I honored that for her. It was also my time with her. While they were at the center, I would go to the cemetery to be with my wife. I took everything the children told me about what they were learning, their favorite games, the foods they liked and didn't, everything I could possibly think of that she would want to know and I shared it with her.

"After Linda disappeared, I only had half as much to tell her. The first Saturday after that day, I brought Gio to the center for his lessons just like always, trying to keep his life as normal as I could. I went to the cemetery. I told my wife that Linda was missing and I realized I couldn't tell her anything about what happened that day. After that, every Saturday, all I could tell her was that I was still looking."

"I'm looking, too," I tell him. "I'm going to do everything I can."

I've said the same thing so many times. I hope it still means something to the people who hear it because I mean it with all that's in me.

"Thank you," he says. "What happens now? Are you going to talk to Richard Smith about what happened?"

I shake my head sadly, not liking what I'm about to have to say. "Angelo, Richard Smith is dead. He died in a plane crash several years ago."

I watch the information sink in. His eyes narrow slightly and his head twitches like he's starting to shake it to refute what I'm saying but stops himself because he knows just wanting something not to be true doesn't actually change it. His mouth opens, then closes again. After a few seconds he seems to come back into the moment and looks directly into my eyes.

"He's dead?" he asks.

"Yes."

"So, he can never tell us anything. He can never tell the truth."

"Maybe he already did," I say.

"And maybe he didn't."

CHAPTER THIRTY-SIX

THE NOTES IN FRONT OF ME CONFIRM THE SUSPICION THAT HAS been pricking at the back of my mind since I first noticed Edgar Brandt standing among the onlookers outside of the school. It wasn't just curiosity that brought him there. Years ago, not long before his death, Richard Smith carried on quite a bit of communication with someone I know to be personally connected to Brandt.

Carver Meachum was a major target of the Bureau well before I even joined up. My father didn't work on his case, but he often talked about it. The guys who were on the investigation hunted him like an animal, trying to get the sadistic trafficker off the streets and away from society. It took many years and during that time, he recruited quite the network of other criminals to aid in his efforts. One of them was Diego Brandt, an older relative of Edgar's who introduced a young Edgar to the life.

I don't know for sure what Meachum and Smith talked about, or why they were in communication with each other so frequently over a relatively short period of time, but it can't be a coincidence. And I have a very strong feeling that he didn't come to the school because he was just feeling nostalgic thinking of his old friend.

The information Eric got me shows the two men exchanged multiple phone calls and were also seen together or in the same location many times. The researcher went over all of the information available and pinpointed two separate occasions when both men had rooms in the same hotel over similar windows of time. In one instance, Diego Brandt checked in two days before Smith and stayed a day longer, and in the other, Smith arrived on the same day but stayed three days longer.

There's nothing clear cut that shows why the two men were in the same location or in what way they may have interacted with each other during those times, but it's the kind of situation that makes me think of one of my husband's most steadfast philosophies in life: there is no such thing as coincidences.

Those men were there at the same time for a reason. Even if no one overheard the conversation they had or even saw them together, I know they were. And it brings a new layer to the investigation. I just don't yet understand what it means.

It's a long shot, but I hope talking to Vincent Broddeus might give me some of the insight I need to find those answers. I want to know if Richard Smith means anything to him and what he can tell me about Brandt's association with him. It was a long time ago, and the connection between the men is tenuous. I can't make any direct links between Vincent and Richard. Only the tangential thread that goes from Richard to Carver to Diego to Edgar and then eventually to Broddeus. It's shaky at best, but there's enough there that I'm not ready to just put it aside and ignore it.

I don't want to leave the area for long enough to travel all the way to the facility where Broddeus is being kept pending his hearings, so I've arranged for a phone call instead. It isn't ideal. I would prefer to be able to look at him and read his facial expressions and body language while we talk. But this is better than not being able to talk to him at all.

"I wish I could say this is a pleasant surprise," he says sarcastically when he gets on the line. "Didn't you get enough amusement out of our last encounter?"

"Amusement isn't the word I would use," I reply. "But that's not what I want to talk to you about. I'm working another case and I think you might have information I could use."

"Oh, really?" he asks, sounding pleased at the thought of me coming to him. "How the tables have turned."

We are on the phone, so I don't even try to cover up my eyes rolling. I didn't realize people actually say things like that in real life. Unless Broddeus has convinced himself he is living in his own movie, which is entirely possible.

"This is an investigation, not a friendly conversation. I want to know what the name Richard Smith means to you."

"Richard Smith?" he asks. "Doesn't ring a bell. Who is he?"

"He was a teacher at a place called the Dawn Day School," I say, trickling out little bits of information to see which details he might react to. "About thirty years ago."

"Thirty years?" he asks with a scoff. "Digging way back, are we? I can't help you with that."

"I know you've had dealings in McCutcheon, Maryland. It's in your record."

"I might have," he hedges, still denying everything and not incriminating himself even though he's sitting in a jail cell waiting to be tried on enough charges to keep his skeleton incarcerated until it turns to dust. "But that doesn't mean I know a Richard Smith. You say he was a teacher?"

I can't tell if he's genuinely trying to reach around in his memories and find anything he can about Smith or if he is just trailing me along because it amuses him to have me sitting here on the other end of the line, waiting for his next words.

"Yes."

He seems to think for a few seconds. "What did he do?"

"You know I can't give you all the details of an active investigation."

"Then I don't think I can help you. You're asking me about somebody from three decades ago. Check my records, Agent Griffin. That's well before anybody started misconstruing me as a criminal of some kind," he says.

The simpering tone he adds to the proclamation of innocence sets my jaw on edge. He's goading me, trying to work me up, and I have to stay steady if I'm going to have any hope of getting any kind of information out of him.

"Have you ever heard of a girl named Linda Carmine?" I ask.

"Another one that doesn't sound familiar," he says. "How old is she?"

"She was nine when she went missing."

"A kid? No. I don't mess with kids. You should know that. When have you ever seen anything connecting me to kids?" he asks, all of the sarcasm and arrogant taunting gone from his voice, replaced with fierce defensiveness and anger.

He's right. In the years of investigation that have gone into his crime rings, there's never been any indication that he had anything to do with child abduction, child sex trafficking, or even black market adoption. He has done horrible things but always to adults. Even among criminals, there are codes of ethics and a sense of honor. Broddeus has drawn the line at harming children.

"How about Edgar Brandt?" I ask.

There's a beat of silence and I know he's surprised to hear the name. "What about him?"

"I know he has connections to you. He's done jobs for you. He's known to be a go-between for you and has been under suspicion for harboring evidence for you. Don't act like you don't know him."

"Alright," he finally relents. "I know him. What does that have to do with anything?"

"He showed up at the school during my investigation. He said he was only there because of curiosity, but I don't believe him. I think he knows something. And I think you do, too," I say.

"What are you investigating?" he asks.

"Mass murder," I say.

"Go big or go home," he chuckles.

⌐

My jaw and the muscles along the side of my neck are still tight from the conversation with Broddeus when Sam comes into the conference room a little while later. I'm standing in front of the large pieces of paper I've taped up to the wall, a black permanent marker bouncing in my fingertips as I review the notes written along the length of the paper.

"How did the call go?" he asks, handing me a cup of coffee.

I thank him and take a long sip.

"It was pretty useless. Broddeus says he doesn't know anything and insisted he wasn't even active yet when Linda Carmine went missing. He said he didn't know the name Richard Smith and tried to act like he didn't know Edgar Brandt. But when I called him out for that, he admitted to knowing him, but said he didn't know why he'd be here," I tell him.

"Do you believe him?" Sam asks.

"I think he knows more than he's saying," I say.

"Maybe he's holding onto it for leverage in his case," Sam offers.

"Or maybe he just thinks it's funny and is trying to piss me off," I say.

"Also a possibility."

"And now I have no way of getting in touch with Brandt to talk to him more."

I let out a sigh and Sam's eyes scan the paper on the wall.

"What's all this?" he asks.

"I'm trying to construct timelines. The day that Linda Carmine disappeared. The night the Berkeley couple was at the school. The night of the most recent murders." I indicate each of the lines as I name them off. "When I was talking to Angelo Carmine he said that he just wished he knew more about what happened that day. It made me think about the parallels in what Sasha and Mark Berkeley said compared to what we've gotten from the evidence the paranormal team gathered. There are things that are very similar."

"What about the day Linda disappeared?" Sam asks.

"I've been going through all the information we have—which, admittedly, isn't very much—and trying to piece the day together. I was able to find a schedule from that time that shows when the different bells rang, lunch, recess, all those things. I also went through the clinic records and wrote down who was in the clinic and when."

"What's this?" Sam asks, pointing to one of the lines.

"This is when the morning bell rang," I tell him, pointing to Linda's line. "And in the recordings from the night the team was murdered, there's a sound in the background that they note but don't give any explanation of what it might be. It's not really a bell, I wouldn't say, but it's a high-pitched trilling kind of sound. They happened at opposite times. Seven-thirty in the morning, seven-thirty in the evening. Then right here," I say, pointing to another note I've written on all three lines. "This is when the bell rang for the younger classes to have recess."

"The playground balls," Sam says.

I nod. "They Berkeleys didn't know for sure what time it was, but there's a recording of one of the paranormal team talking about the balls, and then also a video that seems to show one rolling up at the top of the frame. It coordinates with the time, again on an opposite schedule, but the same time."

"It sounds like whoever did this was familiar with the schedule of the school," he notes.

"Yes, it does." I lean back and stare at the timelines again, trying to make something else stand out to me. "What time is it?"

"Almost three," Sam says.

"Damn. I didn't realize it had gotten so late. I've got to go. I got through to Will Baylor."

I set my coffee down so I can pull on my coat, then pick it back up along with a notepad and pen.

"The survivor?" Sam asks.

I nod and he follows me as I head out of the conference room and through the precinct building toward the parking lot.

"Yep. They still have him in the hospital, but he's willing to talk. He hasn't been interviewed yet. I'm hoping he can fill in some of the blanks and tell us what he knows about what happened. It might help make sense of some things," I say.

"Do you think he could have anything to do with it?" Sam asks. "There is the recording of one of the victims shouting his name right before his death."

"David," I say. "I know. And I'm going to keep it in mind."

"But you don't think he did," Sam says.

He knows the changes in the sound of my voice and can tell when I have a feeling about something.

"I don't want to discount any possibility. Obviously it doesn't look good for him, but the fact that he was found with injuries outside the building makes it seem like he was trying to escape. Officer Chapell has some of his people on researching the group to find out if there's anything that might have caused the crimes, but they haven't really given me anything new. David and Will were best friends. They started the team together, with the others coming later. Maybe there was something going on that people didn't know about."

CHAPTER THIRTY-SEVEN

WILL BAYLOR LOOKS ON EDGE WHEN I WALK INTO HIS HOSPI-
tal room. He's sitting up in the bed but propped with several
pillows. He's covered in bandages, including a gauze pad and
tape on the inner part of his elbow where an IV was recently removed.
There's a tray off to the side with food on it, but only a few bites have
been taken out. Though the TV is on, he is staring at the wall rather than
watching it.

"Will?" I start as I step in.

He looks up and stares at me for a second before answering.

"Yeah. Agent Griffin?"

I nod. "Yes. How are you feeling?"

"Like shit," he responds.

Straight to the point. He has set the tone for the conversation.

"Well, I can understand that. I'm just going to go ahead and get
right to it, if that works for you," I say.

"Go ahead. I'll tell you whatever I can."

"Alright. First, I want to let you know that I am leading the FBI investigation into this case, but we are working alongside the police department. You might need to speak with them as well," I clarify. "We're looking at many different angles of this situation and investigators might need different information from you."

"That's fine."

"Okay. Good. As far as I know, no one has talked to you yet."

"Right," Will says.

"Which means I need to ask you… how much do you know about what happened?" I ask.

I don't want to feed him any details that might sway what he's going to tell me. I need to know right from the beginning of the conversation how much he knows about the carnage so I can then gauge how he talks about his experience that night.

"I know you're trying to be careful but you don't have to be," Will says. "I know that I'm most likely the only one of us who survived."

He doesn't hesitate and I hear very little, if any, emotion in his voice. He speaks calmly and openly. There's nothing about him that seems like he's trying to concoct a story or like he plans on hiding anything from me. His body language shows anxiety and trauma, but that's to be expected from someone who has endured something so horrific. I don't feel like I need to be on my guard talking to Will.

That isn't always the case when I sit down to talk with a witness. Even when I have no reason to suspect that person had anything to do with the crime I'm investigating, if they project a sense of defensiveness or deceptiveness, it puts me on edge. I immediately distrust them and cast doubt and suspicion over everything they say.

"Yes," I tell him. "You are. I'm sorry for your loss."

"Thank you," he says.

"Before I ask you any questions or say anything else, why don't you go ahead and tell me what you remember from that night? Just start from when you decided to go into the school and go up until the police found you. Everything you remember."

"Alright. Well, you probably know by now that we were a paranormal investigation team."

"Yes," I nod, trying not to let any of my own thoughts on the topic filter into my tone. "I heard that you were in the school doing an investigation."

"We've been talking about investigating Dawn for years but could never get permission. Now that they're planning to demolish the school, it was our last opportunity, so David decided we needed to take the chance," he says.

"'We, as in, you and David?" I ask.

"Yes. We used to be best friends. But recently, I guess you could say there wasn't any love lost between the two of us."

"Why is that?" I ask.

Will explains the breakdown of their friendship over their diverging views on their investigations and the evidence they gathered. He tells me that the conflict came to a head the night of the murders, which was why he wasn't with the rest of the group with the killings started.

He starts telling me about that night, his hopes for the investigation, and the plans he had for gathering evidence of all the different eras of the school.

"I don't really know a lot about the history of the school," I tell him.

He gives me a brief overview of the building from the time it was built as a private home through its dark years as the problematic boarding school, and then finally the Dawn Day School.

"All those years and all that emotion is a prime situation for hauntings," he says. "One of my primary focuses is to investigate the concept of spiritual energy and why the energy of some individuals remains in certain places while others seem to completely dissipate at the time of death. I believe that intense emotion generates greater energy and some of that energy is so intense it allows the entity to remain as an intelligent being. Meaning it can engage with the living."

"Do you believe that it was an entity that was responsible for what happened?" I ask.

He looks at me with a hint of disgust. "No. I don't think that ghosts murdered all those people. Whoever did this was very much alive."

"I had to ask," I say. "Just to make sure we're on the same page."

"Agent Griffin, I want to make this clear. I am aware of what people think of what I do. It's not like I'm oblivious to people thinking I'm crazy or that my work is ridiculous. But I am a scientist. I explore possibility. There was a time when people didn't know what germs were, or the thought of electricity was far beyond comprehension. That's what science is. Going beyond what is on the surface. Believing the unbelievable and striving to discover the undiscovered. But being a scientist also means I approach things with scrutiny and skepticism. The simplest explanation is the one I go with first and then I search for what else it can be. When I tell you about what happened that night, I need you to understand I am not elaborating. I'm not dramatizing. I am telling you facts."

"I understand," I nod. "And I appreciate that. It makes my job much easier."

"Alright," he says. "Then let's do this."

I listen as he recounts the entire night for me. The details he's able to recall are impressive, but I remind myself he was there to collect evidence. Observation is a central part of that. It makes sense that he would be vigilant. One part of his story in particular stands out to me, but I tuck it aside as he finishes.

"We recovered several pieces of video and audio recording equipment from the school and have been going through the recordings. We've gotten quite a bit of information from them, but there's something in particular I wanted to bring up and see what you have to say about it."

"Sure."

"One of the audio recordings is of David when he was doing his solo investigation. He describes what he's doing as he walks around. Then the batteries in his flashlight die and he has to go back to the kitchen. He talks about the fire and asks who started it, and if it was meant to be a joke."

"There was a fire in the kitchen when David was there?" Will asks, sounding both confused and surprised.

"Apparently. He calls out asking who started it and accusing them of trying to get his reaction, then shifts into talking about providing heat and energy for the spirits. Does that mean anything to you?"

Will nods and explains the concept of the spirits using the fire for energy to communicate.

"But there shouldn't have been a fire there," he says. "We'd talked earlier about starting one, but David was adamant that there shouldn't be one going when we weren't in the room because it could be dangerous. And it couldn't have been the same fire at the back of the building that was going when I escaped. There was no fire in that fireplace when I was back there later in the evening, before I found Lila."

I make a note of that so I can compare it with my timelines and other evidence to see if I can corroborate it.

"That actually isn't what I wanted to talk to you about. In the recording, David gets fresh batteries and goes back out. He goes to what used to be the ballroom and is talking to the spirits about the parties that used to be thrown there. Then it seems that someone comes into the room. He interacts with them briefly and the recording does seem to capture his murder. But right before that, he shouts your name," I say.

I watch Will's face to see how he reacts. He looks confused, his eyebrows pulling in tight together and his eyes narrowing.

"My name?" he asks.

"Yes. You say that the two of you were arguing that night. You told him that you didn't want to be a part of the group anymore and that you were planning on exposing him as a fraud," I say. "And he threatened to discredit you in the scientific community."

"I was angry with him. I hated what he turned our investigations into, and that the team had turned into some ridiculous song and dance number for the entertainment of his groupies rather than any kind of genuine learning or insight. He was wasting my time and damaging my reputation. That wasn't something I was going to tolerate anymore. But that doesn't mean I was willing to kill because of it. I'm in the business of searching for spirits and trying to understand them, not creating them," he says.

His flippant comment makes my eyebrow raise.

"It doesn't seem to be bothering you very much knowing what happened to him," I note.

"Of course, it bothers me," he says. "David and I knew each other for a long time. Like I said, he was once my best friend. It's horrifying knowing what happened to him. But I can't let myself think too much about what I saw that night. Or the things I know happened but I didn't see. If I do, I don't know if I'll be able to take it. For right now, I have to keep it at a distance for as long as I possibly can and try to help you figure out what happened. I want answers as much as you do. I want to know what happened to my friends and make sure that the person responsible is held accountable."

"Do you have any idea why he would call out your name right before being attacked?" I ask.

Will thinks for a few seconds and I watch his shoulders lower slowly, almost like he's gradually deflating.

"When we first started, David wasn't at all like he was in the last year or so. He didn't try to pretend he was super brave or like he had any kind of special sensitivity or power. He would get scared, and if we weren't in the same room, he would yell for me."

Sadness finally appeared in his eyes as he realized that in the last moments of his friend's life, he was afraid and reaching out for him.

I give Will a couple of seconds before continuing.

"You said you went through the servants' passages in the school," I say. "What can you tell me about those?"

He's still staring ahead and I can almost see the events of that night playing out across his eyes, but my voice seems to jostle him and he looks up.

"What? Oh. The servants' passages. They're hallways designed into the building when it was a home. Secret passages, so to speak. They let the servants move around the house without being detected and made it easier to get from place to place," he says. "I found out about them when I was doing research into the history of the building."

"Were they used by the school staff?" I ask.

"I don't know. I didn't find anything about that in my research. But they weren't sealed off, so maybe they were."

"Thank you," I say. "I'll let you know if I have anything else I need to ask. If you think of something else, don't hesitate to get in touch with me."

"I won't," he says.

I make a stop at a courtesy phone outside a waiting area so I can call Sam before leaving the hospital.

"I just wanted to let you know I'm going to be a bit longer," I tell him.

"Is everything okay?" he asks. "Did something happen?"

"Everything's fine. Will Baylor just gave me some information I want to go check out. I'm going up to the school."

"Do you want me to come with you?" he asks.

It's cold and the hospital is closer to the school than the hotel is, so I'm about to tell Sam to just wait for me, but my fingertips lift almost involuntarily to the slight scar across my neck and a voice from the past hisses in my ear: *I know you're alone.*

I'm not afraid. But I also know there's no need to put myself in danger.

"Sure," I tell him. "Meet me there."

"I'm leaving now. I'll see you soon."

CHAPTER THIRTY-EIGHT

THE ONLY POLICE AT THE SCHOOL NOW ARE THE ONES STATIONED at the end of the driveway to prevent the curious mob from returning and going inside. The team has removed everything we've requested, but the building is still considered an active crime scene. There's still a lot of evidence that we weren't able to remove from the building that still needs to be looked over.

The emptiness makes the building eerie and strange as we step inside. Officer Chappell tried to have the electric company return power to the building so we'd have light for the investigation, but they told him that wasn't an option. The wiring is far too old and after so many years of going untouched, suddenly turning it back on could be very dangerous. To make up for that, the team set up generators and strategically placed floodlights at points throughout the building. They don't provide the total illumination of overhead lights and still cast shadows and leave dark stretches between them.

But I don't really care. I have a flashlight with me and I don't need much light. I ask Sam to get the floodlight in the entryway going, but other than that, I'm not going to bother. I'm not here to look through the hallways and classrooms I've already seen. I want to see the hidden passages Will told me about.

He described how to find the access point closest to the entryway and Sam and I use those instructions to find a panel in the wall. I move it out of place, revealing a narrow, dark corridor behind the wall. I step inside and shine my flashlight around. There are old metal sconces positioned at regular intervals along the wall, showing how the household staff once illuminated the hall so it could be used to traverse the house.

I'm fascinated by the network of passages as Sam and I explore them. It's an entire world hidden behind the walls, kept out of sight like the complex networks concealed within beehives.

"Look," he says when we turn a particular corner. "That looks like blood."

I look where his flashlight is shining and see dark staining on the floor and on one wall.

"It does," I nod. "We need to make a note of that and let the crime scene investigation unit know so they can come in here and collect a sample."

We continue through the corridors, taking note of other potential blood stains.

"It looks like we know how David got from the ballroom to the classroom," Sam notes. "His killer moved him through these passages."

"Come on," I say, feeling emboldened and something close to excitement at the appearance of the new information. "There's something else I want to look at."

We leave the servants' passage into a darkened hallway and I take a second to orient myself so I know where we are, then lead Sam deeper into the school.

"Where are we going?" he asks.

"The basement. I didn't get to see it the first time I was here and after talking to Will, I want to make sure I look at it. It's how he was able to escape, but I want to see if there's anything that indicates it could be part of the crime scene," I say.

"What kind of part of the crime scene?" Sam asks.

"Storage," I say. "The bodies in that classroom weren't there three years ago, when Sasha and Mark Berkeley stayed the night at the school. But several of them are far older than that. Which means they had to be kept somewhere during that time. Maybe it was the basement."

We go down into the basement and I see the boxes and tarp-covered furniture just the way Will described it. Nothing seems to be out of place and the fine layer of dust on the floor and on all the surfaces is undisturbed except for the footsteps I'm assuming belong to Will and the investigators. I go up to one of the tarps and pull it back. It looks to be a dining set. The next is an empty aquarium and a cage that could have once held a bird.

"It doesn't look like any of these things have been moved in years," Sam notices. "I don't think somebody was stashing bodies under these tarps or in any of the boxes."

"Neither do I."

I stop in the middle of the room and look around. Shining my flashlight from side to side, I take in the dimensions of the room and how it is laid out in the context of the rest of the building. Ahead of us I see the cellar door Will used to escape. Investigators secured it closed, but the damage, along with the blood he left behind, is still evident.

"What is it?" Sam asks.

"There's something about the room that's bothering me. I'm not sure what it is. It just doesn't look right."

"Maybe it's that there's stuff down here? The school closed. It always bothers me when abandoned buildings still have things in them."

"I mean, that's strange, but… I don't know. There's just something about this room that isn't sitting right with me."

Before I can say anything else, we hear a loud thud overhead. I meet Sam's eyes for only a second before running to the staircase. The officers assigned to guard the outside of the building didn't come inside. There's no reason anybody else should be in here. Prepared with my flashlight in one hand and my gun in the other, we emerge from the basement and head in the direction we heard the sound. I can't be positive but it sounded like a door slamming.

As we turn a corner into the main front hallway, I notice the floodlight isn't in the same position it was in. It hasn't been moved drastically, only a few inches like it had been accidentally bumped. I hear another sound—this one softer, but still distinct. I nod in the direction of the main office. Sam returns the gesture and we head for the room.

The front part of the office with the receptionist's desk is dark, but it only takes a few steps to notice a flickering light coming from it down the hallway to the side.

"Someone's in the principal's office," I whisper to Sam.

"Could it be one of the detectives from the police department?" he asks.

"I don't think so. They would tell me if they were coming here for something. And they would probably have more lights on."

With my gun still held in front of me, propped up by the arm holding my flashlight, I make my way quickly down the hallway. The door to the principal's office is mostly closed. I dispense with formalities and kick it the rest of the way open. A man standing behind the desk lets out of startled cry and steps back away from the door.

"FBI. Hands up," I call out. He immediately complies. "This building is an active crime scene. What are you doing here?"

I get closer and my flashlight illuminates his face. It takes a few seconds for me to notice he looks familiar and as he speaks, I realize who I'm looking at.

"I—I'm sorry. I'm just here looking for something. I don't mean any harm," he stammers.

"Richard Smith," I say.

He looks a bit startled to hear me say his name but quickly adjusts. "Yes. I was a teacher here."

"I know who you are. I also know you're supposed to be dead."

CHAPTER THIRTY-NINE

"LIFE WAS HELL AFTER LINDA CARMINE'S DISAPPEARANCE. The town turned on me and I had to leave my home, my career, everything. Even after I left and tried to start a new life in another town, the people here continued to torment me. They tracked me down and made sure everybody in my new town thought the same thing about me that they did. It didn't matter to them that they weren't telling the truth. That they were lying about something so horrific. All they wanted to do was ruin my life. After a while, it didn't even seem like they cared if they got answers about Linda. They just wanted me to suffer," Richard tells me.

I glance at Sam, still keeping my gun trained on the man. I nod for him to continue.

Richard keeps his hands up above his head and sighs. "I kept moving around, and eventually I did find a place where it seemed like they couldn't find me. Things were quiet and I was able to establish a new life where nobody had heard my name and nobody thought I was involved in something as reprehensible as what the people around here accused me of. But I never felt completely confident. I never felt completely at peace. I always felt like at any moment somebody was going to show up and it was just going to start up again. So, when that accident happened and I was listed among the dead, I saw an opportunity. I could have contested it but I didn't. Instead, I let Richard Smith die and I moved farther away and started again."

"Why were you listed among the dead in the first place?" I ask.

"I was supposed to be on that flight, but I got sick the day before and couldn't make the journey. The damage to the aircraft was so extensive that many of the bodies were unrecognizable. Many were burned or crushed, and all that could be used for identification was personal effects. Some weren't even connected to remains. It was just assumed that if they were not found among the very few survivors, a person whose name was on the manifest had died. My name was listed and I wasn't among the survivors at the crash scene, so I was considered killed by the crash," he explains.

"Weren't records kept of who boarded?" I ask.

"Apparently there was an error. One of the survivors was listed as not having gotten on the plane while I was listed as having boarded. They believed that the survivor being overlooked was the only error, so I was officially declared dead. And I went with it. I thought it was my fresh start. And for thirty years, it's worked for me. I haven't been bothered. No one is accusing me of anything. It doesn't mean that I've been at peace. I have to live every day with the memories of Linda and the aftermath of her disappearance. But, I'm alive and I'm free, and that's far more than what I expected in my life," he says.

I lower my gun and he relaxes.

"Why are you here? After all this time, why did you come back here?" I ask.

"I heard that the school was going to be demolished and I felt the compulsion to say goodbye. Despite all the terrible things I went through, this place is extremely important to me. I've missed it more than I could possibly tell you in the years that I have had to be away. I wanted to come back and see it one more time. Then I heard what happened and I couldn't believe it. I was going to cancel my visit and stay away because the last thing I figured I needed was to be around town after another tragedy happened here."

"But you're here," I say.

"Yes. I couldn't give up my last chance to see this building. And I wanted to get what I left behind."

The words sound slightly ominous in the context of his history with the school and the community.

"What did you leave behind?" I ask.

"When I was forced out of here, I wasn't even allowed to take the time to get any of my personal belongings except for my jacket and a couple of things that I was able to pick up from my desk. Everything else I was forced to leave. Most of it I didn't care about. But there was a scrapbook."

"A scrapbook? The one that was given to the principal?"

"No. It wasn't given to him. It was given to me. At the celebration for the staff members honoring us for our years of service to the school. I was recognized for all the extra work that I did establishing programs, leading clubs. I put my entire heart and soul into this school, and they wanted to recognize that. So, they created a scrapbook for me. I had dedicated a lot of time to researching the history of the building and the Boudreaux couple who'd built this house originally, as well as some of the long-standing stories about the grounds.

"I had uncovered a lot about the children the Boudreauxs lost and became fascinated with finding where they had been laid to rest. Everything I read about the couple seems to indicate they were kept here on the grounds rather than being buried at a church, but no grave-yard has been identified. I created a club with some of the older students to continue my research and work to find that graveyard and make sure it was properly marked and shown its appropriate respect. My belief is that the family cemetery was on the grounds, but when the building was turned into the boarding school, those in charge felt having a visible graveyard nearby would be disturbing to the students and so all markers were removed.

"The scrapbook given to me contained documentation of the history of the building and some of the relics I found during my searches of the attic and servants' passages. I didn't get as far into the research as I wanted to before everything happened," he says. "There are still areas of the school I was never able to fully search and I never got to look at original plans of the home and its grounds. Now I never will. But having that scrapbook would mean the world to me."

"Why are you searching for it in here?" I ask.

"After I was forced out of the school, I know some of my belong-ings were disposed of, but I heard some things, including some of my book collection and lesson plans, were kept. I hoped my scrapbook was among those things. I know the school didn't survive very long after the scandal and I thought perhaps it would have been left behind. But I don't see it."

"How did you get in here?" Sam asks. "There are guards in place at the end of the driveway."

"I came through the back. The way I used to when I was teaching here. When the school was active, there were small living quarters for some of the teachers in the woods and a walking path that led to the grounds."

"Living quarters?" I ask.

"Just small cabins. But they were comfortable and well-equipped. Everything I needed as a single man, anyway. I believe they were all destroyed when that land was taken to be added to the park."

"Were they searched after Linda Carmine disappeared?" I ask.

"Yes. Extensively. Those of us who lived in them were brought down there and the police searched through every inch. It wasn't much space so it didn't take them long. Nothing was found in any of them. Including mine."

"What can you tell me about Edgar Brandt?" I ask.

His eyes narrow briefly. "Edgar Brandt? I don't know anything about anyone by that name."

"How about Vincent Broddeus?" I ask.

He shakes his head. "I'm sorry. I'm not familiar with those names."

"I have information that shows you were in contact with an associate of both of those men in the months leading up to your untimely death," I say. "A man by the name of Meachum."

"I did used to have a friend by that name. Many years ago. We met through an old college friend of mine. We shared a lot of interests. But I don't recall ever meeting anyone by either of those names," he says.

He watches me with unflinching eyes as I stare at him, waiting for something else, but nothing comes.

"The scrapbook was found during the initial investigation," I tell him.

His face lights up. "It was?"

"Yes. It was assumed it belonged to the principal. It was taken into evidence. For now, that's where it's going to stay. Until this is over and everything is released, it will remain at the precinct in storage."

Richard nods. "I understand. Thank you."

"I need you to stay in the area for the time being. You have to understand that you are still a focus of this investigation, but you might also have more details that could help us answer some lingering questions we've had. I need to be able to get in touch with you," I say.

"That's fine. I'm staying in a hotel in McCutcheon and I'll just stay there."

"Good. Also, don't come back here. You are trespassing and interfering with the investigation of not only multiple murders but also the continued investigation into the disappearances of Linda Carmine and Alma Mulroney."

Richard's face drops. "Alma? What happened to her?"

I realize there's no reason he should have heard about the other girl's disappearance. It was never put in the media, and without any contacts with the people of this community, he wouldn't have gotten that information.

"She disappeared eleven years after Linda. She left her college campus telling everyone she was going to California. Her mother heard from her a few times but has not been able to locate her and has not been able to confirm she is still alive in quite a while. Five years after that, three more female students disappeared from the same college campus. They may be related," I say.

Richard looks stunned. "I can't believe Alma is gone, too. Those little girls were the cutest things together."

"Were they particularly special to you?" I press.

He gives me a withering look. "I have spent thirty years trying to escape accusations like that. I have never and would never harm a child. Especially in the way you're suggesting. I did take a shine to Linda Carmine, but all teachers have students that they connect with more than the others. It's part of being a teacher. We take on this role so that we can nurture young minds and help them to become what will make this world better.

"Linda was an incredible child. Bright, intelligent, friendly, talented. She was truly something amazing. And I hoped to see her grow into her full potential. I would never have done anything to hurt her. Nothing," he says. He takes a breath. "I need to get in touch with Carla."

"Carla Mulroney?" I ask. "Alma's mother?"

"Yes," he says. "I'd like to express my condolences to her. We didn't always see eye to eye, and I know she was uncomfortable with me teaching her daughter, but she was still someone I saw regularly."

"When she was picking up Alma after school?" I ask.

He shakes his head. "No. Because she worked in the clinic."

CHAPTER FORTY

"DO YOU BELIEVE HIM?" SAM ASKS AS WE LEAVE.

"I want to. But I can't just pretend I don't recognize how suspicious this entire situation is. I need to keep a close eye on him. Tomorrow morning I'm going to see Angelo Carmine and let him know that Richard Smith is still alive. He deserves to know. He was really upset when he heard that Smith was dead, thinking that meant he would never be able to get any information from him about his daughter's disappearance. I need to tell him that he's alive and what he told us," I say. "I'm also going to talk to Carla Mulroney. I can't stop thinking about the fact that she worked at the clinic and didn't mention it to me."

"Maybe she didn't think it mattered," Sam offers. "Since you were investigating something having to do with the school, she might have assumed you knew. Why would it make that much of a difference?"

"If she worked at the clinic at the school, she was there when Linda disappeared." Saying that makes me remember my conversation with Carla and I realize the way she worded things. "She said she saw Linda on her way out of the building. That's because she was working inside. And when Angelo arrived to pick Linda up and couldn't find her, he went to the clinic. He wouldn't have done that for no reason. It was because he thought she might be in there with Carla."

I let out an exasperated sigh. I can't believe I missed that. It changes how I would have approached my conversation with Carla, especially considering the records that I've been using to build the timeline. Dean and Xavier left to continue on with the road trip, but if they hadn't, I would have sent Dean to talk to her. She seems to trust him and I feel like she might have been more open with him than she has been with me.

The next morning I go to the office where Angelo Carmine works and knock on his door. He looks up from his desk and beckons me inside.

"Good morning, Agent Griffin," he says.

"Good morning."

I glance at the papers on his desk. They appear to be handwritten memos from several different people along with manila folders with notes attached to the front with paper clips. It's barely past the beginning of business hours and it looks like he has already put in an entire workday.

"If you'll just give me one second," he says. He signs one of the memos in front of him, gathers all of the papers up into a stack, and tosses them into a wire basket at the corner of the desk. "There. I'm sorry, I just needed to get that finished. I don't like leaving things unfinished."

"I can see that," I say.

He chuckles as he stands, but there's no humor in it. "You know, all my colleagues who I started working with right out of college are talking about retiring now. I guess I'm just a few years away from being that age. But I haven't started planning for that at all. I really don't have any interest in retiring. What would I do? My career is basically my entire life. I don't have any grandchildren. Gio has made it clear he has no intention of getting married or having children, and I would never pressure him into doing something he doesn't want to do. I've spent all my free time the last thirty years trying to find out what happened to Linda, so I don't have hobbies or pastimes I want to devote myself to. This is what I do. So, I'll just keep doing it." He gestures toward a seating area to the side of his office. "Coffee?"

"No, thank you. I'm not going to take up much of your time." We sit down and he pulls close to the edge of the seat cushion, leaning toward me like he wants to keep the space between us small so he gets the words I'm about to say as soon as possible. "Richard Smith is not dead."

Angelo stares back at me blankly like he can't process what I've just told him. Finally, he blinks and draws in a breath.

"He's alive? But you told me he died in a plane crash."

"I know. And that was the information we had. There is a death certificate for him and everything. News reports listing him as one of the victims of the crash. But it was a misunderstanding and he elected not to correct it so that he could start a new life outside of the shadow of what happened here thirty years ago," I explain.

"So, he's just been allowed to roam around without anybody even knowing who he is?" Angelo asks.

"Yes. But, again, he isn't a fugitive. He never faced any charges. He was never even arrested. He wasn't hiding from the law. He was hiding from the people of this community and the reputation that they made sure followed him. I am still looking into him. I don't want you to think I'm just giving him a pass because of what he went through. But I also can't just assume he did anything wrong. I need you to understand that I am taking this investigation piece by piece. It's a complicated situation because of the different elements and how many years separate the incidents."

"But you do believe that they are linked."

He says it not as a question but as a confirmation that I am on his side. That I see things the same way he does. He wants to make sure there isn't yet another person who has forgotten about Linda, or who is going to put her aside to focus on something else.

"I think I would be remiss to not consider the possibility." I stand up. "Thank you for your time. If I find out anything else, I will get in touch with you. And you are always welcome to reach out to me if you have any questions or if anything comes to mind that you think might be important."

"I will. Thank you for letting me know."

We shake hands and I leave the office. There's a chill along the back of my spine left by the look in Angelo's eyes. I purposely didn't mention that Richard Smith is in the area. No matter how much Angelo says that he and Richard got along and that he wasn't among his accusers in the past, the expression on his face and the tension in the muscles running down the sides of his neck say otherwise.

Carla Mulroney is getting ready to leave for work when I arrive at her house. I hadn't called ahead of time and she looks taken aback when she opens the door and sees me coming up the front walk.

"Agent Griffin?" she asks. "What are you doing here?"

"I'm sorry to just show up like this, but there have been a couple of changes in the case and I wanted to talk to you about them. Do you have a few minutes?"

She looks at her watch and seems unsure but eventually concedes. "I have a few. Would you like to come in?"

"Yes. Thank you." I follow her in and go to the living room, sitting in the same place I have each time I've been here. "There are two things that I need to discuss with you."

"Alright," she says. "Go ahead."

"Did you work at the Dawn Day School when Linda Carmine went missing?" I ask.

"Yes," she says without hesitation. "I worked in the clinic."

"I wasn't aware of that," I say.

"I'm sorry. I thought that would be something that was in the records. I didn't mean to keep it from you. Is that a problem?" she asks.

"It just changes how I interpret some of your statements. Knowing you were inside the school when you last saw her rather than being outside on the school grounds. That kind of thing. Did you know that the medical records were left in the clinic when the school closed?"

"I guess I didn't really think about it," Carla replies with a shrug. "There really wouldn't be any use for them anywhere else, and no one intended to use the building for anything, so I guess it was just decided that it would be easier to not bother with them."

"You made notes of everyone who came into the clinic, right?" I ask.

"Yes," she says. "Each child who came was recorded. Their name, what time they came in, their complaint, any treatment offered, and whether they went back to class or were collected by a parent. There was a new record for each day."

"I've used those records to create a timeline of the day Linda went missing. Do you think if I brought them to you, it might jog your memory of anything else that happened that day?" I ask.

"It might. It was a long time ago. I don't know if there's anything else I can remember that I haven't already told the investigators," she says.

"I'd just like you to look," I say.

She nods. "Alright."

"Great. Thank you. I also wanted to let you know that Richard Smith is in town."

Carla's face drops. "Richard Smith? I thought he was dead."

"I did, too. But I encountered him last night and he explained that the reports of his death were a misunderstanding he chose not to correct," I tell her.

"Why is he here?" she asks. "Why did he come back?"

"He said there were things he wanted to get before the building is demolished."

"Do you think that's true?" she asks.

"Right now I don't have any reason to think anything else."

"Oh."

She looks away, her gaze sliding over so she stares at the cushion beside me, like she's getting lost in her thoughts.

"Carla?" I say a few moments later. "Are you alright?"

Her eyes lift to mine. "Can you give me one moment?" She gets up and walks into her kitchen. I hear her pick up the phone and dial, then tell someone on the other line that she will be late. She hangs up and comes back to me. Her eyes are bright. "I need to tell you something."

"Okay. Go ahead."

"Now that Richard Smith has shown back up, I can tell you something I've been keeping from you. I know Alma is alive."

I stop short in my tracks and it's all I can do to keep my jaw from hitting the floor. I'm not sure how to react to the revelation. But I don't need to. Carla rushes on without my input.

"She's been writing letters to me. She asked me not to tell anybody about the letters and to keep acting like I thought she was missing."

"Where is she?" I finally ask.

"I don't know for sure. She never leaves a return address. Only that she is still in California."

"I don't understand. Why doesn't she want anyone to know that she's alive?" I ask.

"She is afraid. Because of what happened to Linda. She says she knows something awful happened to her and is afraid that the same thing might happen to her. She has always felt like she was being watched and targeted, and that she was supposed to go at the same time Linda did. They did everything together and that was supposed to be the same way. But she didn't. Something happened and she was spared, but she doesn't know what it was," Carla explains. "She's afraid that if she returned or if people knew where she is, she would be in danger."

"Why are you telling me this?" I ask.

"She said the only way that she would be able to come home is if we found out what happened to Linda. Once she's found and we know what happened, then she'll feel like she can come back. Now that you're here investigating Linda's case and that teacher showed back up, I know you're going to figure it out. It's all coming together. It's all going to be worth it. You're going to find out what he did to her and my baby is going to be able to come home. I'm going to have her again."

She sounds almost giddy and her hands tremble as she reaches out to take mine. She squeezes them.

"Can I see the letters?" I ask.

"Of course," she says. "I have all of them. Take them with you. Do whatever you need."

She hurries out of the room and comes back a few moments later with an accordion-style file. She hands it to me and I unwrap the closure cord to look inside. There's a large collection of letters and postcards inside. I scan through them briefly before closing the file again.

"I'll go over these at the station," I tell her.

"Thank you. Thank you so much."

CHAPTER FORTY-ONE

HOURS LATER, I'M SITTING AT THE TABLE IN THE CONFERENCE room going over all the correspondence from Alma. The earliest ones are just as Carla described them, talking about her personal journey and what she wanted to find for herself, talking about the charismatic man she met and the group she was committed to. She chronicles some of their travels and her heartache over "her Charlie" being "persecuted." There's a long stretch of silence for a few years, but when they begin again, the intention seems to have shifted.

There's more clarity in the communication, as though Alma had come through a fog and was ready to confront things about her past that she hadn't really talked about before. She acknowledges her reluctance to revisit anything about Linda's disappearance and to acknowledge everything that happened during that time, then hints at secrets that she never shared. These letters are tight with anxiety and fear. Sometimes they share memories and emotion about her lost best friend, others just beg for her mother to find out what happened.

Officer Chappell comes in as I'm taking notes on a series of post-cards that all arrived within a few days of each other. Their postmark was from California, just as Carla said.

"Hey," I say, sitting back and arching slightly to stretch my tired muscles. "What's up?"

"How are you doing?" he asks.

"Great," I tell him, and he laughs.

"Convincing. I have some notes for you."

"Notes?" I ask.

"The medical examiner was able to connect a couple of the bodies to missing persons' reports. And I have some identifying information on others. Still a lot of work to be done to identity all of them, but we have a few positive IDs."

"Okay," I say, taking the paper from him. "At least that's a start."

"I also have some notes from interviews with Linda Carmine's classmates."

"Have you found them all?" I ask.

"Most of them. There are still two we're working on tracking down. Another two have passed. But the rest have been found and interviewed. Most of them didn't have much to say, but we compiled comments we thought you might want to see," he says.

"Great. Thanks."

"Is there anything else I can do?" he asks.

"Not that I can think of right now. I'll let you know."

"Okay. I'll be around."

I nod and he leaves. Pushing the letters from Alma aside, I stack the notes in front of me and start going through them. There isn't a lot. Recollections thirty years later are hazy at best, especially with something so traumatic. Most of the statements share essentially the same memories. They outline the activities they remember doing that day. The lessons they learned. Linda playing hide and seek after school. A couple remember some of her hiding spots. One remembers seeing her running toward the back of the school the last turn she played.

Then there are the wild theories and accusations. A few predictably point to Richard Smith and the rumors of his fascination with the girls. Some mention people I've never even heard of. I finally stop when I read the one that claims the ghost of Mrs. Boudreaux came back and snatched Linda as a way to replace one of the children she lost. I set the notes aside and prop my elbows on the desk, running my fingers back through my hair as I squeeze my eyes closed to combat the tired feeling stinging at the back of them.

As I'm sitting there, fighting exhaustion and frustration, a thought pops into my mind. I go back through the statements from the classmates, noting the ones that mention remembering Linda in class with them that day.

She sat beside me.

She sat in front of me.

She sat on the other side of the room.

I get to my feet and walk over to the board where I've posted pictures of the crime scenes. Going over to the door, I lean out of the room and call out to the receptionist not far away, asking her to get Officer Chappell. He comes in a couple minutes later.

"Hey. You needed me?" he asks.

"Yes. Could you get me that scrapbook that was in the principal's office? And anything you can find me about the other bodies that were found on the grounds of the school," I say.

"Any time frame?" he asks.

"All of them. Anything you can find with pictures or investigation sketches of bodies found anywhere around the school from the time Linda disappeared until the most recent murders," I say.

"You got it. I'll be back as soon as I can," he confirms.

"Thank you."

He walks out of the room as I continue staring at the images, trying to make the tenuous connections starting to form in my head link together. There's something here. I just need to figure out what it is.

A knock on the conference room door breaks my concentration a few minutes later.

"Yes?" I call out.

The receptionist sticks her head in. "Agent Griffin, there's a phone call for you."

"Thank you, Amy. I'm coming," I say.

I take one more look at the pictures before heading to her desk.

"This is Agent Griffin," I say into the phone.

"This is Edgar Brandt. I need to speak with you."

I'm surprised but try not to let it come into my voice.

"Can you come down to the station?" I ask. He hesitates. "Listen. Nobody here cares who you are. I'm the only one who knows. I'm up to my eyeballs in this investigation and I frankly don't want to lose the time going anywhere. I'm not trying to trick you or trap you or anything like that. You're going to walk out of here when you're done talking."

I know I'm potentially letting a major witness in a massive crime ring slip through my fingers, but at this moment, that isn't my priority. I already have Broddeus on ice. I don't really need anything Edgar Brandt has to say about him. I'm more than willing to turn a blind eye to him for right now if he's able to give me anything I can use in this investigation.

And if what he has to say doesn't ring true or he doesn't offer me anything of value, there's a window of time when he can't get but so far away. I can still get him in custody.

"Fine. I'll be there in ten minutes," he says. "Meet me at the door."

It takes him twenty and I'm about to crawl out of my skin by the time Brandt shuffles up to the door to the precinct, his head tucked down low in the collar of his coat and his hands plunged deep in his pockets. I step out of the door before he gets to it.

"Hands out," I say.

He looks up at me. "What?"

"I want your hands out of your pockets," I say.

He scoffs and pulls his hands out, taking the pockets along with them. "You think I'm going to show up to a police station for a conversation with an FBI agent armed?"

"I've seen crazier things."

"Are you satisfied?" he asks.

"Mmhmm. Come with me."

We go inside and I bring him to an interview room near the conference room. I don't want him in the room with all the evidence on display. No matter what it is he wants to talk to me about, he shouldn't be given access to that kind of information. I sit down and gesture for him to sit across from me.

"I'm going to start right off telling you I don't have all the answers. I know some things and I think some things, but I can't give you full details," he says. "Not because I'm trying to hide them. At this point, I'm done covering for him over this. I just don't know. But what I can tell you is that you need to look more into Vee Broddeus and his connection to all this. Look at his associates. The people he dealt with then. I don't know all the details about what went down, but I know I've heard that teacher's name. And I know there was some shady shit going on around this place back then. Now, I can't abide that kind of thing. I know you probably disagree with me, but I do have my standards. There are some things I just won't tolerate."

"I don't disagree with you," I say. "Morality is subjective. What is right and wrong is up to a person, but that doesn't mean it doesn't exist."

"Exactly. And I've done some stuff, but there are things I just won't do."

It's the same sentiment Broddeus had when I talked to him, but I feel like this time it's different. I take notes on what he has to say and walk him back to the door.

"Thank you for talking to me," I say. "I appreciate it."

Brandt looks like there's something else he wants to say, but he stops himself, nods once, and hurries away.

CHAPTER FORTY-TWO

T HE WOMAN BEHIND THE DESK AT THE HOTEL WHERE RICHARD Smith is staying takes several steps backward when I storm into the lobby the next afternoon.

"What room is Richard Smith staying in?" I demand.

"I'm sorry, I can't give out that information," she says in a shaky voice.

I pull out my badge and hold it up as I continue my way across the lobby toward the elevator. "What room?"

"109," she says.

"Thank you."

I decide to forgo the elevator, not having the patience to wait for it, and go for the stairwell. I take them two at a time and push open the door to the hallway. When I get to the door, there's a Do Not Disturb sign hanging from the doorknob, but I don't care. I pound my fist on the door without stopping until I hear the throw lock disengage.

"Can't you read? The sign says…" Smith says as the door opens.

I slam my open palm against the door to shove it open further and walk toward him, forcing him backward into the room.

"I don't give a fuck what the sign says," I snap. "Where do you get off lying to me?"

"What are you talking about?" he asks. "And I don't think that I invited you into my room."

"I don't need an invitation into your room," I say. "You're lucky I don't drop you right now and drag your ass into jail. You're welcome to leave that door standing open, but I don't know if you want everyone staying here to hear what I have to say to you."

He stares at me for a brief second like he thinks he might be able to break me, but then realizes he's no match and closes the door. He's shirtless and wearing nothing but a pair of sweatpants, so he goes for a stack of laundry sitting on the corner of the dresser. He grabs a shirt and tugs it down over his head.

"I don't know what you're doing here," he says.

"I'm going to ask you a question I already asked you, and this time you need to think really carefully about whether you're going to lie to me. What do you know about Edgar Brandt?"

He draws in a breath through his nose, his chest lifting and then lowering slowly.

"I don't want to talk about this," he says.

"I don't give a shit what you want. Do you understand what is happening right now? I talked to Edgar Brandt. I know you were tangled up with his associates. I thought it was Vincent Broddeus. But Vincent wasn't active thirty years ago, just like he told me. But his father was. Vincenzo Broddeus. Known as Vee. Now, tell me you don't know that name. Think about it for a few seconds. Make sure you're willing to stand behind what you're about to say to me," I say.

Richard Smith's jaw sets. "Yes. I knew Vee Broddeus."

I throw my hands up in the air, growling with aggravation. "Do you understand how bad this is? You faking your death was problematic as it is. I can understand you wanting to escape the shit that these people threw at you if you actually didn't have anything to do with Linda Carmine's disappearance, but that doesn't mean accepting people saying you're dead. Especially when you have personal links to criminals known for crimes associated with children. Vincent doesn't mess with kids. Edgar doesn't mess with kids. Meachum and Vee, though, were *known* for trafficking. So, what is it? Were you selling girls? I bet the children of wealthy families would catch a pretty penny out in the black market."

"No," he says, his voice low and gritty.

"How about drugs? Getting the teenagers hooked on drugs Vee provided you so that you could get the girls under your control and feed them to the ring?" I ask.

"No," Smith repeats.

"Then maybe you thought you could make even more by combining your efforts. Linda was a pretty little girl. Bright and special. You said so yourself. With a wealthy father and a best friend who you could just as easily grab. You thought you could take them and raise up your own little stable."

"I didn't do that," he snaps. "I would never do something like that."

"How am I supposed to believe that when you admit that you had dealings with Vee and Meachum?"

"I didn't have dealings with them. Not like that," he says.

"Then why would Brandt bring you up? Are you going to tell me that the three of you were just old friends and you had no idea? You've already tried that. I'm not buying it."

"Look into the accident," he tells me.

"What accident?" I ask.

"The aircraft. The one I supposedly died in. Look into the accident. Check the records. You'll find that every single person, alive or dead, is accounted for," he says.

"You already told me that there was a mistake on the manifest," I tell him.

He shakes his head. "The names were accurate when the plane took off."

The realization of what he's saying hits me in the center of the chest like a punch. I take a second to catch my breath.

"You turned state's evidence," I say. "You knew what they were doing. You witnessed it. And you became an informant."

"Yes," Smith says. "The other witnesses started dying at an alarming rate and nothing was being done about it. I already had the people from Gordon and McCutcheon wanting to skin me alive for something I had nothing to do with. I wasn't about to let someone else put my name on their hit list. I told the authorities I wasn't going to cooperate anymore if they didn't do something to protect me. So they came up with the idea of having me die. The next week, I went down with the aircraft. At least, that's the official word."

My mind is spinning. Colors dance in front of my eyes.

"Why didn't you tell me any of this? When I first talked to you, why didn't you make sure I knew what's really going on?" I ask.

"I didn't know if I could trust you. I've gone for this long having to conceal my real identity under threat of being killed. It's how I've survived up until now."

I shake my head. "No. There's something else happening here. If you were that afraid, you wouldn't just show back up at the school because you were upset that it was going to be demolished and feeling nostalgic. That's not enough to make you break your story and put yourself at this much risk. Why are you *actually* here?"

"I want my name cleared. Linda's disappearance has followed me for three decades. It took my career. My home. My future. And I was never even allowed to grieve for Linda. The rest of the community was able to come together and feel sad about her loss and worry about her together. That was taken from me. When I heard this happened, I knew it was my chance. This has to do with her. I want the truth to be told," he says. "I want the chance to live again."

"I've thought that the murders have had something to do with Linda's disappearance since early in the investigation. But my most compelling suspect was eliminated," I say.

"Who?" he asks.

"You."

"Me?"

"You have an extremely strong motive for wanting to seek revenge on this community. Like you just said, you were wronged all those years ago and have suffered because of it. The only reason I stopped considering you was when I found out you were dead. Now that I know that's not true, and that you have a troubling link to some serious criminals, even if that did result in you becoming a witness, you are right back on the list," I tell him.

"I didn't do this," he insists angrily. "I didn't do any of it. Yes, they tormented me. Yes, they ruined my life. But what good would it do me to kill… anyone? People I don't know. People who had nothing to do with it. And the bodies found in the classroom have been dead for years, but they weren't found until just now. If the point was to punish the community, what good would that do? What sense does it make?"

"None. Which is why you're going to help me find out what does."

CHAPTER FORTY-THREE

I T TAKES UNTIL THE NEXT MORNING FOR ME TO GET ALL THE
information I requested from Officer Chappell, but when it comes
in, I'm ready. Spreading everything out on the table in the conference
room, I take my marker up to the fresh pieces of paper I've attached to
the wall opposite the timelines. I make a few notes, then go back to the
table to look at the pictures.

The first picture I look at is of Linda Carmine's class from before
she disappeared. The photographer was standing at the front of the
classroom and had obviously told the class to pose and smile because
all of the children are smiling politely and have their hands folded on
top of their desks, the girls with their ankles crossed beneath them. It's
such a stark difference from images of contemporary elementary school
classrooms. This black-and-white image shows little girls in dresses and
ruffled socks, boys in slacks and collared shirts. Pristine. Everything in
its place. Classrooms today are all bright colors, silly faces, and struggles
just to keep everybody sitting still.

I push the picture across the table toward Richard Smith.

"Is this what they always looked like?" I ask.

Looking at the picture of his class seems to take his breath away for a brief second. I realize this is probably the first time in many years that he's seen that room or the smiling faces of those children. Somewhere in his mind he probably still thinks of them that way. They are frozen at nine years old, perfect in their clothes and their smiles. But still children. Still full of energy and life and laughter. It would be a shock to him to see those children now full-grown adults with children of their own.

"Yes," he finally says in a soft, powdery voice. "I assigned seats at the beginning of the year and that was where they sat every day."

"No variation?"

He shakes his head. "None."

"I don't want to show you the actual crime scene image of the corpses because it's pretty intense. But I have a sketch I'd like you to look at." I put the sketch in front of him, lining it up next to the photograph. "The desks were set back up the way they were when there was class. Look at the rows. But there are empty seats." I point out the few desks that don't have bodies in them. "I don't think this is by chance."

Richard points to one of them, then to the face in the photograph. "That's Linda." He points to the one beside it. "And that's Alma."

The observation aligns with the thoughts going through my mind. I point to another empty desk.

"How about this one?" I indicate the boy in the photograph. "Him?"

"Jack Meadows. Good at math. Hated reading. Started talking about the science fair on the first day of school."

It's an incredible ability of teachers to retain their students and recall details about them even many years after they left the classroom. But it's exactly what I need right now. There's information I can't get anywhere else. I need it from his memories.

"Do you remember if he was in class the day Linda Carmine disappeared?" I ask. "I know it was a long time ago and a serious longshot for you to actually remember something like that, but I was hoping…"

"He wasn't," he confirms. "I remember because we had a reading quiz that day and my first thought was that he was trying to get an extra day to study for it by pretending to be sick and then having to take a makeup the next day. It was something he had done before."

I go over to the paper on the wall and make a note of that, then go back to the picture.

"How about this one?"

He looks at the boy's face.

"Dandridge Cooper. Very quiet. He was a little bit of a wallflower. He just kind of blended in. I honestly can't remember if he was there that day," Richard says.

I feel discouraged for a brief second before a thought comes to mind.

"What did you say his name was?" I ask.

"Dandridge Cooper."

"I've heard that name. Or seen it." I think for a second, trying to remember why it sounded familiar, and it occurs to me. I go to the stack of records on the other side of the table and pull out the clinic registration form. "Here. He went to the clinic that day. In the middle of the morning. His mother picked him up."

"So, the empty desks are students who weren't there that day. But Linda and Alma both were."

"But they are both missing now," I say.

I'm about to put the clinic record back when Richard stops me.

"Hold on. Let me see that." He turns the form toward himself. His eyes dart back and forth over it for a few seconds and his head begins to shake. "This isn't right."

"What do you mean?" I ask.

He points out a name beneath Dandridge Cooper's.

"Sarah Grier." He shows me a girl in the image of his former class. "This is Sarah Grier."

I look at the sketch from the crime scene. "There's a body in her desk." I check the clinic form. "It says she was given a bandage and then returned to class."

"Right, but that didn't happen. This time that's listed was during our lunch. The younger students had lunch in the classrooms rather than in the dining hall like the older students. I remember her crying because she got a stain on her dress while she was eating and it was her favorite dress. One of the other girls comforted her and said that her mother would be able to get it out, and that calmed her down. But look at the record. It says that she came in with a cut on her arm. There would be no way for her to get an injury like that in the classroom during lunch."

I look through a few more papers before looking at him again.

"You said you had a reading quiz that day. Do you remember anything else about the lessons you were teaching? Classwork they did? Anything?"

Richard looks confused but seems to think about the question.

"We had the reading quiz. We were working on fractions."

"What kind of fractions? Multiplying? Dividing?"

"No. We hadn't gotten to that yet. I think we were reviewing adding fractions and whole numbers that day."

"What did you use to teach? Did you use a lot of worksheets? I'm a few years younger than these students would be now, but I don't remember using worksheets very much in my math classes. My teacher would write things on the board and we would copy them into our notebooks," I say.

"That's how I taught," Richard confirms. "Occasionally we'd have a worksheet but not very often."

"So, you didn't use any visual handouts? Like a picture of a pie or a cake or anything?"

"No. I used to draw things like that on the chalkboard, though. It was an easy way for them to start to recognize the concepts of fractions. Why do you ask?" he asks.

I show him one of the papers in my hand. "These were found in the top drawer of the desk in that classroom."

"My classroom?" he asks, sounding surprised and a little bewildered as he takes the paper from my hand and looks at it. It's a math worksheet depicting a cherry pie and an apple pie with various fractions questions. "This isn't mine. I never used anything like this."

"Are you sure? Look at the date."

"I see that. It's the date Linda disappeared. But I know I never used this kind of worksheet." He turns it around and runs his fingers over the paper. "This doesn't even feel like the paper I would have used then. This is photocopied. We didn't have a photocopier in the school at the time."

I realize he's right. Photocopying machines weren't available back in the fifties. Even in as elite an educational environment as the Dawn Day School was, the technology wouldn't have existed. These papers can't be from that day.

So, why were they there?

The incongruent details in the evidence is troubling. I make another note on the paper on the wall and turn to the sketches of the other bodies found over the years.

"I want you to look at these," I tell Richard. "Again, it's just sketches. These are illustrations of the grounds and locations of where bodies have been found in the years since Linda disappeared. There have been several deaths outside of the school that have never been linked to anything. So far, they haven't been considered suspicious. Drug overdoses, exposure. That kind of thing. Unfortunately, that happens near abandoned buildings. It doesn't necessarily have anything to do with each other or with anything else that might happen around that area. But when looked at in the context of everything else, they might mean something. I've tried to find any of those links in the locations of these bodies, but nothing has stood out to me other than one. And it's shaky at best."

"Which one?" he asks.

I point out the sketch that shows the body of a man who had a heart attack outside the door to the shed at the front of the property.

"This is the shed where the teacher got locked in and was found dead," I say.

Richard doesn't look convinced. "That was years before Linda disappeared. I don't think that fits."

"That's what I thought, too." I let out a breath. "How about any of the rest of these? Does anything strike a chord with something that happened that day?"

He looks over the papers spread out in front of him, occasionally pulling one closer or shifting another further away to focus on each individual sketch.

"This one," he says, pointing out the depiction of a woman who was found after what appeared to be an overdose near the playground equipment. "This would be where one of the playground monitors would have been after school. As long as there were children playing, one of the staff would have been standing in that spot." He looks at the sketches again. "Did you notice that these two are different?"

"What do you mean?" I ask.

"The letters on the outlines of the bodies. I'm assuming they are the initials of the people."

"Or the letters used to identify them if they are still Does," I tell him.

"So, there aren't going to be duplicates, right? They wouldn't identify two bodies with the same letters?" he asks.

"No. Each one is unique."

"Look at this." He points at two sketches, showing me outlines of what at first looks like two different bodies, but then I notice they have the same letters written beside them. "They have the same label, but they aren't in the same place. This is the school, right?" He swirls his fingers over the rough outline of the school made on each page to give context to the rest of the sketch. "Well, this one is drawn to the left, closer to the old conservatory. This one is drawn further to the back of the building, near the cellar door. It's basically the same place, just flipped."

"That's really strange," I say. "I'm going to have to find the original crime scene photos and see which one of these is accurate. Thanks for pointing that out."

I look back over at the notes I've written across the wall and then the timelines across the other.

"Is something wrong?" Richard asks.

"No. I was just thinking about something my friend Xavier said when we brought him to the aquarium. Everything seems so perfect. It's right and wrong at the same time. And the animals are just there, pretending to be living normal lives."

CHAPTER FORTY-FOUR

T HE DOOR TO THE CONFERENCE ROOM OPENING JOLTS ME OUT OF
my thoughts and makes me turn. Carla Mulroney is standing at
the doorway, her eyes sparkling and a piece of paper clutched in
her hands. The receptionist comes up behind her and looks over her
shoulder at me regretfully.

"I'm sorry, Agent Griffin. When she asked where you were, I didn't
realize she would just come down here. I tried to tell her to stop."

"I need to speak with you," Carla says.

"It's alright, Amy," I say. "Thank you."

The receptionist glares at Carla and huffs as she makes her way back
toward her desk. I don't want Carla to see sensitive elements of the case,
so I walk around the table and hold my arms out to her, trying to gather
her up and guide her back out into the hallway.

"Is that…" she starts, her voice trailing off as I notice her eyes are
locked on Richard Smith.

"Yes," I say. "He's assisting me with some pieces of evidence that needed context."

"Hello, Carla," Richard says. "It's good to see you again."

She bristles, but the tears coming to her eyes tell me there's far more to that reaction than anger or distrust. I reach for her shoulders, hoping the squeeze of my hands will help her focus.

"Carla, what is it?" I ask. "What do you need?"

She keeps staring at Richard for a beat, then turns her attention to me. "I got another letter from Alma. I brought it right to you."

She holds the paper out and I take it.

"Did you check the postmark?" I ask. "Is it from California, too?"

"I didn't," she admits. "But I'm sure it is. She'd tell me if she'd moved somewhere else. She wants me to know she's safe. She wants to come home. And she's going to. You're going to find out what happened to Linda."

She's speaking in a slightly hushed tone, like she doesn't want Richard to overhear.

"I'm trying, Carla. I'm still…"

"Agent Griffin?"

I look up and see Officer Chappell coming toward me with a gray, drawn expression on his face.

"Yes?"

"I need to speak with you for a moment."

I take a few steps away from Carla and notice Richard coming out of the room.

"Emma, I'm going to leave," he says. "I need to make some calls."

I nod. "Thank you for your help."

He walks away, Carla refusing to look at him as he passes. I turn my attention back to the officer standing in front of me.

"Edgar Brandt was found dead in his home earlier today," he tells me. "He was murdered."

"Oh, god," I say. "Has anyone…"

"Broddeus has already been interviewed. He didn't come right out and admit to setting it up, but he did say that Brandt shouldn't have gotten involved with that teacher. And he never should have done what he did."

I run my hand over my face. "Alright. Thank you for letting me know."

Chappell clears his throat. "I also wanted to let you know that Will Baylor called. He wants to talk to you."

"Thanks."

He pats my arm and walks back down the hall. I take a second to compose myself and go back to Carla.

"Is everything okay?" she asks.

"Just an unfortunate development with one of my cases," I say. "Anyway, about the letter. Does Alma say anything new in it?"

"She says that Linda came to her in a dream. She was older and looked like she'd been through something awful. She told Alma that she needs her help now more than ever. That she has to be careful when listening to friendly words and know when she's hearing lies," Carla says.

The message doesn't sit right with me and when Carla leaves, I find myself pulled back to the rest of the letters and all the notes Carla took from the handful of phone calls she'd had with her daughter over the years she's been missing. I pull my notepad closer to me and write down a few bullet points, then grab my keys and head for the door. I need to visit the library.

I've been in the research room for more than an hour before I remember Will Baylor's phone call. I go to the office and ask to use their phone, first reaching out to the hospital to see if he's still there. When they tell me he was discharged, I call the department again. Will doesn't live in the area, so he wouldn't be in the phone book. Fortunately, he left the name of a hotel with Amy.

The front desk connects me to his room and he answers on the second ring.

"Will, this is Agent Griffin."

"Thanks for calling me back," he says.

"Absolutely. What can I do for you?" I ask.

"I want to go back to the school and I figured you would be the one who would be able to give me permission to do that."

"Why would you want to go back there?" I ask.

"Unfinished business," he says. "No one will give me all the details about what happened to Jonathan, David, or Lila. I watched Charlotte die. I know what happened to her. But I need to know what happened to the others. I want to see if I can contact them."

"Will, this is a crime scene. These are real deaths of real people. It's fine if you want to listen to ghost stories and go take tours and try to talk to spirits or whatever it is that you do, but I'm investigating multiple murders and the disappearances of at least two people. This isn't the time to play," I say.

"It's not play," he says, sounding obviously offended. "I never finished searching the annex in the attic or the basement. You say you listened to the evidence we got. Then you know there are compelling moments that suggest someone is trying to communicate. If I can just get back in there, I might be able to contact one of the team and they could guide us to who did this."

"I appreciate you wanting to help. But..." I stop myself. He could actually be right. Maybe he does need to go back there. "Actually. Yes. I can get you in there. But I have to be with you, and you have to follow every one of my instructions while we're there. This is still an active scene and I don't want it compromised."

"Of course."

"Alright. I have a few things left that I need to get finished and then I can come get you. I'll pick you up in two hours," I tell him.

"I'll be ready."

I go back to the research room and finish reading through the weather reports and news clippings I'd located. With my notepad full of notes, I go back to the conference room and pull out the picture of the bodies in the classroom and then the class as it was before Linda disappeared. I compare them, looking more closely at each of the bodies.

Words keep repeating through my mind. My heart beats faster in my chest as the fragments start to come together. I check the time and realize it's getting late. Before leaving, I stop by the desk and call Sam.

"Hey, babe. I need you to do something for me. Would you go by Richard Smith's hotel and pick him up, then meet me up at the school? I'm going to call him to let him know you're coming," I say.

"Sure. What's going on?" he asks.

"I think I figured something out, but I need him to verify a couple things. I'm going to get Will Baylor and I think with the two of them comparing notes, I could narrow down what happened that night."

"Alright. I'll see you in a bit. I love you," he says.

"I love you." I hang up and call Carla. She sounds slightly breathless. "Carla? Are you okay?"

"Oh, I'm fine," she says with a little laugh. "I was walking out the door when I heard the phone ring and had to come run back and answer it. I was just leaving for work."

"I'm not going to keep you. I just wanted to ask if you could find the envelope that letter you brought me today came in and just drop it by the police station tomorrow."

"Of course," she says.

"Great. Thanks. I also have a question. What did Alma want to do with her life? Why did she go to college?" I ask.

Carla stammers for a second like she wasn't expecting that question. "Oh. Well, she had so many dreams."

"I remember you telling me that. Did she choose anything specific?"

"She had a few ideas but before she left she hadn't settled on anything. She always said she knew life is short and unpredictable..."

"And everything worthy in it takes sacrifice," I finish. "I read that."

"Yes," Carla says.

"Alright. That's all. I hope I didn't make you late."

"Oh, no. I have plenty of time before the day starts. I just wanted to leave early because of the weather. It looks like it's going to rain. I hate driving in the rain," she says.

"Be careful."

"You, too."

CHAPTER FORTY-FIVE

WILL IS ALREADY STANDING OUTSIDE THE HOTEL WHEN I PULL up. He has a bag over his shoulder as he stands beneath the portico to stay out of the rain that has started to fall. The sky overhead is blotted out by dark, thick clouds and a threatening energy is in the atmosphere. It feels like a storm is coming. It's too warm for snow, but that almost makes it worse. It means the rain will soon turn to ice.

"Thank you for being willing to do this," Will says when he climbs into the car. "I really feel like I can make a difference."

"I do, too. I brought some of the recordings from that night. When we get to the school, I want you to listen to them and try to tell me where each of you were when you got those recordings. Most of them have markers that say where you are or what you're looking at, but some of them don't. It can help me identify some of the sounds in the context of where they are happening in the school."

"I can try," he says.

THE GIRL AND THE WINTER BONES

The rain is getting more aggressive as we get closer to the access road behind the school. A light rumble of thunder rolls in the distance.

"Are you sure you're up for this in this weather?" I ask.

"Yes. It was worse the night I was here," he says.

When I spoke to Richard he told me he was catching up on a few things for work while he was in the hotel and needed a little time. It means Sam should be getting to the hotel right around now and be on his way, giving Will and I twenty minutes or so by ourselves. As we pull around to the front of the driveway, I notice the officers are no longer positioned there. Chappell had mentioned ending the guard now that the team has finished removing the evidence from the building and everything has been photographed. There would still be regular patrols, but the school is alone again.

I step out into the cold rain to use my key to open the lock securing the gate. The chill runs down my spine and I'm eager to get back in the car and drive up as close to the building as I can.

"Did you bring a flashlight with you?" I ask.

Will holds up his bag. "I have everything."

I grab my own flashlight, and we get out of the car and dart for the front door. Inside, I see the floodlights are still in place. I'm grateful for them as I get the generator going and light up the front hall. I look over at Will to check on how he's doing. People react very differently when they're brought into a place where they've experienced extreme trauma. Some are perfectly fine, while others have an intense emotional response and can't handle it.

Will appears calm as he looks around, his flashlight burrowing into every corner and cutting through the darkness across the ceiling. He draws in a breath.

"Are you alright?" I ask.

He calmly looks over at me. "I'm fine."

"If at any point you want to leave, just tell me. We can come back when the weather is better. In the daylight. Or not at all. You don't have to do this."

"Yes, I do," he insists.

"Walk me through what you did when you first got here that night."

Before Will can say anything, a sound somewhere in front of us stops us. It's not loud but it's distinct. Like the sound of a cabinet closing. I hold up a finger to my mouth. Everything stays silent. We wait for a few more moments before we continue. Will guides me through their steps and I ask him to bring me along his own path, where he went when he separated from the others. I have a recorder in my pocket and want to play some of the evidence for him.

We go into the hidden passage and have only taken a few steps when I hear another sound. A low scratching, it seems to be coming from somewhere ahead. Will and I exchange a glance, but before I can even ask if it's one of the same sounds he heard, the loud smashing of glass behind me gets me running back to the front foyer.

The darkness envelops me as soon as I step beyond the movable panel. I shine my flashlight into the entryway and see the floodlight has been destroyed, glass scattered on the floor around it.

A crash of thunder is accompanied by a flash of lightning, briefly making the hallway glow. I see something move out of the corner of my eye and chase it with the beam of my flashlight. I don't see anything and turn back to Will. His eyes are wide, his expression like stone.

"Someone is here," he stammers.

"It's going to be alright," I whisper to him. "I need you to take my keys and go back out to the car. Wait there."

He shakes his head. "No. I'm staying with you."

"Will, I told you that you have to follow my instructions. I know you want to help, but right now, I need to know you are safe. Go to the car and lock the doors," I order.

The silence of the building breaks with the shrill sound of a bell ringing. Will's knees buckle and he sags down toward the carpet. I grab him with my free hand and pull him back to his feet, dragging him toward the door. Pressing the keys into his palm, I shove him out onto the porch. He hesitates for a second, then heads for the car. I watch until he gets inside and locks the doors. My pager beeps on my hip and I look down at it. It's a message from Sam.

The long string of numbers reminds me of the messages that come from Xavier. It's the alphanumeric code, a simple translation of number to letter that allows them to send me whatever message they want to. I just have to interpret it. With Xavier's tendency to try to carry on full conversations over pager, I have had enough practice for the words to form fairly quickly. My stomach drops as the message appears in letters across my mind.

Richard not here. Blood in room. On my way.

I'd considered waiting for Sam so he could radio for additional backup, but now I know I can't. I take out my gun and slowly, cautiously, head back inside. The beam of my flashlight is enough to illuminate a strip of the hallway and I make my way down it carefully but without hesitation. I know exactly where I'm going. The bell has gone silent, leaving only the sound of my footsteps and I count them as I move toward the corner.

I hate the darkness behind me. I hate the secret passages I know could have someone inches from me without me knowing. They're like veins, hidden, carrying blood throughout the school.

"Emma!"

My name exploding in the silence makes me whip around. My flashlight beam falls on Sam's face, his wet hair clinging to the sides of his head. I rush back to him, holding up a hand to quiet him.

"Sam, I need you to get Will out of here. Get backup to come get him," I say.

"Where is he?"

The question is like a rock plummeting into my gut.

"In my car. Right outside."

Sam shakes his head. "No, he's not. That's why I shouted for you. When I pulled up, the driver's door was standing open. No one is inside."

"Shit. Radio the precinct. Get guys here. Now. We're probably going to need an ambulance."

Sam takes his radio and calls for backup. I keep my flashlight moving through the dark to see anything that might be close, hoping for lightning to aid the brightening.

"Richard..." Sam starts, but I shake my head.

"I know where he is."

We move quickly down the hall and around the corner to the classrooms. A slight flickering light is visible under the door to Linda's classroom and I can hear a muffled voice from inside. With Sam behind me, I force open the door and rush in. A lantern sitting on one of the front desks is enough light to show Richard Smith bound, standing with his back against the chalkboard. A noose is around his neck, secured through a hook in the ceiling and attached to the far side of what used to be his desk. It makes it so he has to stand on his toes, keeping himself taut and upright so the rope doesn't tighten.

I run for him, tossing my flashlight onto the desk and putting my gun back in its harness so I can take the rope from his neck. As I'm fighting through a thick layer of tape around his wrists, I notice a piece of chalk taped to his hand.

"Are you hurt?" I ask when the tape is taken from his mouth.

"My leg," he croaks.

I look down and see blood pooled beneath him.

"Emma, it was..."

Sam lets out a grunt behind me and when I turn, he's on the ground, Angelo Carmine's foot pressing down on his throat.

"Agent Griffin, how nice of you to join us. You're just in time for today's lessons. Now that we have our teacher, class is ready to start."

Beneath him, Sam shifts enough to get his arm out from under his body. One swift movement cracks his flashlight against Angelo's leg, making him stumble. I surge forward, slamming both of my hands into his chest so he crashes back into the desks and onto the floor.

"That's what this is, isn't it?" I ask, pinning him down with one knee on his chest and the other on the floor beside him. "You told me you don't like leaving things *unfinished*. That you wish you knew what happened that day."

"He knows," Angelo says. "He knows what happened to her. I've spent thirty years recreating this day. Over and over. Trying to understand what happened. He was the last piece."

"Emma," Sam says, but he's not fast enough.

Angelo takes hold of the leg of the desk beside me and yanks it forward, making the wood crack against the side of my head. My vision blurs and I drop down to the side. Angelo scrambles to his feet and stomps on me as he heads for the front of the room. I roll over and see him dig into his pocket. He pulls out a knife as he lunges for Richard. Sam catches him around the waist and tackles him, sending the knife skittering across the floor. I get up and grab the handcuffs from Sam's belt, securing Angelo to the desk. He rages and tries to yank himself free, but he's not going anywhere.

I help Richard out of the room and lower him to the floor.

"Wait here. We have help coming," I say.

"Someone else is here," Richard manages weakly. "It's not just him."

"I know. Stay here." I tear off part of his shirt to tie around the gash in his leg. "Keep pressure on this. You're going to be fine."

Sam comes out of the room and hands me my flashlight.

"The guys are almost here," he says.

"We need to find Will."

"The cellar," Richard says. "Look at the cellar door. The caretaker was at the door."

I start running, Sam close behind me. We burst through the door to the basement and nearly slide down the steps.

"What is he talking about?" Sam asks.

"The sketches of the bodies," I say. "Two of them didn't match up." I see rain pouring in through the open cellar door. A hand is hanging in from the ground overhead. "Angelo corrected it."

THE GIRL AND THE WINTER BONES

I climb the steps and find Will lying on the ground, the side of his face pressed into the dirt. Blood rolls down his other cheek from a cut across the bone. I check his pulse.

"He's alive. We need to get him inside."

Sam and I pick Will up and carry him down into the basement. He groans and I see his eyes flutter open.

"Agent Griffin?"

"It's alright. What's hurt?" I ask.

"My face," he says.

"Not your back or your neck?" I ask.

"No," he says. "Just my face."

"Okay. Sam, put him over your shoulder. We need to get him upstairs to the clinic," I say.

"The clinic?" he asks.

"This   isn't   over."

CHAPTER FORTY-SIX

PUT ON MY BEST LOOK OF CONCERN AS I GET TO THE CLINIC. JUST as I'd expected, I find Carla sitting behind the desk. She looks up as I rush to her.

"Carla, we need help. A student got hurt."

She immediately stands up and gestures to one of the cots.

"Lay him down there."

Sam follows the instructions and Carla walks over to a large medicine chest on the wall. She opens it and starts pulling out first aid supplies.

"Do you want me to fill out the registration form?" I ask.

"Yes," she says. "Make sure you put down the time."

Sam meets my eyes and I feel an unexpected tightness in my throat.

"Like you've done for all the students?" I ask. "The ones Angelo has you take care of? I noticed a bandage on the arm of one of the bodies in the classroom. She was sitting in Sarah Grier's desk." She pauses and looks over at me. "Carla, those supplies are new. Why are they here?"

She glances down at the bandage in her hand. "He said it was the only way to find out what happened to Linda. You have to finish what you start."

"And until he knew what happened to her, he wasn't finished. And you believed Alma would never come back," I say.

Her eyes snap to me. "Her letters. She told me. You read them. You know how scared she is and that she can't come home until we know what happened to Linda and hold him accountable."

"Richard Smith?" I ask. She nods. "Carla, Richard didn't do anything to Linda."

"Then what happened to her?"

"I might know," I say. "But I can't look until this is over. You told me earlier you were leaving for work. You were coming here. You've always been committed to taking care of people."

"I still am," she says. "I've been taking care of them. All of them. This had to happen."

I draw in a breath. "It was the sacrifice that had to be made."

She nods and starts to gently clean the cut on Will's head. Behind me, I hear the team crash through the front door.

"The letters from Alma at first were authentic. But there was a break of a couple of years when she didn't hear from her. After that, everything was from Angelo. When I went to his office to tell him Richard Smith is alive, I saw memos from different people on his desk. At first, I thought he was just approving them. It didn't occur to me until later that he signed one of them with a different name. He wrote in different handwriting and signed different signatures to make it look like memos were coming from various executives in the company. And they probably were. He just didn't have the patience to wait for them to actually do it, so he did it himself."

I explain how comparing details about the weather and news events in Alma's letters with their timing along with ticks in the wording convinced me that Angelo had written the letters. I believe he'd sent them to an associate in California, then had them individually mailed so that the postmark would show that's where they were from. I don't know who was helping him, but I doubt they have any idea what they were actually aiding. The clinic records and classwork that didn't fit only underscored my belief that Angelo was responsible.

"Carla was so convinced Alma would come home if someone found out what happened to Linda that she would do anything that seemed like it would make that happen. Even be his accomplice to years of murder. She believed it was the sacrifice that had to be made for something worthy," I say. "Angelo has been waiting thirty years to know what happened to his daughter that day. Both of them were willing to do whatever they needed to do to get their answers."

Will is back in the hospital, but this time I've made sure he has books and all the evidence gathered at the school with him so he can work while he's here. It doesn't matter what I think. This is what's valuable to him, and that's not for me to decide.

As Sam and I leave, I check my watch.

"We should hurry. They should be there soon."

We pull up to the school under a vibrantly sunny sky. The building looks less foreboding, but there's still a sense of sadness around it. A team is gathered at the back when Sam and I walk around. I reach out to shake the hand of the contractor who approaches me.

"Thank you for coming," I say.

"Of course. Explain to me again what we're doing."

I give him a brief overview of everything.

"Richard Smith pointed out that there was a caretaker outside the cellar the day Linda disappeared. Will was beside the door, recreating that moment. It means someone else saw it and Angelo felt it was important. I remembered being in the basement and the dimensions felt off. Then I remembered a receipt for a coal delivery that was in the scrapbook made for Richard before Linda's disappearance. It was from when the building was still a private home.

"That made me curious about the original layout, so I found the blueprints. There was a coal chute on the side of the house that was removed and sealed over. But when it was still used, it led into a dumb-waiter-type elevator that brought the coal down to the basement but could also bring it to other parts of the house to be used in the fireplaces. The elevator was located in a coal room at the side of the basement. I realized when it seemed that the dimensions were off it was because it was too small. I found out the coal room had been sealed off, but it was still accessible through the servants' passages.

"Most people didn't know about those passages, but the people working here did, which means their children would. When she was young, Alma wrote about her secret world. I think she was talking about the passages and that she shared them with Linda."

"And you think that might be where she's been all this time?" the contractor asks.

"The caretaker's statement about that day was that he was working on the grounds like he always did and left the cellar door open. One of the children made the statement that Linda was seen running around to the back of the building. Investigators at the time said that the building was thoroughly searched, but they may not have thought to search secret passages and a sealed-off room."

Sam and I stand back as the team descends into the basement and starts to dismantle the wall that blocks off the coal room. When it's revealed, they open it and I go inside. The dust and dirt from years of abandonment are suffocating, but I'm focused on the heavy iron elevator in front of me. My heart thuds against my ribs. I open the door and at first see nothing. I'm somewhat relieved that my theory was wrong until I realize the platform of the dumbwaiter is elevated just slightly and the wire that should be holding it up has been snapped. I touch it.

"After years of neglect, the wire broke," I say. "Somebody help me lift the platform."

We slip our fingers into the gap between the platform and the bottom of the elevator. As we lift it, pink fabric comes into view, then bones.

"Find something to prop this up," Sam commands.

I kneel down and reach out to run my fingers over the cracked skull. An old, battered book and a small flashlight rest under the bones of a tiny hand. It looks like she crawled inside looking for a good hiding place and entertained herself reading while she waited, only to fall asleep in the warm, dark space. I can only pray she didn't know what was happening when the wire broke and the metal platform came down.

"Linda," I whisper to the bones as Sam goes to call for a team. "I'm going to go tell your Mama about your day. And I'll bring your teacher with me. He'll tell her everything."

A month later Sam and I are back on the grounds of the Dawn Day School watching as machinery rolls in to take the building down. He wraps his arm around my waist and pulls me close to him.

"You did it," he says.

"No, I didn't," I say. "There are still four women missing. We weren't able to link the three girls from the Conway campus to anything and haven't been able to trace Alma."

"But you found Linda. You were able to give her back to her mother."

I think of the funeral held for the little girl just a week after her bones were removed from the basement of the school. It seemed like the entire town came out to say goodbye to her. Tears spring to my eyes as I think of the students reuniting with Richard Smith, the parents asking for his forgiveness. I know he's not completely innocent. He's committed crimes and done things he never should have done. But that doesn't matter. He isn't who they thought and now, in their minds, he can go back to being the teacher they loved.

"This will be a gorgeous park," I say. "And Richard already has permission to find the cemetery and make sure it's properly memorialized. It will be a wonderful place to visit."

"We'll come back when it's finished," Sam says.

I hum in agreement. "Let's go."

"I thought you wanted to watch," he says.

"I think I've seen enough."

We turn to walk away and a breeze touches my cheek. I turn toward the sound of a soft giggle behind me.

"What is it?" Sam asks.

I shake my head, a smile coming to my lips.

"Nothing. I just thought I heard something."

"Come on," he says. "Let's go find Dean and Xavier. We have a road trip to finish."

AUTHOR'S NOTE

Dear Reader,

Thank you for choosing to read *The Girl and the Winter Bones.*

For many people, the start of the new year is important because it's a reset. An opportunity to start a few good habits, and start off on the right foot. I hope that you enjoyed reading this murder mystery and that I'm starting off my 2023 writer's journey on the right foot. There is so much that I want to accomplish this year and I want this year to be better than the last! I'm so excited to share with you all of the projects and ideas that I have planned for the new year!

Thank you for all of the support that you have shown my retro series project. If you can please continue to leave your reviews for these books, I would appreciate that enormously. Your reviews allow me to get the validation I need to keep this limited series going as an indie author. Just a moment of your time is all that is needed.

My promise to you is to always do my best to bring you thrilling adventures. I can't wait for you to read all the books I have in store for you!

Yours,
A.J. Rivers

P.S. If for some reason you didn't like this book or found typos or other errors, please let me know personally. I do my best to read and respond to every email at mailto:aj@riversthrillers.com

ALSO BY
A.J. RIVERS

Emma Griffin FBI Mysteries

Season One

*Book One—The Girl in Cabin 13**

*Book Two—The Girl Who Vanished**

*Book Three—The Girl in the Manor**

*Book Four—The Girl Next Door**

*Book Five—The Girl and the Deadly Express**

*Book Six—The Girl and the Hunt**

*Book Seven—The Girl and the Deadly End**

Season Two

*Book Eight—The Girl in Dangerous Waters**

*Book Nine—The Girl and Secret Society**

*Book Ten—The Girl and the Field of Bones**

*Book Eleven—The Girl and the Black Christmas**

*Book Twelve—The Girl and the Cursed Lake**

*Book Thirteen—The Girl and The Unlucky 13**

*Book Fourteen—The Girl and the Dragon's Island**

Season Three

*Book Fifteen—The Girl in the Woods **

*Book Sixteen —The Girl and the Midnight Murder **

*Book Seventeen— The Girl and the Silent Night **

*Book Eighteen — The Girl and the Last Sleepover**

*Book Nineteen — The Girl and the 7 Deadly Sins**

*Book Twenty — The Girl in Apartment 9**

*Book Twenty-One — The Girl and the Twisted End**

Ava James FBI Mysteries

Book One—*The Woman at the Masked Gala*
Book Two—*Ava James and the Forgotten Bones*
Book Three —*The Couple Next Door*
Book Four — *The Cabin on Willow Lake*
Book Five — *The Lake House*
Book Six — *The Ghost of Christmas*

Dean Steele FBI Mysteries

Book One—*The Woman in the Woods*

Emma Griffin FBI Mysteries Retro - Limited Series

Book One— *The Girl in the Mist*
Book Two— *The Girl on Hallow's Eve*
Book Three— *The Girl and the Christmas Past*
Book Four— *The Girl and the Winter Bones*

Other Standalone Novels
Gone Woman
* Also available in audio

Printed in Dunstable, United Kingdom